COLD
FLASH

Also by Carrie H. Johnson

Hot Flash

Published by Kensington Publishing Corp.

COLD FLASH

CARRIE H. JOHNSON

KENSINGTON PUBLISHING CORP.
www.kensingtonbooks.com

DAFINA BOOKS are published by

Kensington Publishing Corp.
119 West 40th Street
New York, NY 10018

All Kensington titles, imprints, and distributed lines are available at special quantity discounts for bulk purchases for sales promotion, premiums, fund-raising, and educational or institutional use.

Special book excerpts or customized printings can also be created to fit specific needs. For details, write or phone the office of the Kensington Sales Manager: Kensington Publishing Corp., 119 West 40th Street, New York, NY 10018. Attn. Sales Department. Phone: 1-800-221-2647.

Dafina and the Dafina logo Reg. U.S. Pat. & TM Off.

ISBN-13: 978-1-4967-0401-6
ISBN-10: 1-4967-0401-0
First Kensington Trade Paperback Printing: June 2017

eISBN-13: 978-1-0402-3
eISBN-10: 1-4967-0402-9
First Kensington Electronic Edition: June 2017

10 9 8 7 6 5 4 3 2 1

Printed in the United States of America

Dedicated to my sister, Roberta Johnson,
who always has my back.

ACKNOWLEDGMENTS

Many thanks to Anika Nailah for continuing to give me the kind of support, clarifying and thought-provoking comments needed to empower the story. Thank you to my sister, Roberta, my first reader, toughest critic, and drum major. And always a special thanks to my partner in crime, Adrienne Lloyd, firearms examiner—retired, without whom none of this would be happening. A special thank you also to Selena James and the rest of the Kensington/Dafina Books team for all their hard work.

CHAPTER 1

Lord only knows the things we'll do or how far we'll go for the people we love.

Flailing around in the pool at the Salvation Army Kroc Center this Friday morning was my "thing" I was doing for my girl Dulcey. She has breast cancer. I committed to doing a triathlon, as in a quarter-mile swim, twelve-mile bike ride, and three-mile run. Mind you, I am scared to death of the water, have not been on a bike since childhood . . . that would be forty-plus years . . . and have not run with any speed since the police academy more than twenty years ago.

The SheRox Triathlon Series raises funds for breast cancer research. I admit the whole triathlon thing is a smoke screen for coping with the fear of losing Dulcey. Somehow my crossing the finish line will turn the nightmare into a fairy tale, with a happily-ever-after ending.

So here I am, three months into my training. It's not like I never work out. At five foot three and 140 pounds, it is necessary to keep all my parts in check. I work out on a semi-regular basis, three or four times a week for a month or two, then I'm distracted by any good reason. Not this time. At least not for another month until after the July event.

I learned to swim five weeks ago and have since mastered a slow, steady stroke. Grab the water, push it away in an S motion with flat hands. Turn my head, suck in air, put my face in the water, blow out air. Each time I turned my head to gulp air, I saw this guy whipping the lifeguard, Pam, with his pointer finger. White guy, six feet, 250 pounds maybe. He was wearing a green, black, and silver sweat suit and a black Eagles cap pulled low on his brow. At first I thought maybe he was a disgruntled parent of an eel, pollywog, or fish—names that indicated a child's level of swim achievement.

Children's squeals bounced off the pool's dome, signaling the end of adult swim time. The sounds were muffled each time I put my face back in the water. I dug deep to squeak out the last lap, which totaled sixteen, a half mile. I got to the deep end and flipped to retrace my path for the final length.

When I reached the shallow end and walked up the stairs, the guy had Pam's arm pinned behind her back. He pressed against her body, talking into her ear, red-faced like a heavy drinker or druggie. His other hand was stuffed in his pocket, which bulged with what I suspected was a gun.

A quick check had the children on the opposite side of the pool with their instructors, making enough noise to part the waters.

Pam wriggled under his hold. Her wide eyes darted in every direction until they set on me. She watched me walk past them and sit on the bench. I dried my feet, my arms, and my head, the whole time pleading with the good Lord to move this guy along or grow me large enough to pound him.

He yanked Pam's arm backward. Pam yelped like a hurt puppy. Damn. I approached from his blind side, aware of my inadequate clothing and dwarfed size in comparison to him.

"Is everything all right here?" I asked, my voice steady, my nerves shivering.

"Mind your damn business, lady," the guy said, twisting Pam's arm harder.

"You're hurting me, Bunchy," Pam whimpered.

"Shut up. Do what I'm telling you or I really will hurt you."

Pam pulled away from the guy and screamed. I pushed her to the side and stepped in front of her.

"Easy, mister. I'm Philadelphia Police. Take your hand out of your pocket, slow."

He pulled his hand out, holding a Beretta. I rushed in with one shoulder down and grabbed his arm. He got off a shot. Loud screaming. I knocked the gun from his hand, spun around, grabbed his wrist, spun around again and twisted his wrist, bringing him to the floor. I jammed my foot into his neck. He squirmed, trying to get loose.

"I'll break it if you don't keep still," I said.

"You stupid bitch. I'ma kick your ass. I'ma kill you." Spit sprayed from his mouth with each word.

I twisted his wrist a little harder and stepped into his neck a little deeper. "Not today," I said.

Pam came up the stairs from the pool with the gun in hand. She walked over to us and pointed it at Bunchy.

"Put the gun down, Pam. He's not going to hurt you or anyone else. Believe me, you do not want to kill him. He's not worth it, Pam."

"He'll just come back. I tried to get the police to do something. A restraining order doesn't do any good. He'll just come back."

"Not this time. This time he'll go to jail. Put it down, Pam. Think about your little girl."

She kept pointing it.

"Don't shoot me, Pam. I'm sorry. I love you," Bunchy

pleaded, relaxing his pull on my hold. I dug my foot deeper into his neck.

She lowered the gun as police stormed into the dome. An officer took the gun from Pam and pulled her arms behind her back for cuffing.

"She's good," I said. He released her.

Three officers gathered to relieve me of my charge. "You sure you need our help with this guy?" one of the officers joked.

I stepped off Bunchy's neck. Bunchy growled as he rose up and lunged forward headfirst, pushing me backwards. I went down.

"Welcome back."

Fran Riley, my partner, put his hand out to stop me from trying to sit up. "You should stay put a few." I brushed his hand away. He sighed a helpless verse and pulled me forward to a sitting position.

I tried to speak, but the words stuck in my throat. I looked around at the uniforms helping the parents and children to calm down. Other uniforms were snapping pictures and asking questions. A little girl lay out on the deck, an EMT bent over her. I stretched my neck to locate Pam. A police officer restrained her, blocking her path to her daughter. I rubbed my eyelids but failed to clear my blurred vision.

"Muriel? You all right? You with me? Muriel?" Fran asked, as he waved his hand in front of my face. I brushed his hand away and nodded. I tried to stand with his help. Halfway up, another EMT interfered and I was back on my butt.

"That might not be a good idea yet." The EMT motioned Fran to move, then knelt and flashed a light in my face.

I could see he was talking to me. The sounds were muffled,

as though I was still under water. My ears popped. I covered them with my hands, a buffer against the sudden loudness of the hollow voices. ". . . a bump on your head. You'll be fine. You're lucky he didn't break your neck." The EMT turned to Fran and said, "Keep an eye on her for a few hours. Precautionary."

Detective Mosher, who I knew from the fifth district, stood in front of me. "What happened here, Mabley?"

I took a deep breath. "Is the little girl . . ."

"She's alive. Now, what happened?"

I settled down. "The guy . . . he was having words with the lifeguard, with Pam." I closed my eyes and put my head down to ward off a rush of dizziness.

"You good, Mabley?"

I looked up and continued. "I was in the water doing my last lap. He was cursing her out. I noticed a bulge in his jacket pocket that appeared to be a gun. I got out the water, dried off . . ." Dizziness blurred my vision again. I bowed my head and closed my eyes against the desire to puke.

"Big guy," Mosher said.

I took a deep breath. "Yeah, but he went for his gun." I nodded toward the little girl. "What happened? Where's the guy?"

"After you went down, he pulled an officer's weapon and tried to shoot the lifeguard but hit the little girl instead. Grazed her head. She'll survive. She's their daughter. Took six officers to bring him down." He shook his head. "You had him on your own. I need to invest in some of that kung fu stuff." Mosher moved his arms in a chopping motion.

My fuzzy thoughts repelled the humor. "Where is he?"

Mosher put his arms down and got serious again. "He had some kind of seizure. Hopped up on drugs, didn't make it. I would bet some junk—heroin, fentanyl, cocaine, a mix. You know. Mother said the guy is her ex-husband. He's an army vet. Suffered from PTSD, spazzing over custody of the daughter. She's seven. She could have been killed." Mosher walked away, barking orders.

Fran helped me up. "Nice suit." He half-ass smiled, trying to rile me. I had on one of those triathlon suits that cover everything, including thighs. I had no room for his humor either. I cut my eyes and sucked my teeth as loud as I could.

Fran wrapped a towel around my shoulders. "C'mon, I'll help you outta here," he mumbled.

I let him lead me out holding my arm, like I was an invalid unable to do or say anything but what I was told.

"Can you handle dressing yourself? I can come in and help."

I pulled away from him and gave him a sideways F-U glance and leaned on the door to the locker room. "Don't get your brain in a knot about it."

The locker room was quiet. Clothes, towels, flip-flops strewn in the aisles between the lockers. I sat on the bench and closed my eyes. The uneven quiet seeped in and calmed the tension that squeezed my temples.

I was startled when Fran yelled in, "Hey, Muriel, you about done?"

"Yeah. Out in five."

When I finished dressing, I met Fran back in the pool area. Parents were gathering their children and moving toward the locker room, police were leaving. Fran insisted on driving me home and picking up my car later. I conceded.

"Why were you at the Kroc anyway?" he asked, on the way.

"I'd rather not say, you know."

"No, I don't know."

Fran had been my partner for three months; blond-haired, blue-eyed, Mark Wahlberg–faced Fran. Before him I had the same partner for seventeen years. Laughton McNair. Suffice it to say that Fran is at the opposite end of the spectrum of cool,

color, and charisma from Laughton. Laughton[   ]
ners, friends, and for a time, lovers. I shake[   ]
feel every time he invades my thoughts, like now.

We are firearms examiners in the Philadelphia Police[   ]
partment. We examine, study, test, and catalog firearms confiscated from criminals and crime scenes, and testify in court
about the findings.

"My best friend, Dulcey, I think you know her; she has breast
cancer. I'm doing a triathlon in her honor."

The few moments of uncomfortable silence made my insides
boil. Really, it wasn't the silence that had sweat dripping off the
tip of my nose. While the silence was indeed uncomfortable,
the heat was a part of the aging process that came on now and
again and made me want to jump out of my clothes; that or
punch something or someone. I glanced over at Fran with
balled fists.

"Yeah, I met her at your house. We'd just finished our first
tour together, remember? Damn. I'm sorry to hear that." He
hesitated. "You got a call from a Detective Burgan after you
left last night. Said she had some information for you."

"She could have called my cell. Thanks. I'll call her when I
get home."

"What's it about, Miss M?"

"It's a personal matter."

That is, unless Hamp got his butt thrown in jail, I thought.
Hampton Dangervil—Dulcey's husband, aka Hamp or Danger. You think you know a person and then you are slapped
upside the head for thinking. I got slapped when Hampton
confessed his transgressions to me like I was his priest and
could offer him divine mercy. He said he lost some money
gambling. He said he was trying to make enough money to
keep Dulcey living in style. Silly man. Dulcey loves his dirty
drawers no matter rich or poor, right or wrong. I asked Burgan, who runs the Mobile Street Crimes Unit, to do some

checking on two characters Hamp said he owed money to. He only knew their street names—Bandit and Muddy—laughable if it weren't for the gurgling in my gut pushing out sharp pangs, which always meant something messed up was ahead.

"I'm not going to push, but if you need me you know I'm right here."

I shifted in my seat and rolled the window down.

"I can turn on the air if it will help."

"Damn it, Fran. Stop trying so hard. We're partners and that doesn't mean you need to be patronizing about everything or try to be inside my head. I'm over everything that happened. I'm over it, despite what you heard before you decided being my partner was right for you."

I cringed at my outburst. I guess you could label me still in recovery. It had not been quite a year since I shot Jesse Boone. Boone was a psychopath responsible for twenty-plus murders dating back twenty years. He almost took my life and my sister's. His death still sparked much discussion among police officers, with a positive vibe. For me it sparked emotional torment.

Fran kept face forward and did not respond. When we pulled up to the house, Fran opened his car door to get out.

I said, "I can make it on my own."

"Yes, boss," he said in a playful subservient tone.

"Sorry, didn't mean to sound so righteous." I moved to get out and he pressed my arm, stopping me. I turned to match his stare.

"I took this job because it is exactly where I wanted to be. I wanted to learn from the best, which I understood to be Laughton McNair, if he was still around, and you. If there's an issue with me, either embrace it or request another partner."

I wanted to exit the car and slam the door. I wanted to tell him to go to hell, not because I was angry but because a rookie had put me in my place. I felt like I was moving fast down a slope that meant I had no good nerves for police work anymore. Instead all I could muster was "I'm good" as I pushed the door open.

"I'll pick you up in an hour. We can pick up your car on the way to the lab. You have court at one o'clock."

"Yeah, yeah," I said before I closed the door. I turned back and bent down to peer at him through the window. "Thank you."

"No problem," he said, flashing me a cheeky grin.

I waited until he pulled away from the curb before I limped up the walkway to the door. It opened before I got to it. My nine-year-old twin nieces, Rose and Helen, jumped out. The twins are my sister Nareece's children.

Only nine months earlier, the twins lived in a million-dollar home in Milton, Massachusetts, with their mother and father. Now their father was dead, murdered, and their mother was in a semi-unresponsive state at Penn Center, a long-term care facility, the result of being raped and tortured by Jesse Boone, before I killed him.

"Hi, Auntie," they said in unison. The twins are best described as striking. Their father was Vietnamese. Their dark skin, almond-shaped gray eyes and jet-black, crinkly hair, turns heads.

Rose took over. "Travis left us here with Bethany cuz he said he had to go do an errand and he'd be right back, but he didn't come back."

Fifteen-year-old Bethany is our neighbor and the backup sitter. The twins begin attending camp next week. Until then, Travis, my twenty-year-old son, is the designated babysitter. Travis is a sophomore at Lincoln University, home for the summer.

"What do you mean he didn't come back? How long has he been gone?"

"He left at seven. He didn't even fix us breakfast. He should have taken us with him. He left you a note on the kitchen counter," Rose said.

"Calm down. Nothing happened, right?"

In unison they chimed, "Yeah. We're big enough to care for ourselves. We are on the case to find out where he went and why."

My nieces took on more of me than I sometimes could handle. They started the Twofer Detective Agency in my honor. As investigators, they question, research, and detect everything, and I do mean everything. I liked that they wanted to be "like me" in that way.

Rose said, "We know he got a phone call from Uncle Hamp. After he talked on the phone to Uncle Hamp, he left. From what we heard, we speculate that Uncle Hamp has troubles."

"You speculate, huh. Enough of the speculation."

"Yes, ma'am," they said in unison, standing at attention and saluting.

"Hi, Miss Mabley," Bethany said, emerging from the den. "It wasn't nothing for me to come over," she said, sashaying her way to the front door. Bethany's round baby face—big wide eyes and dab of a nose—made her appear younger than fifteen. She was another version of striking, having a German father and Haitian mother, both musicians. "I'm usually available anytime, so just call when you need me."

Bethany agreed to come back in an hour if Travis had not returned. After she left, the twins sang, "Bethany likes Travis, Bethany likes Travis, and Kenyetta's going to be pissed."

Kenyetta is Travis's girlfriend since freshman year in high school. She ran away from her foster home and was living on the street when Travis brought her home and asked for my help. We found her a better living situation. Their friendship blossomed, not surprising since Kenyetta is a beauty—dark skin, long, thick coiled hair, and curvaceous frame. They have been bound together since.

"Enough. Besides, how do you know Bethany likes Travis?"

"We've been watching them talk to each other and interrogatin' her and Travis, separately of course, about their associations."

I was sorry I asked as soon as the words escaped my lips. "C'mon. I'll fix you breakfast," I said, moving toward the kitchen while checking my phone. There were four missed calls from Travis. I tapped his name in my phone and waited. No answer.

"We already ate. Bethany made us pancakes. We're watchin' *Transformers*," they said, running back to the den. Their voices and footsteps echoed through the large newly remodeled five-bedroom Colonial that we had just moved into a week ago, which was still mostly decorated with unpacked boxes. Nareece and I had grown up in the house. I rented it out after my parents died, until the last tenants moved out a year ago. After everything that happened with Jesse Boone, I decided to re-model it so we could all live here together.

I went to the kitchen and found Travis's note on the floor. Bending to pick it up made me dizzy. I grabbed ahold of the counter and inched my way to an upright position.

```
Moms, I'm sorry I had to leave
the kids with Bethany. Uncle Hamp
called and said he couldn't reach
you and he needed help. I had no
choice. Travis.
```

Considering Hampton's earlier call to me, for help with his gambling debt, my feelings of relief at having arrived home curdled into worry.

CHAPTER 2

It was eleven o'clock by the time we got to the lab. The Firearms Identification Unit, aka "the lab," is housed in the basement of the Forensic Science Center located on the southwest corner of Eighth and Poplar Streets in North Philly. The center also includes a crime-scene group for gathering evidence, chemistry labs for drug analysis, and DNA labs for hair, fiber, and blood analysis.

The firearms lab is a maze of eight-by-eight cubicles with desks on three sides, allowing each examiner to section off their space to fit their needs. In mine, a library of research materials collected over the years is crammed on one side desk, tools for bench examinations—a stereomicroscope, magnifying glass, pliers, grips, screw drivers, wrenches, bullet pullers, hammers, and mallets—are cluttered on the other side desk, and two computers sat on the center desk.

Fran owned the cubicle across from mine, Laughton's old chair. Officer Benjamin Parker owns the cubicle next to mine. He's the longest-reigning member, with twenty years. I'm second in that category with eighteen years as an examiner, twenty on the force. The other six members, including Fran, are newbies with two years or less of service. Three examiners are civilians.

"Mabley, Parker, my office," Lieutenant Pacini barked. Pacini is our commanding officer. He's a bear—big, burly, and brash; at least that is what he puts out. I suspect his more bear-cubbish side surfaces for a chosen few. He stepped in nine months ago.

Parker raced me to the lieutenant's door—childish play spurred on by years of working together. I won.

"First, Mabley, I know it's been a long time coming, but you're cleared of any wrongdoing in the death of Jesse Boone and one of our very own, Captain Butler."

I cringed. He was talking about his predecessor, Captain Iverson Butler, who I had known since my childhood. He was my father's best friend. He saved my life more than once. In my obsession to put Jesse Boone in prison, I stumbled on Cap's illegal activity of getting payoffs from Boone and other gangsters dating back twenty-plus years.

"I'm sure it's been the longest year of your career with Internal Affairs poking around anywhere and everywhere in your life to clear you of knowing about and participating in the captain's illegal activities. That's what happens when you go off on your own rather than going through the proper legal channels, like keeping the higher-ups informed and calling for backup."

In the few moments of silence that followed, Parker and I just ogled the lieutenant, as though what he said made all the sense in the universe. Not.

Pacini cleared his throat, then continued. "Not judging, just saying. Make sure nothing of that nature happens on my watch, meaning you will keep me abreast of everything that goes on having to do with this department." Another pause where I guessed he was waiting for an affirmative from us. None given. "Well, Mabley, you're going to receive a commendation for taking down both men. Deservedly so, I'm sure."

Parker gave a few claps and said, "Yep, that would be about right. The department wants the publicity and does not care how it all went down, since Boone is dead and the whole police corruption piece can be squashed."

The lieutenant sat forward in his chair and clasped his fingers together in a pyramid-type fashion. "Because of your previous commander's indiscretions, there'll be an Internal Affairs investigation into the possibility that evidence in a number of cases was shipped directly to City Hall before being examined. The other examiners are new. Hell, there's no one been around longer than a few years but you two. So Internal Affairs is going to be looking to you two for information and possible blame." He bowed his head and nodded sideways. "A commendation in one hand and a complaint in the other."

"They can complain all they want. This office does its work," I said.

"We've been working like crazy to finish the examinations," Parker chimed in. "It's not like we've been shipping weapons to evidence storage without examining them. We do our job. No—we do our job and that of a dozen others that should be working here. The city can't see its way to fulfill their end by hiring more people, but we're expected to do all the work." Parker plopped down in one of the chairs in front of the lieutenant's desk. "This is not good for us. Sounds like the consensus is we don't do our jobs."

"Nobody's saying you don't."

"That's exactly what they're saying." Parker pushed back with a scowl that caused Pacini and me to turn our attention to him with raised brows. Parker being defiant? Mild-mannered, Mr. Peabody–style Parker? I have never in eighteen years seen Parker angry. It's hard to imagine what his angry expression would look like. Parker's eyes are close together until he looks cock-eyed. He also sports blow-fish cheeks and a mole that graces the tip of his nose.

"What?" Parker said, staring us down. "Well, it is."

Pacini broke his stare and continued. "They want intel about how a case backlog of four thousand dropped to six hundred in a few years."

"So we should be getting praise rather than being investigated," Parker said.

"It appears the real issue here is some stolen gun parts. Allegations of a cover-up are surfacing in language that alleges your ex-partner, Laughton McNair, incited it."

"What stolen gun parts? We have not had any cases about that. Why would Laughton cover up something like that?" My voice escalated more than I intended.

"An intriguing question," Pacini said.

Feeling a pinch of anger escalate to a full punch, I got louder. "Let them come, damn it. No one is doing anything wrong except working too many hours and getting punched in the face because of it. I have no knowledge of stolen gun parts, and Laughton McNair didn't steal any. He wouldn't."

I regretted the outburst. I got up and went for the door. "I got court," I mumbled.

Parker was at my back. When we got back to our desks, Fran was hunched over his with a bullet casing in one hand and a caliper in the other.

"Parker, how many cases have you completed in the past couple of years?" I asked.

Parker cocked his head to one side and did this thing with his mouth that changed its position to the side of his face. "Five hundred, give or take."

"Me too. And maybe another thousand, give or take, completed by everyone else."

"Yeah. The backlog should be a lot more than six hundred. Man, if the captain had some of these guys ship evidence right to City Hall . . ."

"Could mess up a lot of prosecutions. But why the hell

would Cap violate protocol unless he was covering up something?"

"Damn, Muriel, the whole unit could be under scrutiny. All the cases we've worked on for the past few years could be jeopardized." Parker scrunched his nose as though smacked with a putrid smell.

"Pull Forrester in on this. He's been here longer than the rest and can help you go through the logs if we can get our hands on them at this point."

"I'll get them," Parker volunteered.

I knew he would.

The US Courthouse was a seven-minute drive down Eighth Street from the lab. I pulled into the Bourse Garage on Fourth Street, and walked the quarter mile, stopping on the way for a coffee and bagel at the Bourse Café.

I was testifying in the shooting death of Jennifer Humphries. Her boyfriend, Joseph Bonanno, said Jennifer committed suicide. The forensics evidence I was to testify about told a different story.

Joseph is the youngest son of Angelo Bonanno, a hit man for the Cosa Nostra. Joseph says he was meeting Jennifer at the Windham Hotel. When he got to the room, the door was ajar, he went in and found her dead on the floor. The prosecution contends that Joseph blew Jennifer's brains out.

I sat outside the courtroom and pulled my phone from my purse to shut it off as the bailiff opened the courtroom door and called for me. I stood up and adjusted my skirt. My normal work dress is Dickies-style work pants and a golf-type T-shirt with the FIU emblem on the left chest area, and ankle boots. For court I believe the first impression of the jury and the defense attorney happens with my first step into the courtroom. So courtroom dress is a tailored suit and three-inch heels.

"Officer Mabley, do you swear or affirm that the testimony you are about to give is the truth, the whole truth, and nothing but the truth."

Before I sat, and with my right hand raised, I replied, "I do."

The DA approached the stand. "Officer Mabley, you are an officer of the Philadelphia Police Department?"

"Yes, I am."

"To which unit are you assigned?"

"The Firearms Identification Unit."

"Officer Mabley, a position in this unit requires a considerable amount of training?"

"Yes, it does."

"Can you give us your background and training?"

I should make a recording for every time I've had to present my qualifications to the court, I thought. In eighteen years, I had testified hundreds of times and regurgitated the same spiel each time. New court, another spiel.

"My training began in the police academy, where I received extensive training on operations and care of my service revolver, with weeks of live-fire drills designed to build skill and knowledge in handling my weapon.

"My duties as a firearms examiner are to process all firearms and firearm-related evidence that is turned in or confiscated within the City of Philadelphia. All evidence is examined and compared against all like evidence. My training is a three-year process of everyday on-the-job training, which includes the history of firearms and the invention of gunpowder. During this time, I worked under a senior examiner learning the makes, models and caliber of many different firearms, the proper assembly and disassembly of many types of firearms, revolver pistols, shotguns, and rifles, along with the operation of each firearm. A mandatory part of the training is to tour the New England area to visit gun manufacturers to witness the manufacturing process from the beginning: from raw steel that is formed through the heating and cooling process to add strength to the metal, to the shaping and cutting of the lands and grooves into the barrel, which gives the bullet stability in flight and makes it possible to identify a particular projectile back to one gun, to the exclusion of all others.

"Some of the other areas I have been trained in and am considered an expert in are microscopy, which is the use of a comparison microscope, serial-number restoration, trajectory, blood-spatter analysis, distance determination through gunshot residue, and wound ballistics.

"I am an armorer for Beretta, Smith and Wesson, Sig Sauer, Hi-Point, Ruger, and Colt. I am a member of the AFTE or Association of Firearm Tool Mark Examiners, an international organization.

"I have studied with examiners from across the world and trained with the FBI, ATF, and the DEA. I have been an instructor at the Philadelphia Police Academy, the Philadelphia Office of the District Attorney for all new DAs, the Philadelphia College of Osteopathic Medicine, and Widener School of Law."

"Is there any objection to accepting this officer as an expert?" the judge said.

"No, Your Honor," the defense attorney said.

The DA approached the witness stand again. "Officer Mabley, did you have an occasion to examine the firearm that was placed on property receipt number 09572894312?" He handed the firearm to me.

I looked over the firearm. "Yes, I did. Submitted on this property receipt was a Sig Sauer forty-five-caliber ACP with a serial number of FLD-28945."

"It has been previously testified that this firearm was collected from the scene in the area of Ms. Humphries's body by Officer Ortiz of the Crime Scene Unit. What conclusion did you come to from your examination?"

"I determined that the projectile submitted on property receipt number 26454768847 by Detective Barrows of the Homicide Unit was found to be a forty-five-caliber projectile weighing 185 grains and was fired from the firearm placed on property receipt number 0957289431 2."

"And you make that determination to the exclusion of all other firearms?"

"Yes."

"Officer Mabley, you also visited the crime scene and did other studies that led to a conclusion of how Ms. Humphries died. Is that true?"

"Yes, it is."

"Can you tell us about the crime scene and then tell us about your testing and conclusions?"

"The crime scene was contained to room number 809 at the Windham Hotel at 400 Arch Street. The firearm was found near the left side of the head of Ms. Humphries."

"Where were the injuries to Ms. Humphries?"

"The projectile entered the left side of her head in the area of her temple and exited on the right rear side of her head.

"Since Ms. Humphries was shot on the left side of the head and was right-handed, it was likely that a person wanting to commit suicide would use their dominant hand. We wanted to know what would happen to the firearm if a small-framed woman used her nondominant hand to fire a large-caliber firearm. So, we used a police officer of the similar height and build as Ms. Humphries and using her nondominant hand, she tried to duplicate the incident."

I looked from the district attorney to the court and squirmed a bit when my gaze met with Angelo Bonanno's. Like I said, he's a hit man for the Cosa Nostra. This was a first for me, testifying in a case involving known Mafia members, so, yes, I squirmed.

"We found that even though Ms. Humphries was familiar with the firearm, which was in the household, it would have still been impossible for her to fire the gun and have the action cycle complete. By that I mean, the firearm goes through a process each time the trigger is pulled, and at the end of the cycle the firearm is ready to be fired again. But, our test officer, an officer trained to shoot all calibers, could not maintain the grip on the firearm to allow the energy to be properly distributed and allow the firearm to recycle.

"Second, our test officer could not duplicate the angle in which the bullet entered Ms. Humphries's head. The bullet entered the left side and traveled in a slight downward angle. Due to the size of the firearm and the length of Ms. Humphries's arm, it would have been impossible for this to have happened as the defendant stated."

The defendant, Joseph Bonanno, popped up from his seat and snarled at me. "She's lying. Jennifer killed herself." Bonanno is a short, beefy guy—standard Hollywood mobster issue. His legs barely cleared the table when he vaulted over it. The courtroom erupted in shouts and screams against the banging of the judge's gavel. Officers wrestled Bonanno to the floor as he hurled death threats toward me. When they got him settled back in his seat, he blubbered like an angry child. His glare ripped through me with all its fury.

"Mr. Bonanno, another outburst like that and you will be removed from this courtroom," the judge commanded, hollering above the roar of the audience.

When I got in my car after testifying, four missed calls showed on my cell, one from Detective Burgan and three from Hamp. I called Hamp first and left a message. I waited until I returned to work to call Burgan, who I hoped would provide information about the two guys Hamp said were hassling him about his gambling debt.

Detective Zoila Burgan runs the Mobile Street Crimes Unit, where members of FBI, DEA, and PPD work together on gang issues. We went through the academy together. I helped her through the physical challenges where she was lacking. Since then, we've seen each other at a few gatherings, and spoke by phone a few times.

Zoila bypassed any pleasantries. "Pebo 'Bandit' Miles and Murray 'Muddy' Wilson are badasses, wannabes," Burgan said. "They have been on our watch list for a while. Both have long rap sheets."

"What's their thing?"

"They're part of Berg Nation, a gang out of the Blumberg in North Philly. They are capitalizing on the heroin epidemic. Mercy, Lord." I heard her breathe in and let out a sigh. "Anyway, I'm sure you know about the violence. They murder anyone who steps out of line. Black Mafia style. We like them for three murders in South Philly, but can't prove it. Back in the nineties the Junior Black Mafia were ruthless, leaving dead bodies everywhere. It was like some Wild West antics around the Norris and Cambridge homes. They've demolished all of them now, and Blumberg is next." She hesitated, seemingly contemplating the justice in the demolitions.

"I'm aware of the history," I said. A flicker of gut-wrenching memories peeped through. My first year on the police force, I was recruited to work undercover in the Black Mafia, one of the deadliest organizations in American history. I was not recruited for my experience but rather for my young age and appearance and for being stupid enough to do it. That same innocent stupidity is what had me jumping at the "opportunity." Six months in, my cover was blown, I was turned into a heroin junky, rented out to so many men I lost count, and then dumped in an alley around the Norris Homes and left for dead. I wished I was dead during the severe, uncontrollable cold flashes, vomiting, and shitting on myself during the days before the police found me in a dumpster. I closed my eyes to the memory—seventeen years, three months, and twenty-eight days later, and still I feel the warm sensation of drugs penetrating my veins. Once an addict, always an addict.

Burgan interrupted my thoughts. "Girl, I grew up in Passyunk on the south side. Raised my kids up in the projects too. Thank God they are grown now."

"Thanks for the information on Miles and Wilson, Zoila."

"What are you into, girl?"

"I'm not sure yet, but I might be calling you again."

"No problem. I got you."

I called Travis, Dulcey, and Hamp's cells again. No answer. I left a message on each of their phones, then organized my desk and headed out.

It was four thirty when I pulled out of the parking lot, calculating twenty minutes to Dulcey's house, some time to check things out since Dulcey, Hamp, and Travis weren't answering their phones, and twenty minutes home, in time for Bethany to leave for her regular babysitting job. I jumped on I-676. Dulcey lived at 4604 Locust Street in West Philly, in a neighborhood of twin row houses, most of which needed face-lifts and paint. Dulcey's was the exception. I parked in front. Neither Dulcey's or Travis's car was there.

Her neighbor, Mrs. Harris, whose house is connected to Dulcey's, was watering flowers that lined her walkway. She used a bucket, swinging it back and forth so the water splashed out, hit the ground, and splattered mud on the hem of her pant legs. Mrs. Harris had to be crowding eighty, I guessed, and had lived next to Dulcey for the eighteen years Dulcey had been there. When I got out of the car, she took notice.

"Hi there, Muriel."

"Hey, Mrs. Harris. How you doing?"

"Oh, girl, you know, the best I can. Gettin' old and doing the best I can." She gestured to the flowers with the hand she held the water bucket in, causing water to splash over her shoes. "These flowers the only young things around here." She chuckled.

"Pretty."

"You know that Dulcey got everyone trying to make their houses beautiful. I'm not one for outdoor plants, but they sure do make a difference, I guess." She turned and shuffled back to her house. "Ain't nobody home over there."

"Thanks, Mrs. Harris," I said, getting back in the car.

I decided there was nothing to do but go home and wait for Travis. If it was something important, dangerous, worth worrying about, Travis had sense enough to call me. One of them would call.

CHAPTER 3

When I put my key in the door, screams came from inside. I dropped my bag, fingered my gun, and pushed the door open. A moment of silence gave way to fits of laughter. I exhaled. I holstered my gun and stepped back outside to retrieve my bag, dropped it by the stairs, and went down the hall to the kitchen. The twins and Bethany were putting on a freak show at the kitchen island counter.

Rose's ugly face—wide eyes, scrunched nose, and bared teeth—amplified the horror of green, brown, white, yellow, and red mush spewing from her mouth. Bethany led the gruesomeness with an uglier face and a double mound of putridness, which dripped from her mouth, accompanied by screeching and growling.

The twins squealed with delight. They covered their mouths when they saw me, unsure of my reaction to their nauseating play.

I feigned puking, to more squealing.

"We're pretending to eat humans," Helen explained. "Want to have some?" She scooped up the last spoonful of the mixture from her bowl and held it up to me.

"Humans are not my favorite," I confessed, "unless, of course, they are little girls with big eyes and ponytails cut up into tiny pieces and doused with hot sauce." I made my own ugly face and growled at them, to their enjoyment and my mortification.

Bethany's recipe included Kraft macaroni and cheese, tomatoes, spinach, chocolate chip cookies, and cherry Kool-Aid. Yuck. What else could I say? They cleaned their bowls.

Fact is, the twins were spindly. They did not eat or like anything edible except chocolate chip cookies, so seeing them fill their mouths with any kind of food that had some nutritional value registered as a blessing.

"Travis hasn't called, Auntie," Rose said, slurping up the last of the mush from her bowl.

"We tried to call him but he didn't answer, so we left a message but he hasn't called back," Helen added.

"He'll be home soon," I said, more to myself than them.

Satisfied with my answer, the twins charged into the den to watch a most appropriate television program for nine-year-old girls who want to solve all the crime in Philadelphia, then the world: *Cops*. I could hear Nareece in my head ranting about my selfishness for letting her little darlings see such a perverted program that only encouraged their demonic behavior.

"How about some plain macaroni and cheese, Miss Mabley?" Bethany offered. I sat at the table and watched her pull a plate from the cabinet and fill it with macaroni and cheese. "Here you go, plain."

Unconvinced of its purity, I moved the food around on the plate a few times before deciding it was safe for eating. A spoonful ignited my hunger, the slop taking on flavors of filet mignon and mashed potato. If only it were true.

Bethany cleared the table and filled the dishwasher. She left, vowing to help the twins solve their latest case the next time she babysat.

Halfway through the second bowl, the macaroni and cheese

regained its true flavor and got dumped down the garbage disposal. I wiped down the counters and stove, then went into the den. The twins were stretched out on the floor, now engrossed in *Terminator Genisys,* their chins resting on upturned palms.

A dull ache crept up the back of my head. My fingers grazed over a small lump where my head had slammed into the pool deck. It was sore. I attempted to stretch out on the couch; instead jumped up, having been speared in the butt by the handle of a magnifying glass stuck between the cushions. The twins stayed glued to their movie, oblivious to my plight. I felt around for other Twofer Detective Agency paraphernalia. I settled back down and closed my eyes to the sounds of explosions, machine-gun fire, and loud voices swearing death to the bad guys.

I press my sweaty finger against the trigger. My arms shimmy under the weight of the .44 Magnum. A cold breeze presses against my shoulders. I twist around, and back and around again, and drop my gun. A twisted, snarling face floats in suspended light, toward me. I fall to the floor and feel for my gun. Hands grab at my body, pull my hair. I slide across the floor. My fingers feel the cold metal. I pull the trigger.

I bolted upright and jerked around in every direction, whipping through the uneasiness of not remembering where I was. The muted light from the television gave a spooky aura to the surroundings. The familiar sound of news anchor Monique Braxton interviewing witnesses to a shooting in North Philly eased my tension.

Twenty years on the force and I had never fired my gun. That is, until I killed Jesse Boone. Even though I celebrated his death, a boulder of guilt pressed squarely on my spirit.

The psychologist had said something about me being human, that the worry would be if it did not phase me at all. For me, I wanted uninterrupted sleep, without it being plagued by nightmares.

My phone buzzed on the glass coffee table. Calvin's name showed on the screen—my love, all five foot ten, 210 pounds of gorgeous, sexy, courageous, passionate, luscious man. Did I mention the man makes me scream in glorious, agonizing ecstasy when we make love?

Calvin owns a nightclub—Calvin's Place—where we met almost a year ago. Sometimes he headlines as the entertainment, showboating his Barry White–sounding self. Hmph. Hmph. Hmph. Make a woman of sound mind and body faint.

"Love that sleepy voice. Sounds like I woke you." His voice sparked goose bumps.

I took a deep breath and got comfortable. "I just woke up. I called myself watching TV with the twins. What time is it?"

"Going on eleven thirty. Long day, huh?"

"Crazy day. I tackled this guy at the pool this morning and he tackled me back."

"Baby, how you gonna tackle some guy, as little as you are?"

"Thanks for the compliment. The little part. But hey, I'm a hundred and forty pounds of might."

"I'd love to tackle those hundred and forty pounds of might."

"I could handle that right about now; long, slow, gentle tackling."

"A romantic dinner, sweet aromatic wine to tantalize your taste buds and satisfy your animal cravings before I ravish your body."

"Mmm, I am incapable of resisting that offer."

A few more minutes of sexual banter before making a dinner date for Saturday, left me relaxed and horny. I slid off the couch in slow motion to avoid a resurgence of head pain and tripped up the stairs to check on the twins. They were in their beds reading.

"Why didn't you wake me before you came up?" I asked.

"We didn't want to disturb you, Auntie. We know you had a

long day and are worried about Travis. We were waiting for you, though, so we could say our prayers," Rose said.

"Well, that's very thoughtful, but you-all don't have to worry about me. It's my job to worry about you guys and Travis. Now c'mon, prayers." We knelt beside Rose's bed, one on each side of me, and began.

They said in unison, "Now I lay me down to sleep. I pray the Lord my soul to keep. If I should die before I wake, I pray the Lord my soul to take. God, please make Mommy better and bring her home. And give Daddy a kiss and hug from us, and keep Auntie and Travis safe. We love you. In Jesus's name we pray. Amen."

I kissed them and tucked them in, before I closed the door and returned to lying on the couch. A check of my phone showed 11:50 p.m. Worry resurfaced. I tried Travis's phone again. Still no answer. The same with Dulcey's and Hamp's phones.

An hour later, Travis stumbled in.

"I must have called your phone ten times," I said, trying to temper my tone. "What the hell is going on? Hamp and Dulcey didn't answer their phones either."

"My phone didn't have any juice." Travis plopped down at my feet and rested his head back. "Ma, Aunt Dulcey and Hamp got serious problems. Why he called me I don't know since they're telling me not to say anything to you cuz they don't want you to get involved."

"What do you mean they don't want me involved?" I sat up and swung my legs around, ready to pounce.

"Don't go off on me, please. I spent hours dealing with the two of them. I had to keep Aunt Dulcey from killing Uncle Hamp." He gave me a sideways look. "David against Goliath."

Dulcey was six one and a half, 200 pounds. Hamp was five eight, 160 pounds soaking wet. Travis was a little taller than Dulcey at six two, 180 pounds, but still no match. Yep, my girl had them. I know even if they attacked her together they would get pounded. What Dulcey wants, Dulcey gets, except for what she had now.

"Can we do this in the morning, please?"

"Boy, you better start talking and hope I don't have too many questions when you're done." I massaged my temples in anticipation of a tale that would only escalate the throbbing.

Travis pushed back on the couch and put his feet on the coffee table. "So I was messing around with the twins when Uncle Hamp called. It didn't even sound like him. He sounded high. He talked all crazy—said Aunt Dulcey was dying and he would die without her. Said he needed to handle some trouble. I'm thinking it's seven thirty a.m., how bad can he be? I picked him up at the Red Star, a dive on Mifflin on the south side. I picked him up cuz I thought he wanted me to take him home. I would have brought Rose and Helen with me, but I know that area definitely ain't cool and like I said, Uncle Hamp sounded off the chain. Anyway, I figured I wouldn't be gone more than an hour—pick him up, drop him off. He cussed me out for taking so long getting there, then begged me not to take him home. Said Aunt Dulcey would kill him if she knew what he did, only to keep her happy, especially now, since she's so sick. I did not plan to go up against Aunt Dulcey, no matter what he said."

"What's he into? Drugs again? And where the hell else would you take him?"

"Just hold on, Ma. Chill and let me finish. When he got in the car he was real nervous, like he was scared. Directed me down back roads and alleyways, and through parking lots. Said he thought someone might be following us. When we got to the house the first time, Aunt Dulcey wasn't home. He asked me to wait while he changed and then take him to a meeting or something. It took him forever to get ready. Man is worse than a woman, I swear."

"Where'd you take him?"

"Will you please just let me finish?"

"Well, go on then. Finish."

"I took him to some joint on the north side. We sat in there for hours waiting for somebody who never came."

"What do you mean you sat in there for hours? Doing what?"

"Nothing. Uncle Hamp had a few drinks. We shot some pool. Ate some chicken wings."

"And never once did it occur to you to call me?"

"Mom, my phone was dead."

"Hamp has a phone."

"Don't you think I asked him? He said he left his phone at the house. And the pay phone was busted."

"Right."

"Do you want to hear the rest of the story or are you just going to jam my behind?"

"Go ahead."

"When we left, I took him home. Aunt Dulcey was waiting at the door. Going in did not even enter my brain, but Uncle Hamp wouldn't let me leave. Said I was the only thing that was going to save him from Aunt Dulcey killing him. It took everything I had to keep her from backing up on him. And I do mean she was seriously going to kill the man."

"Why was she so upset?"

"She thinks Uncle Hamp is using again," Travis said.

"Shit, I was afraid of that."

"She said she'd rather see him dead than stuck in that game again. The neighbors must've called the cops with all the hollerin' and cussin' going on, and Aunt Dulcey almost got hauled off to jail. She was crying and promised not to bother Uncle Hamp anymore. Said she's too sick to care, which is a lie. She cares. Then you know Aunt Dulcey had to cook some food, and made me eat. When I left she was in one room sleeping and Uncle Hamp was in another."

"What is Hamp thinking with all this nonsense, when Dulcey is fighting for her life?"

"Ma, I actually had a good time hanging with Uncle Hamp. He is my godfather, after all."

"Yes. What was I thinking."

"I think Uncle Hamp got more going on than he's talking. I ain't never seen him freakin' out like he was." He hesitated before asking, with a brighter tone, "My girls are good?"

"Yeah, your girls are fine."

"Well, I'm wiped, so I'm saying good night." He got up and bent down to kiss me. "I love you."

"Love you too. Good night."

I toyed with calling Dulcey, then decided I would wait for her call in the morning. I shut the television off and went to the kitchen for a glass of water, shutting the lights on the way. When I got to the stairway, Travis sat on a step halfway up.

"Ma, that ain't everything. I wasn't going to say anything about this, cuz I didn't want Uncle Hamp to be salted, but . . ."

"Travis, baby, just tell me."

"When I drove away I passed this hooked-up Beamer 650 coupe, parked down the street. A woman was behind the wheel. When I got to the corner, I checked my rearview mirror. She pulled to the house and Uncle Hamp came out and got in and they split. I turned around and drove back by the house but the house was dark, so I figured Aunt Dulcey's resting, right? I didn't want to, you know, make anything more of it and get her riled up again."

For a moment I couldn't speak, so we both hung out in the silence, staring at each other until I worked through my disbelief and waved at him to go on to bed. I let Travis's words hammer my brain for a few minutes before I shook them off. I shut the lights out and went upstairs. Hamp having an affair? Ridiculous.

CHAPTER 4

The ringing grew louder and louder. I rolled over, refusing the nudge to wake up. The ringing stopped. A blissful sigh turned into a moan when it rang again. Dulcey at 5:30 a.m. As soon as I answered, she started crying, only the second time I ever heard tell. The first time was when Travis said she cried the night before.

"Muriel, the man has lost his ever-loving mind." Dulcey sniffed so hard her nose honked. "I swear I woulda killed him last night if Travis had not a been here. The boy musta tole you all what went on here. I'm sorry he had to be a part of all that."

"Dulce, Travis is good with all that, I mean being able to help, but you can't be worrying about Hamp's mess now. You got enough to do."

"How can I not worry about the man when he's up in my face, actin' the fool?"

"Where is he now?"

"He's gone. Where else but at the boat most likely, where he always runs to. And I'm up here sniveling like some schoolgirl. I need to go to the shop and focus on hair, get my mind off that fool."

Hamp and Dulcey owned a twenty-eight-foot cabin cruiser,

the *Dulcey Maria*, which they moored at Penn's Landing. Dulcey owned Dulcey's Beauty Spa, a hair, nail, and skin salon at Fairmont and Fifth Avenue.

"You can run but you can't hide," I halfheartedly joked.

"I know that's right. I'll see you later. I'll be by about two."

I fell back to sleep until the twins came bounding into my room and turned the television to cartoons. They slipped under the covers, one on either side of me, and got comfortable. I dozed a few more times before the alarm went off at eight thirty.

By ten, we were on our way to Penn Center, the long-term care facility on Chestnut Street, to see Nareece.

When we arrived at her room, Nareece was sitting in a wheelchair pushed up to a table, eating breakfast—or brunch, given the late-morning hour. Rather, she was being fed by Nurse Diana.

Not that she can't feed herself; more like she chooses not to. Physically there is nothing wrong with her. Emotionally, she's racked with guilt, shame, horror, and God knows what else because of Jesse Boone. And so she's vegging, mostly unresponsive. Doctors call it conversion disorder and say she could recover and be back to her old self at any time—that is, when she decides.

The small, private room had a large window at the far end that brightened the room and made cheery the otherwise drab décor that included putrid-green walls and old-fashioned flowery curtains from great-grandma's house. The good news: Her room faced west, so sunshine filled the space most of the day.

The twins bounded into the room, disrupting the feeding process, though not because Nareece made any moves toward them. She remained still, like a statue, while food dripped from her bottom lip to her lap. Rose picked up her napkin and dabbed at her mouth. Usually, I fed her while the twins jabbered on about events that had taken place since their last visit. Today we were late. I got up to her face, nose to nose. Somehow her blank look held a glint of recognition, distant yet there. I swear I saw a flash of anger—because of our tardiness, maybe.

"Hey, sis. Sorry we're late."

"She's been a little resistant this morning," Nurse Diana said, trading places with me so I could take over the feeding. "She's only had a few mouthfuls."

I filled the spoon with some oatmeal and put it to her mouth. Nareece clamped her lips shut and tightened her fists, a sign her awareness had improved, even if it was to blow me off.

"I guess you've had enough, huh?" I pulled her wheelchair away from the table. "We'll get you cleaned up and go for a walk outside, get some fresh air. Can't stay long. The girls are going to spend the day with Mr. Kim, from my old neighborhood."

"Yeah, Mom. We're going to go sightseeing with Mr. Kim and Hana. Mr. Kim is going to take us to the aquarium," Helen said. Rose continued to dab at her mother's mouth and wipe her chin. She cleaned off her nightgown too, where some oatmeal had spilled.

"C'mon, baby." I tapped her forehead. "You're in there, listening to me and the kids. It's time to come out of there. It's time to move on."

Silence.

I left the girls to talk to her and went into the bathroom to draw a bubble bath. When I came out, Nareece held Rose in her lap and Helen stood behind her chair, brushing her hair. I turned the television on and changed the channel to cartoons.

The twins stopped what they were doing and got comfortable on the bed, while I helped Nareece up and guided her to the bathroom.

"Pretty soon you'll be home with us. You'll see, everything will be right again," I whispered to Nareece.

I slipped her granny nightgown off over her head and eased her skinny frame down into the warm bath water. The twins weighed more than she did. Scars spanned her chest and down the center of her body to her groin. My eyes watered. Not because of the look of them, but because of the memories they evoked. She took the soap and facecloth from me and began washing herself. I went to grab the facecloth back, then realized what was happening. After she wiped her face, she dropped the facecloth in the water and stilled her movements again. I helped her out of the tub, dried her, and rubbed lotion over her body.

After I dressed her, we all went for a walk around the hospital grounds. Nareece walked part of the way with a twin on either side of her holding her hand, while I pushed the wheelchair. Halfway around the hospital grounds she dropped anchor and took to the wheelchair. That was the thing—she moved around when she wanted to, but she wouldn't look at you, or speak, or even look like anything anyone said was getting through. The good news was, she was becoming more active with each visit.

The twins pushed her in the wheelchair, talking to her as though she'd respond. And then she smiled. We all saw it. We exchanged gazes but did not say anything. By the time we got back to the room, her blank expression had returned.

❧ ● ☙

We arrived at Mr. Kim's at one thirty. Mr. Kim, my neighbor for fifteen years, also held the distinction of being my self-defense instructor, the neighborhood security, and my friend. I owned the vacant twin house a grassy yard away from Mr. Kim's house. We moved out a week ago. The decision to sell or rent waged war in my brain. I'm not sure why I hesitated selling since housing prices were up more than they had been in a decade. Still, I needed more time.

Our houses looked the same on the outside. Inside, Mr. Kim's took you on a journey, which beckoned at the opening of the front door.

Hana, a tinier version of Mr. Kim, answered the door and bowed to welcome us. She grabbed a hand of each twin and pulled them in. Stepping across the threshold, shoeless, was stepping into a sanctuary of calm. The open space of shiny blond hardwood floors and sleek modern and antique pieces of Korean-style furniture created an elegantly sparse chamber. My favorite was an antique two-piece stacking chest made of elm wood with persimmon-wood panels. Mr. Kim had promised it to me when I reached black belt status.

I had been doing Tae Kwon Do with Kim for five years, the last year as a black belt apprentice, harboring much anxiety over the looming black belt test, despite Mr. Kim's assurance of my readiness.

Mr. Kim stood center room. The twins, at nine years old, were bigger than Mr. Kim, but Bruce Lee could not match the man's might and skill as the ultimate grand master of martial arts.

"Welcome."

"Hi, Mr. Kim," the twins said in unison, bowing simultaneously.

The twins kissed me goodbye and followed Hana upstairs, giggling all the way. Not running and howling in their home way, but walking and covering their mouths to muffle the sounds of their giggles.

I turned to Mr. Kim. It was weird how he knew things.

"Come, sit," he said, ushering me into the dining area.

The cherrywood table was long and thin with wide, short legs. It was flanked by four low, cushioned chairs. When I sat, or rather fell, into the chair, I was Mr. Kim's height. Mr. Kim approached from behind and pressed his fingers into the sides of my head and temples. The relief was immediate. I closed my eyes and let the glimmer of peacefulness take me away, for a moment, before Mr. Kim's voice registered.

"Miss Muriel, I have a favor to ask of you. I am ashamed . . ."

"Mr. Kim, we've been friends too long to talk about shame." I modulated my voice so as not to disrespect. "You got my back, I got yours."

"Yes." He hesitated while moving his miracle fingers to my shoulders. A deep sorrow hugged the silence. I reached up and stopped his hands. I shifted around in my seat to face him.

"It's Karin. She left two nights ago to go out and has not returned. I am concerned." Like me, he had begun a new phase when his daughter, Karin, and granddaughter, Hana, moved in with him. They had arrived from California six months earlier.

Even Mr. Kim's strength was no match to the challenge of Karin, who had come home way harder and more haggard than the bright-eyed, spunky, ready-to-take-on-the-world twenty-year-old who left five years ago. This was the third time Karin had disappeared.

I knew that my best advice to call the police and report her missing was not acceptable. It was not the Mr. Kim way.

"The child has been very upset about her mother. I am sure that the twins being here today will help her. However, without her mother here . . ."

I struggled to stand until Mr. Kim reached out a hand and touched my fingers. I rose from my seat without a hitch.

"She needs to go into rehab, Mr. Kim. You can't help her unless she decides that's what she wants to do." He turned his back to me. "It's the only way she'll even begin to recover." I walked around to face him.

Mr. Kim's stoic expression did not waiver.

"I'll check around for Karin. Where was she going when she left?"

"She was going to a nightclub downtown, but I am not aware of which one."

"Who'd she leave with?"

"I believe a gentleman picked her up. But he did not come in. I have called all hospitals. The possible outcome of my request may be difficult to hear. It will be more comfort than not knowing."

"I'm sure—"

"Let us not speculate about those things that we do not know but can only hope."

When I returned home, Travis and his friends, Elijah and Sam, were in the living room preparing to leave. Sam walked up on me and kissed my cheek. Sam had been coming around since first grade.

"Good to see you, Miss M. My mom says hello."

"It's been awhile, Sam. Everything good?"

"Yes, ma'am."

Elijah bolted up from the couch and stepped in front of me, blocking my path. "Hey, Miss Mabley. Nice to meet you again." He bowed as though honoring a queen.

"Elijah."

"You look lovely as usual," he said with what I categorized as a devious smirk.

"Thank you." I moved toward him. He moved aside.

"Where are you guys headed?" I said to Travis.

"We're going to play a little basketball and hang out for a while," Travis said, planting a kiss on my cheek.

"I'm sure I'll see you again soon," Elijah said, backing out the front door.

Ah, the simple joy of being home alone. I giggled my way to the kitchen and snagged the container of watermelon sherbet from the freezer, a bowl, and spoon. My plan included being couch comfortable and bingeing on movies until Dulcey arrived.

Bingeing on movies lasted a minute before I clocked out. I woke to Dulcey pounding on the door and yelling my name. I felt groggy, in a dreamlike state. I checked the time on my phone: 2:38. I slid off the couch, stubbed my toe on the leg of the coffee table, and hopped the rest of the way to the door before Dulcey broke through it.

"I was about to break the damn door down," Dulcey huffed, blowing by me. "I'm late, as usual, but my baby called and we talked for a few hours," she said. She unpacked a bottle of Sauvion Vouvray and uncorked it, then poured me a glass, while I set the teapot on the stove. Tea had become her drug of choice since the onslaught of chemotherapy treatments. I watched her twitch around in silence, the sound of her flip-flops snapping against the floor and her heel, checking out the boxes in the kitchen that needed unpacking. She finally took a seat at the island.

"I can't believe you're not unpacked yet. Looks like you're getting ready to move out." She cackled for a second before she got serious. "You need some Dulcey help around here so you can put your head on straight. Besides, I might have to take up residence with you if that Negro of mine keeps up his nonsense." She stopped moving around and looked at me with her hands hugging her hips. "You are a mess, girl. You look like something left over from the night before."

That was her usual statement to me if I had not seen her in a week's time—that is, allowed her to do my hair in that time period. I had a standing home appointment—one, because I could never find the time to get to her shop, and two, because it was our time.

It was Dulcey who was going through chemotherapy and radiation and the sickness of breast cancer treatment, and here she was making sure I was all good. There was no arguing with her though. Following directions is the best therapy you can offer her.

I took a seat at the counter across from her.

"The man is talking all kinds of nonsense, telling me he's fine and just working out a few problems that I don't need to concern myself about. Says he ain't coming home until he has made things right. Problem is, he ain't tellin' me what those things are."

I stayed silent. When Dulcey needs to talk, you gotta just let her belt it all out.

"I wanted to end his life last night. 'Course, I couldn't live without him. Live and die for that man, no matter. He just gets so crazy sometimes and makes my hair, when I had hair"—she hesitated before continuing—"stand on end, looking like some kind of orangutan." She snorted through tears.

I helped her into the den to sit on the couch. Then I went back into the kitchen and got a paper towel for her. "Hamp is not going to do anything that will hurt you. And he's definitely not leaving you. The man is crazier than crazy about you."

"I can't believe I'm sniveling like this." Dulcey blew her nose, sounding like there was no possible way it would ever need blowing again.

"I can't believe it either," I said. "All these years, I have never seen or heard about you crying until now. Let it go, girl. Let them eyes puff up, those cheeks berry up, and your nose fill up with snot. Go ahead, don't be shy. I've seen everything else you ever put out."

Dulcey slapped at the air in my direction and we laughed.

She almost choked from her cackling, then she got serious and said, "He said he's going to call you."

"I'll help him with whatever I can when he does."

"So now tell me how that man of yours is and how your training for that tree-ath-a-lon is going."

I talked about my training progress, and how my first time swimming in the Schuylkill, or any other body of water besides a pool, was happening in two weeks. I decided it best not to tell her about the incident at the pool, since it would only promote worry and give her reason to mother me.

"Between the training and the girls, my butt be worn out," I said.

"Those young ladies need their momma. How's she doing?"

"The same. We were there this morning. I swear, Dulcey, she looked different in her eyes, like she was hearing me. By the time I got her washed and dressed and we went for a walk, she smiled once, but then she was back looking like she was a million miles away."

"She'll come back. No way she's gonna stay away from her babies for too long. I pray for that girl day and night and I know God is going to help her find her way back. Ain't no Jesse Boone gonna have the last word in this story."

My phone buzzed. It was Calvin.

"Hello, baby," I said in my sweet-lady voice—the kind that says I'm horny and happy to hear from you. Dulcey wrinkled her face and mimed the way I said hello to Calvin, pursing her lips and rocking her arms back and forth. I slapped the air in her direction.

After I confirmed our date and I hung up, Dulcey said, "Sounds like you two got it going on pretty good."

"Sometimes he doesn't hit me quite right. I can't put my finger on it, but . . . maybe it's the secrecy, you know, he's into more than he lets on and won't share with me. 'If I tell you I'll have to kill you' has gotten old. Some mystery about a man might be good for some, but not me. I want to know it all."

"Oh, hush your fuss, girl. You looking for perfection and that ain't happenin' ever. It ain't possible. Except maybe Laughton McNair. Yes, Lord, that man there was as close to perfect as they come."

"Don't start, Dulcey."

"You're right. Men—don't want to live with them and don't want to live without them," Dulcey said and cracked up. I shook my head at her. "So what's he done that's got you tight? Girl, all you talked about a minute ago was how the man made you scream." Dulcey was on her feet, swaying her hips and arms. "What more could a woman ask for?" She plopped down on the couch again. "Hmm. Maybe Hamp is a good deal."

"Ha! Hamp knows that if he doesn't get his act together he won't be around much longer to live up to being anybody's good deal."

"Time for more vino," Dulcey said, getting up. "C'mon, I'll do something with that mop on your head while we sip." She gave me a sideways glance. "While you sip. I bet you been wearing that ponytail all week. You can't go out with that fine thang, looking like who done it."

"I don't have to go out tonight. I can stay here."

"For what? I'ma go home and get in my bed and watch my programs after I fix you up."

"I just haven't had time . . ."

"Shut it and come on in here."

I was blessed with enough hair to provide locks for at least two other women and cursed with the inability to care for it. Without Dulcey, I'd go bald.

A third glass of wine and a head full of curls later, a thud against the front door had us charging to it, braced for battle. When I opened it, Travis stumbled in holding Elijah up, Elijah's face bruised and bloodied.

CHAPTER 5

I buckled under their weight. If Dulcey had not been at my back, we would all have been on the floor. The smell of alcohol and weed pounced on my nose, strong enough to make my eyes water.

I should let them both fall and crack their heads, might slam some sense into them, I thought. Dulcey about lifted both of them off their feet and dragged them to the couch, kicking boxes out of her way as she stepped. Travis mumbled, and Elijah was unresponsive.

I stepped outside the door and saw someone exit Travis's car. Another car waited. At least the boy had sense enough not to drive.

When I went back inside, Dulcey was dabbing at Elijah's face with a wet towel. I raced upstairs and came back with some hydrogen peroxide and a topical antiseptic solution, A & D first aid ointment, Neosporin, bandages, and Band-Aids. What initially looked like someone had ripped the flesh from Elijah's face, with the amount of blood there was, turned out to be a slash across his right cheek—maybe from a fall or a fist. It was not likely we'd find out until tomorrow. While he lay comatose with his mouth spread open, foul breath killing the air,

Dulcey cleaned and fixed butterfly bandages across the cut on his cheek to hold it together and stop the bleeding.

Dulcey stood, shaking her head, her hands planted securely on her hips, and perused the damaged goods. "They are gonna be miserable in the morning," she whispered, as though a louder tone could faze their drunk selves.

"Miserable will be the least of their problems when I'm done with them," I said in a loud voice, almost yelling, wanting them to be fazed. Neither budged. I continued in a softer voice. "The good news is they had sense enough not to drive."

Dulcey gave me a sideways glance of disapproval—of me, not Travis or Elijah—and proceeded to clean up the papers and bloody cloths from the coffee table. "Might as well take them up to bed," I said, ignoring her judgment.

"Muriel, lighten up," she snapped. "So they're a little drunk. Like you said, they had sense enough not to drive, so everybody's all right."

I grunted with disgust as Dulcey helped Elijah up from the couch and I tended to Travis, pushing and pulling him by his arm, shirt, head, until he tackled the bed.

We went back downstairs and Dulcey styled my hair. Just as she finished, Calvin rang the bell. I left Dulcey to answer the door while I ran upstairs to change.

Calvin was an excellent cook, more for me to pine over. Not that I couldn't cook, but I preferred leaving that task to someone else. Eating was my specialty. He also liked to dine at the most elite restaurants in Philly. Tonight it was Vetri, an intimate, five-star Italian restaurant in South Philly. As always, no matter where we went, the doormen and staff knew Calvin. Obama and Michelle would not have fared any better at Vetri.

Calvin had ordered ahead, our private menu of veal tartar

with sweetbreads, linguini with zucchini and *bottarga*—salted, cured fish roe, what Italians call a poor man's caviar—dry-aged ribeye, and for dessert, strawberry zuppa inglese. Ignorance messed with me until each dish was served and I tasted it. Perfect. With Calvin, it was always perfect. I passed up the wine, still woozy from the three glasses I had with Dulcey. After the dinner and drink orders were confirmed, Calvin took my hand and stared at me, as though lost in the pools of my eyes, or something like that, which would have been sensual except I noticed the tension stretched across his brow.

"You are always so refreshing," Calvin said.

"Refreshing can't take away that look behind the one you're trying to pass off as being so into me and my gorgeousness."

"Already you are too in tune to me." He rubbed my hands between his. "I'm thinking of closing the center," he said. He let me go and slugged back his wine.

Besides the club, Calvin operated a center for troubled youth, a safe harbor for kids being threatened by gangs because they didn't want to join or because they wanted out.

"The programs are focusing more on rehab for heroin addicts these days. I can't deal with these kids on that level. They need a different kind of help than I can give them. Besides, I'm getting too damn old."

Two waiters came to the table. One held the tray of food while the other served us. After the waiters left, Calvin continued.

"The strain of heroin out there now is killing them. Heroin mixed with fentanyl and cocaine, a deadly combination. The mix makes it easy to OD. Three kids in one week." He put his fork down and shook his head in slow motion. "The sweetest little lady. They shot her up and dumped her in a pile of trash over off West Jefferson." He teared up, then shrugged it off, and dove into the food.

"I am so sorry, Calvin."

"The way to stop it is not through the center. These kids

need professional, medical help, and I need to do what I do—
bust the flow."

I woke to voices and laughter from the kitchen. Rose and
Helen were eating bacon and eggs that Travis had cooked and
mimicking Bethany and Travis. Rose was Bethany, Helen was
Travis.

"Oh, honey, I think you're cute," Helen said, in the lowest
baritone voice she could put forth.

"I think you're sooo handsome," Rose responded, putting
her hands together under her chin and batting her eyes.

Travis sat at the head of the island, shaking his head and
laughing. "Don't you guys ever let Kenyetta catch you talking
this mess. You-all know she's my girl. Man, I'll have to listen to
her mouth forever," he said.

The laughter subsided when I entered the kitchen.

"Hi, Auntie," they said in unison. "Travis loves Bethany and
Kenyetta."

"He can only have one of them," Rose said insistently. "I
think he loves Kenyetta more, so he should tell Bethany that
she is not the girl for him."

"I think that is enough talk about girlfriends and love. Finish eating and go on upstairs and dress for church," I told
them. They both took another mouthful of food and raced out,
vowing to be the first one in the shower. I sat at the table and
Travis put a plate of pancakes and scrambled eggs in front of me.
I ate while he cleared the twins' plates from the table and loaded
the dishwasher, then took a seat across the table from me.

"Ma, before you even say anything, I apologize. We were
blasted last night and I'm sorry. We were at this mad party and
things just got crazy. Elijah's brother came in with some of his
boys, messin' around and talking shit."

I stopped chewing.

"Talking mess. Sorry, didn't mean to swear."

"Who is Elijah's brother?"

"He's a gangbanger. Runs with Berg Nation. He made Elijah go outside with him, and next thing I know Elijah comes back all beat up. He goes for the drink and smoke getting passed around, and next thing he's acting like a fool. He wouldn't leave until he was so messed up I had to carry him out."

"You weren't in much better shape."

"I swear I didn't have that much to drink. Just seemed like in a minute I was drunk."

"Yeah, it happens like that sometimes," I said, trying to empathize.

"Look, Ma. Elijah's trying to stay out of the gang and his brother wants him in."

"Where're his parents?"

"He said he doesn't have any. Said they died. His father was a gang member and was killed and his mother OD'd on heroin. His brother is the only family he has. He's been sleeping outside because he doesn't want to be in a gang or involved with one. I feel bad for the dude, so I been trying to help him out, let him hang with me. Feed him, give him clothes. I took him to Calvin's center."

"Why didn't you tell me all this before?"

"He didn't want me to tell you because you're the po po, I guess."

"The po po, huh? You put yourself in a dangerous position."

"What am I supposed to do? Dis him and just let the brother die, when all he wants to do is live a normal life, go to school and make something of himself? Is that what you're telling me?"

"I thought you said you met Elijah at the basketball courts."

"I did, but he just kinda kept coming around. He's a good kid, Ma. He just needs somebody to be there for him."

"Be there how, son? You getting between him and his brother could be trouble."

"His brother doesn't care about me."

"If he doesn't now, he will."

"Elijah is eighteen. He's in his senior year at Central High and he's a straight-A student. He wants to go to college and move away."

"Why Elijah? Why you?"

"Maybe cuz all the other dudes bullied him and shoved him around, until I stepped in and got them to let him play. He is a beast at b-ball. Then everybody liked him and wanted him on their team."

"So where did he go last night?"

"He was gone when I woke up."

"We'll talk about this some more later. Is he coming here today?"

Before Travis could answer, the doorbell rang. Travis went to get the door. Elijah followed him into the kitchen. He had on the same clothes as the day before, disheveled, dirty, and smelling like garbage. His face was swollen where the cut was; his eye was black and blue.

"Hello, Miss Mabley."

"Hi, Elijah."

"Please accept my apology for my behavior last night. And thank you for fixing my face."

"Sit down, man. You gotta be hungry," Travis said, signaling me behind Elijah's back to not say anything.

I got up to leave. "Eat, Elijah. You're going to church with us. Travis will give you some clothes."

"Thank you, Miss Mabley. I am very thankful that Travis brought me here. I'm humbled by your kindness."

Always so damn polite, I thought. *Too damn polite.*

Rose won the shower first, since Helen was sitting cross-legged in the middle of her bed, watching Sunday morning news and typing on her computer when I stuck my head in the room.

"Auntie, is it okay to ask God to kill somebody?" Helen asked.

"Who do you want to kill?"

"Just in case, I mean."

"Just in case of what?"

"Just in case somebody threatens Rose or Travis and tries to hurt us."

"What makes you think anyone would?"

Helen raised her arms above her head. "Auntie, someone already tried to kill Mummy."

I went to her and hugged her hard. "Well, nobody is going to kill or even hurt Rose or you or Travis or any of us. And your mom is going to be fine. And, yes, baby, you can ask God for anything. But better you ask him to forgive the bad people and help them be good than to kill them."

"Nope. If someone hurt my family I'd want God to kill them, like you killed the man who hurt Mummy."

What could I say to that? I sat next to her on the bed and cupped her chin so she focused only on me. "First of all, nobody is going to hurt anybody in this house because God's got you. And I got you too."

She kissed my cheek and wriggled in her spot, a slight grin adorning her lips. I sighed and left her resettled into watching television and typing on her computer.

I showered and put on what I call my church suit—a Donna Vinci, mint-green, calf-length fitted skirt with a one-button flared jacket and beige spike heels.

Travis was still helping Elijah find some clothes when I knocked on his door on the way downstairs. Helen was fixing Rose's hair. When I got to the bottom stair, the scratching of someone cranking the doorknob back and forth drew my attention. Thinking it was Dulcey, who probably decided to come over rather than wait for me to pick her up, I yanked the door open.

"Girl, why didn't you . . ." I stepped back and tensed, holding tight to the doorknob. "Can I help you?"

"I'm looking for Elijah."

"And you are?"

He took a step closer. I braced myself.

"Ward Griffin. Elijah's my brother," he snarled.

Of course he was, the same round face accented with dark brown eyes, fine pointy nose and squared chin, perfect eyebrows, and eyelashes the envy of any girl. Different was the scar running across the right side of his face, from temple to jaw.

He squinted and gave me the once-over, as though trying to decide how much force it would take to stomp me. I readied to plant a spike heel in his flesh.

"Look, lady, I don't give a fuck who you are, I want to talk to Elijah. He didn't come home last night and I want to make sure he's good."

"He's good. I'll tell him you were here and have him call you when he comes out of the bathroom." I moved to close the door. He put his hand out to stop it from closing.

"You tell him if he ever shows his face around the Berg again, he's dead." He flipped his head away and spat, then spun around and left.

When I closed the door and turned around, Elijah was at the top of the stairs looking down at me. He sat on the step and held his head in his hands and cried.

"That's my brother and he wants to kill me. He's all I've got and he wants to kill me."

I climbed the stairs and sat next to him, putting my arm around his shoulders. He leaned into me.

"My mother died with a needle sticking out from in between her toes because her veins were shot. I found her." He sniffed.

"My father was an addict. He got killed for a fix. Oh man! My brother's an addict and makes it so other people become addicts. I can't . . . I can't go there. I don't want to be an addict. I don't want to play that."

I held Elijah through his torturous tears.

"You won't have to, son. I got you."

CHAPTER 6

Dulcey was standing on the covered porch outside her house when I pulled Bertha—what I call my 2000 Saab gray convertible—curbside with the twins singing their version of "How Great Thou Art," loud enough to make even God say hush. Surprise, surprise, Hampton stepped out the door, starred and shined in African garb, and grabbed ahold of Dulcey's arm. Dulcey wore African garb as well—a purple George swing coat and pants trimmed in gold, with a matching turban-style head wrap. Girlfriend took the stairs with the swagger of royalty. Halfway down the walkway, Hampton let her go and hustled toward the car, as a gentleman for his queen.

"Hi, Auntie Dulcey," the twins squealed when she approached. She scanned the backseat. "You two are beautiful young ladies," Dulcey cooed. "Where is Mr. Travis?"

"Thank you. Auntie took us shopping for camp next week and bought us these new dresses for church too," Rose explained. She was usually the spokesperson when they weren't speaking in unison. "Travis got a hangover and went to pick up Kenyetta, his girlfriend."

Dulcey laughed and said, "I bet he did," as she turned around and backed her way in, sliding across the front passenger seat.

Hampton bent down and lifted her legs into the car. She brushed her clothing to ensure everything was inside before he closed her in. He opened the back door. Rose got out to allow him entrance, so she could sit next to the window. Hampton obeyed the direction without question.

"You're absolutely stunning, Miss Dulcey," I said.

"Yeah, well, I ain't feelin' so stunning," Dulcey snapped and grunted her dismay. "I guess if I'm gonna be out here lookin' for a new man"—she paused for a second and gave a sideways nod behind her—"I better be looking some kind of stunnin'."

I decided it best to leave it alone.

I kept ogling at her while she pulled her coat together, adjusted her head wrap, pulled her coat together again, checked to make sure her earrings were set firm in her ears, pulled down the visor and checked out her lipstick in the mirror, pushed it up, adjusted her head wrap again, shifted in the seat, then settled with her hands in her lap.

"Well, what you waiting on? We're gonna miss the sermon, you keep messin' around." She hesitated, sucked her teeth, and waved her hand like she was brushing something away and said, "Go on, girl, drive the car."

We attended the First Corinthian Baptist Church on Pine Street in West Philly, with Pastor Dennis Earl Thomas presiding. It was a large cathedral-style church that anchored the middle-class neighborhood peppered with row houses and small family businesses.

The main lot behind the church was full, so I had to park in the overflow lot across and one block down the street. The twins jumped out first and raced to the crosswalk at the corner to push the pedestrian button.

Hamp attempted helping Dulcey with an outstretched hand, which she swiped away.

The light had turned red and the pedestrian light began flashing when we got to the corner. Hamp locked arms with Dulcey on one side and I on the other, as we strolled across the street.

Sounds of beats accompanied by raucous lyrics that included "motherfucker" and "bitch" spewed out the window of a waiting vehicle occupied by four young black men.

My instinct was to check the twins' location. I saw them run up the stairs of the church.

Admittedly, it had been a few years since I had attended church. My attendance ended after he graduated high school and went off to college.

When the twins came to live with us nine months ago, we started attending again. Church members embraced us as though we never stopped. Deacon Bailey had the twins in her clutches when we entered.

Deacon Bailey was a senior deacon who paid special attention to the girls and what was happening with them, and who did not accept anything less than the old-fashioned degree of manners and attentiveness that I remember my parents demanded—addressing elders as ma'am or sir, not interrupting an adult conversation, and only speaking to adults when spoken to.

"Good morning, Deacon Bailey," the twins said. "May we be excused for children's church?" They curtsied and waited a moment for a response.

Deacon Bailey gave them the nod and ushered them to the stairwell that led to the mezzanine level, where children's church took place. I was not so insistent on the discipline of church etiquette, but I appreciated her efforts.

The sanctuary was almost full as we picked our way past patrons already seated in the pew where Travis, Kenyetta, and Elijah sat, saving seats for us.

The sound of the music swirled overhead and rained down a calm that always penetrated whatever crusty exterior had built up since my last visit. I prayed every morning and thanked God for waking me up in my right mind . . . maybe "in my right mind" was stretching it, but I was still here.

My thoughts drifted to Nareece waking up in the confines of the hospital. I glanced over at Dulcey, who sat tall and proud like she had received the best blessing ever. I tuned in to Rev. Thomas singing Kirk Franklin's "Blessing in the Storm." He ended the song with a hallelujah, that was repeated several times by the congregation, before the church quieted, in wait for his next words.

Rev. Thomas paused to allow parishioners a chance to absorb the meaning behind the lyrics, I supposed. He took up his handkerchief from the podium, wiped his forehead, set it back down, and continued.

"Some of us are going through a real storm and we have to drop anchor and pray for daylight . . . Don't drift, don't despair. How you handle that storm will determine a good deal how you live the remainder of your life. Let me leave you with four anchors to help you with the storms of life. Number one, the presence of God. The Word says he will never leave you or forsake you . . . Number two, the anchor of faith. We need faith because of fear. The Word of God will matter little if you do not exercise faith in it . . . Keep hold of that anchor of faith . . . Number three, the anchor of purpose. You must have a sense of destiny about your life and know that God keeps his promises without fail. Number four, the anchor of peace. When we trust God, no matter what the circumstances, we are peaceful. When we are in a storm we ask why. Many times we do not get an answer or the answer we want . . . You need to surrender to Jesus."

At the end of the service, the low hum of voices got loud with greetings and laughter. It took at least a half hour to work our way through the greetings from members to the pastor's receiving line. The twins bounced into the sanctuary from Sunday school as Travis, Elijah, Kenyetta, Hamp, Dulcey, and I escaped our pew row and took up positions at the end of the receiving line. Dulcey and Hampton stood in front of us, holding hands and cooing at each other like newlyweds. *What an hour in the Lord's house can do*, I thought.

The twins were first to greet Rev. Thomas, who stood on the sidewalk in front of the church. Deacon Paul stood beside him, taking notes as the reverend spoke to each parishioner.

The twins wrapped their arms around the reverend from either side.

"What'd you young ladies learn in children's church today?"

"That you should pray about everything and be patient, wait for God to answer," Helen said.

"Very good. Anything else?"

"Oh, Reverend Thomas, you know everything about God without us tellin' ya," they said. They broke their grip and ran down the sidewalk to the crosswalk, yelling their goodbyes behind them.

Next up, Travis and Elijah conversed with the pastor.

"Good to see you in church, son. How you making out your first year in college?" the pastor asked Travis.

"Good so far; a 3.64 GPA."

"That a boy," Rev. Thomas said, pumping Travis's arm with congratulatory strength.

"And this is?" Rev. Thomas said, taking Kenyetta's hand.

"Rev, you know Kenyetta. She's my girlfriend."

"Ah yes, I do remember. It's nice to see you again."

Then he focused his attention on Elijah. "Glad you came, young man. I hope you decide to become a part of our membership." Elijah assured the pastor he would consider such, depending on whether he decided to stay in Philly. My ears perked.

Travis and Elijah moved down the sidewalk to where the twins waited at the corner.

Dulcey, Hampton, and I took turns giving our good wishes. Pastor took Dulcey's hand and pulled her in for a hug. "It's been a long road, Dulcey, but you are looking well now, lady. I will continue to pray for your recovery."

"It was everyone's prayers got me this far. Prayer will take me the rest of the way. Thank you, Pastor." Then Reverend Thomas and Deacon Paul went back into the church sanctuary and closed the doors as we made our way to the corner.

Travis, Elijah, Kenyetta, and the twins had crossed the street and were at the car by the time Hamp, Dulcey, and I got to the crosswalk. Hamp and I took our positions on either side of Dulcey, each holding an arm, and began crossing the street.

Rose ran from the car to meet us. The squealing of car tires caused me to look away from her down the street. When I looked back, Rose froze in place on the sidewalk, her eyes wide with fear. Hamp and I rushed Dulcey to the curb.

A dark-colored sedan sped toward us. A glint of shiny black inched out of the window. My heart raced as I looked to Hamp, who pushed Dulcey behind him, then to Rose, still frozen in position. I ran toward her and yelled for everyone to get down. Several shots were fired as I grabbed Rose and we fell to the ground. I jumped up when the car passed, hoping to see the license plate. The car turned the corner without slowing.

Helen's bloodcurdling scream ripped through the loud silence that settled after the gunfire. I spun around to see her standing over Rose's still body, which lay spread-eagled on the pavement.

CHAPTER 7

Rose was dough in my arms. Dulcey pushed Helen into the backseat and jumped into the driver's seat. I slid in beside Helen. Blood oozed from a hole in Rose's left shoulder. I put pressure on the wound. She did not flinch. Dulcey leaned on the horn as she sped down Lombard Street to Children's Hospital. Hampton hung out the window on the front passenger side, screaming for cars and people to move out of the way. Helen cried, screaming Rose's name. About a block from the hospital, Helen stopped screaming and said, "Tell Auntie Dulcey she can slow down, Auntie. My Rose will be all right."

When we arrived at the emergency entrance, Dulcey got out of the car before I could open the car door. She ran into the hospital and came back with two nurses rolling a gurney. Rose floated from my arms to the gurney. A doctor came as they rolled Rose inside, with us following. Partway down the hall, the doctor stopped, blocking our path, and said, "Who is responsible for this child?"

"I am," I mumbled.

"Who is . . . ?"

"I am," I said louder.

The doctor nodded, then hurried down the hallway while a

nurse took up the duty of blocking our path so we could not follow.

I moved when Helen pulled at my hand, leading me to the waiting room and a chair. Dulcey and Hampton followed. My brain revved with the details—the shooter's car dented on the driver's side, dark blue, three faces, no, four faces, the gun, semiautomatic, the license plate covered or partially covered: 3H or 8H.

Travis, Elijah, and Kenyetta arrived a few minutes later. As soon as Travis came, Helen ran and jumped into his arms. Then she told him the same thing she told us, not to worry because Rose would be fine. I could tell from the relief on his face that Travis bought it. He believed her. He sat down with Helen on his lap and Kenyetta next to him. He rocked Helen while she buried her face in his collar.

Elijah stayed to the rear corner of the room, away from everybody else. Our eyes met and locked for a moment before he looked away, at nothing in particular as far as I could tell. I told myself I did not blame him. His brother may not have had anything to do with it. I took a deep breath and tried to regroup.

"Hey, partner," Fran said, bringing me back. "I was in the neighborhood, heard over my scanner."

Helen jumped down from Travis's lap. She approached Fran with an outstretched hand. "Hi. I'm Helen. My sister got shot, but she's going to be all right."

"I'm sure she is." Fran reached out to shake Helen's hand. "I'm Fran. A pleasure to meet you, Miss Helen."

She giggled. "A pleasure to meet you too, Mr. Fran. Fran is a girl's name."

"It can be." He cupped his hand to one side of his mouth and bent toward Helen. "Between us, I think my mom secretly wanted a girl," he said, which drew another giggle from Helen.

I got up and directed Helen to go back and sit with Travis

while I talked police business with Fran. Helen was resistant, wanting to participate in capturing the bad guy who hurt her sister. I gave her my no-nonsense glare, the same one my mother had given me in difficult moments. She obeyed.

Fran and I left the room and walked down the hall to the door that let us inside the stairwell. I took a seat on a step. Fran stood with his back against the door to ensure our privacy.

"How is your niece?"

"She got hit in the right shoulder." I looked up at him. "Helen says she's going to be fine. So, there you go."

A few moments of silence passed before Fran plowed forward. "Police are interviewing people at the scene. So far, when I left, no one saw anything. They heard noise that sounded like gunfire but didn't see anything by the time they got to their windows or out their doors. The reverend heard the shooting but said the car was gone and you were taking off by the time he got outside. There also were no casings at the scene."

"The question is, who was the target? We were the only ones there—Dulcey, Hamp, Travis, Elijah, Kenyetta, the twins, and me. It had to be . . ." I hesitated.

I decided I needed to slow down and rethink my thoughts before sharing suspicions that I had no basis for. Elijah was a good kid.

"Something you want to share?" Fran quizzed me.

I headed in another direction. "I can tell you it was a dark blue Toyota, a Camry, I think. There were three black men, young, maybe twenties. There might have been a fourth, I'm not sure." Fran pulled a little black notebook from his pocket and scribbled down what I said. "The license plate was covered by something hanging out of the trunk, but two characters were either 3H or 8H. Not much, I know."

"It might take a while, but I bet we can narrow it down."

"I'd also appreciate it if you would pick my sister up from Penn Center and bring her here. I can't leave . . ."

"Done."

"I'll call over and tell them you're coming. Ask for Darla Dawn."

"Darla Dawn? Really?"

"It's a code name so they know you're supposed to be there. Thanks."

Four hours later, Dulcey dozed in a sitting position on the couch in the waiting room, her head hung back, and a full-engine snore going on. Helen was wrapped up in a blanket next to her. I paced between looking out the window and checking down the hall for the surgeon, Dr. Sharma. Another hour passed before he came to the waiting room after five hours of surgery and told us that Rose was in recovery and would be kept under constant watch for several more hours before we could see her. He said the bullet missed bone but damaged some nerves, and while they performed debridement of the damaged tissue, follow-up surgeries might be required.

Helen smiled and said, "See, Auntie, I told you Rose is going to be fine."

I hugged her.

"Twins are spooky like that. Thinkin' the same thoughts, feelin' the same feelin's, knowing what the other one is going to say before they say it. That ain't nobody but God's blessing on them," Dulcey preached.

"Ma, who were they shooting at? I mean, none of the gangs operate in that area. And there definitely wasn't anyone else there but us that I remember seeing," Travis asked.

"Oh boy, what can you tell me about gangs and where they operate?"

"Please. Me and my boys are hip to what goes on in our city, who the players are, where they be hangin' and who not to mess with."

I noticed Elijah did not say anything, just nodded his head

and kept a crooked smile on his lips, not in an evil way, but rather in an awkward boyish manner with an air of innocence.

"Really? That's not at all what I would have thought, the way you came home last night."

"So I got into some stuff. I handled it. I'm your son, ain't I?"

"Damn sure is your boy." Dulcey snickered. "Listen to him, Muriel. Maybe you need to interrogate him. Might learn a few things."

It was going to be a long night.

Dulcey and Hamp took Helen, Travis, Kenyetta, and Elijah out to get something to eat. I was not leaving. They'd been gone maybe twenty minutes when Calvin strode through the double doors, followed by three of his men. I double-timed it into his arms. Caught him off guard. The feel of his hand at my lower back, pulling me into the warmth of his hold, allowed me to absorb all his splendidness and renewed my spirit.

"I came as soon as I found out," he whispered. "How's baby girl?"

"Doctor says she'll be fine."

"Whaddaya know?"

I turned away and sat back down on the couch. Calvin directed his lead man, BJ, to make sure the room was guarded, then he sat with me. I recognized BJ and the other two men from Calvin's club, bouncers who kept the mix of thugs, politicians, and neighborhood folks who patronized the club, at a happy medium.

"Muriel, I can fix this quicker than the police. If you don't tell me I'll find out, it'll just take longer. This is about keeping your family safe. This is about that little girl, your family, needing protection. I'm the best person to make sure that happens."

When I did not say anything, he continued.

"Until it's clear what we're dealing with, you need protection." He gave me a highbrowed look with pursed lips. When he spoke, his tone was soft and even. "Babe, you have to tell me so I can help you."

"I don't even know what I need help with." I hated it when I whined. I sucked it up and told him about Elijah's brother's visit that morning and his threat toward Elijah. I also told him about Hamp's gambling debt and what I had learned from Detective Burgan about his debtors, Pebo "Bandit" Miles and Murray "Muddy" Wilson.

"Yes, it could be a coincidence. It could be a case of mistaken identity or they were aiming for someone else who was passing through the area and who we did not see . . . totally unrelated to Hamp or Elijah."

"Your Detective Burgan is right-on. Bandit and Muddy are members of the Berg Nation gang. Sick dudes. A lot of the young brothers that come through the center are there because they're trying to stay away from Berg Nation and live."

"I hate to involve you in this," I said. "I can't believe my baby got hit for some shit—"

"Shh." He took my face in the palms of his hands and kissed me—a soft, warm, wet, long kiss, the kind that slices into whatever ails you and gives you that blessed assurance that everything will be all right. "Now you need to tend to your family. Like you said, it might be about Elijah or Hamp. Could be both."

"Doesn't matter whether we're talking Hamp or Elijah, seems like it has to do with the same wretchedness."

"Same wretchedness, different solutions. Trust me. I'm meeting with members from Berg Nation at Blumberg. The stuff they're selling now is killing folks and the police aren't making much progress. Seems they want to make some changes since they're the ones contacted me."

"Are you sure it's a good idea to meet these guys on their turf?"

"Babe, I won't be alone. I will definitely be covered."

"You can't play God with these kids."

"Don't worry your beautiful head about what I'm doing." He got up and spun around in a cocky stance, pointing his fingers at me, and said, "I got this."

I laughed at this silliness. He kissed the top of my head and left.

Calvin made me feel safe. It seemed like he was invincible and could do and handle anything and remain unscathed, no matter the weapon. A young girl's idealistic nonsense, I know. An air of mystery surrounded him. I mean, he was a consultant to politicians, PPD, DEA, and FBI, and then flipped and walked a path out in front of gangs and the Mafia. And every time I broached the subject to understand his role better, he'd say, "If I tell you I'll have to kill you or somebody else will."

Not long after Calvin left, Dulcey and the kids returned with cheesesteak pizza. Hampton was not with them. Dulcey said they took him home, so I left it at that. By the time they got back, I had already eaten two bags of cheese popcorn, one bag of chips, and my favorite, a package of red Twizzlers, all washed down with a can of Coke. I could not fathom eating a piece of pizza on top of all that. Travis and Elijah made sure no crumb remained, then decided to go home and come back in the morning.

Three hours later, we were still hunkered down in the waiting room. I had dozed, so surely I was dreaming in blurred Technicolor, streaming from another dimension, the scene of Fran rolling Nareece in her wheelchair into the room. She wore blue jeans, a dark blue blazer atop a white T-shirt with a gray scarf and gray flats, a picture out of a fashion magazine except for her scarecrow hairdo, ashen complexion, and sunken, blank eyes. I yawned, blinked, and rubbed my eyes, trying to work through my drowsiness.

Dulcey popped up like a jack-in-the-box and was on Nareece in one giant step. "My God, my God, he sure is good!"

She squeezed Nareece's shoulders so hard her head bobbed backwards. When she finally released her, Nareece's head fell forward before settling back in a proper position on her neck. Dulcey adjusted Nareece's clothes.

"Child, it is so good to see you outta that hospital and all." Dulcey carried on like Nareece was all the way live and getting it. Nareece sat in her wheelchair, motionless.

Helen sat up from the couch where she had been napping. She wiped her eyes and went from sleepy to awake in a second. "Mommy!" she screeched. She galloped to Nareece and hopped up on her lap. Fran held tight to the chair to keep it steady or they both would have hit the floor. Helen cuddled in Nareece's lap. "Mommy, Rose is hurt but she's going to be all right."

Still, Nareece sat lifeless and expressionless.

"Took a while for them to get her ready," Fran said, stepping down to lock the brakes on Nareece's wheelchair. "She was sleeping when I arrived. They said she had been resistant today, pushed them away and did not want to get out of the bed. Anyway, I left and got caught up in work."

"No problem, thanks."

"Breaking news just in. A nine-year-old girl was shot during a drive-by shooting. The child was taken to Children's Hospital, her condition unknown at this time. We will continue to bring you the latest on this story and the child's condition as it becomes available."

Everyone focused on the news report except Nareece. Helen rested her head on Nareece's chest in a fetal position. Not an easy feat being that she was almost as big as her mother. Nareece turned her head in the direction of the television as the anchorwoman finished her report. She lifted both her arms and wrapped them around Helen, who was still cuddled on her lap. Over Helen's head, her gaze found me. I got up from the couch and went to her. Tears filled her eyes.

Doctor Sharma came in and told us Rose was stable and had

been moved from recovery to a private room. In Rose's room, I stood next to Nareece's wheelchair, holding her hand as she gazed on her little girl, so tiny and helpless, tubes attached to her arms and an oxygen mask over her face.

Dulcey stepped up and stood beside me. She squeezed my hand. Helen slid down from Nareece's lap and climbed on the bed, careful not to disturb any of the tubes, and lay down facing her twin.

While everyone's attention was on Rose, Fran gave me the signal. I gently put Nareece's hand into Dulcey's and followed him into the hallway.

"You should know that the head nurse lady at the rehab place, Ms. Braithwaite, said Nareece had a visitor today."

"What do you mean, she had a visitor? No one should be asking for her. No one but family knows she is in the hospital or even who she is."

"The lady said she told the guy she had no one under the name he gave her, which was Nareece. Black guy, medium complexion, tall, dressed in dark slacks and a dark shirt. Scar or a mole near his lip. Nurse said she was about to call you when I showed up."

As quickly as fear stabbed my chest, it dissipated. Laughton.

CHAPTER 8

Agent Askew of the DEA walked around the table and sat across from me. Agent Rommel stood against the opposite wall from where I was sitting in a small conference room at 600 Arch Street.

Askew leaned forward in his chair and rested his forearms on the table and said, "Can we get you something—coffee, water?"

"I'm good, thank you."

He continued. "Officer Mabley, the city is experiencing a heroin epidemic. People are dying in record numbers not experienced since the sixties and early seventies. Heroin is being mixed with fentanyl, a lethal drug that increases the chance of an overdose. Fentanyl is also being sold in pill form. The pill is made in China, shipped to Mexico, and distributed in the States. The Berg Nation gang is a major distributor."

"What is it you are expecting me to say?" I said, struggling to keep control. "I take my family to church and my niece gets gunned down and you got me in this five-by-seven interrogation room questioning me like . . . like I'm guilty of something. What the hell is going on here?"

"Officer Mabley, what is your relationship with Ward and Elijah Griffin?"

"What do you mean, what is my relationship with them? I don't have a relationship with them. Elijah is my son's friend and his brother is a known member of Berg Nation."

"Is your son involved with Berg Nation?"

"I'm not sure where this is going. My nine-year-old niece is lying in a hospital bed fighting for her life, and instead of trying to find out who shot her and why, you're questioning me about my son's alleged involvement in a gang. Well, no, Agent Askew, my son is not involved with Berg Nation or any other gang." I got up to leave. "I think I need to get to work, so if you'll excuse me. Direct any other questions to my lieutenant," I said, walking around the table and moving toward the door.

I reached for the doorknob, but it seemingly opened on its own, until Zoila, Detective Burgan, came through.

"Muriel, please, have a seat," she said. She held the door open and cocked her head toward the exit. "Gentlemen."

The DEA agents cleared the room. I walked back around the table and sat down.

"Muriel, these guys can be off the charts. It's expected since one of their agents was killed a month back in a failed bust."

"Zoila, what the hell does that have to do with what happened to my niece? I told you everything. Why were we being shot at? If we weren't the targets, then who?"

Zoila spread out some photographs in front of me. Elijah and Travis were in one of them, with Elijah's brother and two other men. Mr. Kim's daughter was in another.

"Travis is not involved with this gang. With any gang."

Zoila gave me the eye that says if he was in a gang I would be the last to recognize it because I'm his mother. It made my skin crawl.

"Damn it, Zoila. I don't wear blinders. If Travis were in with these . . . these . . . guys, he'd be dead by my hand."

"Which is why . . ."

"Which is why I know he's not. Elijah, he hangs out with Travis and comes to the house sometimes. Said his brother hassles him, tries to get him to join the gang. Said his parents are dead and his brother is his only family. Travis befriended him because he felt sorry for him. So I let him stay at the house."

"How long?"

"He's only been there a few nights. Anyway, his brother came to the house Sunday morning and said if Elijah shows his face in the hood again, he's dead."

She flashed me a satisfied look.

"He threatened. Elijah has not gone back."

"But he could be pissed because his little brother, who he has cared for the past five years, is dissing him."

"I don't think so. His brother may be going against him as far as becoming a gang member, but there was something in Ward's manner that said he accepted the idea of Elijah making something of himself."

"You got all that from the guy coming to your door and threatening death."

I twisted my mouth and bore into her. "Yes, I got all that and more, so don't play me."

We sat in silence for a few moments before I went back to the pictures and pulled out the one with Mr. Kim's daughter.

"When was this taken?"

"You know her?"

"She's my neighbor's, I mean my ex-neighbor's daughter. She's been missing for a few days. He asked me to check into it."

"She's new on the scene. It was taken three days ago at the Blumberg."

That would have been Sunday, the day after she went missing.

"Is she on the hook for any illegal activity?"

"Besides hanging out with the likes of that element, no."

"Is this the latest? Any way of knowing if she is still there?"

Zoila stared at me, probably trying to decide if she should give me any more information. It was difficult for me to imagine Mr. Kim's daughter being caught up in the gang activity in the city, but there it was in front of me. The obvious reason was for drugs—heroin, no doubt.

I stared back with a raised brow, challenging her testing me on this. She caved. "I'll make some inquiries," she said.

When I got to the lab, I called Travis. He picked up on the first ring and said he had just returned to the hospital from taking Dulcey home. Rose was doing well. The commotion on his end quieted as he left the room, I guessed.

"Mom, Aunt Nareece is here! How'd she get here? She's acting like nothing's wrong with her, like she's all good."

"I know. She surprised us all last night. I should have called you sooner and told you, but so much is happening, and you were sleeping this morning when I came home and left again."

"It's all good. She's talking like they are going to be moving back to Boston, back into their house, and going on like nothing ever happened. She even talks about Uncle John, going on about what a good husband he is to her and a good dad he is to her babies, like he's still alive. The twins are so happy she's here they're going along with everything she's saying. Helen told her he was dead. She just went on talking about how they would all be together soon."

"I'm asking a lot, but please stay with them and make sure she doesn't do anything crazy."

"Crazy like what, Ma?"

"Just stay close."

"Don't worry. We'll be here."

"We?"

"Me and Elijah."

"Right."

"Mr. Kim and his granddaughter were here for a minute. He

did his mojo over Rose and I'll be damned, I mean . . . after Mr. Kim did his thing, Rose started acting like there wasn't nothing wrong with her. He's definitely the man!"

Parker peered over the partition that separated our desks. "I hope everything is good with your niece, Muriel."

Parker never calls me Muriel. I looked up at his Minion-looking self—eyes too close together and magnified by big glasses—and smiled. "Thanks, Parker. She's going to be fine."

Fran was hunkered over a comparison microscope when I passed the microscope room on my way to the toilet. When I came out, he was in the same position. He waved at me to come in without taking his eyes from his work.

"You got eyes in the back of your head or something?"

"Check this out," he said, pushing his chair back from the table and getting up. I sat down, adjusted the seat, and leaned in to the microscope.

A comparison scope is the same as a microscope that is used in any high school chemistry class, but a comparison microscope allows you to view two separate pieces of evidence at the same time through one set of eyepieces. Then it's a matter of time. It can take days to match up the markings on bullet evidence to a particular gun. If sufficient markings are not present, the findings are inconclusive.

"What you are looking at is the bullet taken from your niece's shoulder and the bullet from the DEA agent who was killed. I'm not ready to call it yet. I want to spend some more time on it."

"So, we find the gun, we find the murder weapon and maybe the shooter," I said. "As much as I want to know about this, it's probably going to turn out we can't connect anyone to the weapon even if we find it. But I hear you. Still, this isn't doing anything to help our caseload."

"I'm working on that as well. I got caught up in your niece's shooting."

Parker stuck his head in the door. "Someone wants to talk to you bad. Your cell won't stop ringing."

It was Dulcey in a panic because her car was in the shop and Hampton, who was supposed to take her to her two o'clock chemotherapy appointment, was a no-show. Parker shooed me on my way, vowing to cover for me with the lieutenant.

When I arrived at the house, it was 1:50. Hampton pulled to the curb behind me. Dulcey charged out of the house, aiming for Hampton's car. Hampton hopped out of his car with his arms raised as though surrendering to the police.

"Baby, baby, I'm sorry I'm late. The traffic . . . You gotta give a brother some forgiveness."

"I'ma give you some forgiveness all right," Dulcey said, wielding her suitcase of a pocketbook.

I jumped out of the car and stepped to Dulcey, redirecting her attention to me before the two collided. "C'mon, girl. You don't have time for this. You're going to be late."

Hampton backed up to the curb and stood with his head hanging, looking drained and defeated. After I had put Dulcey in the car and moved around to the driver side, he made a motion to call him, then clasped his hands in prayer position. I nodded that I would.

Dulcey was silent all the way to the doctor's. I decided it was best to leave the silence be until she was ready to disturb it. The thought wasn't all the way out of my head before she became talkative again.

"Muriel, whatever that man has gotten himself into, he can't fix it by himself. I ain't never seen him act like this before. I'm afraid for him and I can't do a damn thing to help him, especially if he won't talk to me. The way I'm looking . . ." She quieted and went through her ritual of late—pulled down the visor and cringed at her reflection, removed her wide-brimmed sun hat and patted her hair, careful not to tug on it, afraid what little she had left would fall out, then pulled her hat down on her head again and pushed the visor back up. "The way I'm look-ing I wouldn't be surprised if he found him another woman." She sat with that a few moments, then gave it back in force. "I will kill the man if he's messing with someone else. We've been through everything together. I'll kill him."

"You know damn well Hampton ain't messing. You know he loves you and everything about you, no matter what." I pulled into a parking space and shut the car off. "Dulce, I'm gonna find out what the problem is and do what I can to help him fix it. You are going to concentrate on getting better and stop worrying. It's all gonna be good. It all is good. Needs a lit-tle tweaking is all."

She gave me a crooked smile and slid across the seat. I grabbed her arm.

"You hear me, right?"

"Yes, I prayed about it. God got me, you, and Hampton." She rose up out of the car then turned back to me. "That's right, God got you too."

"If you asked him, no doubt he does." I chuckled at her.

Halfway through the two-hour process, Dulcey quieted, re-laxed in the recliner, and fell asleep. I stepped out into the hall-way and called Hamp. No answer. I was about to go back in when my phone vibrated. It was Zoila.

"Muriel, you inquired about your friend's daughter, a young Asian woman."

"Right."

"Got a call from Hayes that a victim matching that descrip-tion was brought into the morgue this afternoon."

Twenty years on the force, I have never even shaped my mouth to say the words, *Your child, the baby you bore, held to your breast, raised up with every speck of unconditional love you had inside, the one with the toothy grin, unkempt hair, lanky physique . . . that child is dead.* Thinking the words, hearing the sound of them humming in my ears—words not yet spoken—my heart ached.

After I dropped Dulcey off at her house, I sped downtown to the city morgue. It was after hours, but Hayes, the medical examiner, lived there. I sat in the parking lot on University Avenue trying to wrap my brain around the fact that Mr. Kim's daughter was lying in cold storage waiting for him to identify her body. "Get a grip, kid."

I pushed the car door open and sat with the task at hand for a few more minutes before I got out and went inside the building. I took the elevator to the basement. My footsteps echoed down the empty hallway that led to the inner room. Hayes was performing an autopsy when I entered. The smell of antiseptic mixed with the repugnant odor of decomposition pushed me back outside the door, retching. It took a few minutes to readjust and go back in.

"Hispanic female, age thirty-five to forty, scar on left shoulder . . ." Hayes stopped mid-sentence when he saw me. "Detective Mabley, how nice of you to visit," he said, his craggy teeth beaming in a jack-o'-lantern kind of smile.

"Doc. I got a call that you had a young Asian woman brought in this afternoon."

"Yes, I've been expecting you." He snapped off his latex gloves and spun around toward the cold chambers. The release of suction and thud of rollers being disengaged to allow the drawer to move gave me pause. "You can't identify the victim from over there," Hayes mused, motioning me forward.

I stepped forward as he pulled back the sheet that covered her face, and nearly fell forward on the corpse had not Hayes put his arm out to stop my stumble. I regained my footing and backed away.

"Tha . . . that's not her," I stammered, turning to leave.

"Wait, Detective. The victim's belongings included a business card for a club named Calvin's Place. The card had your name scribbled on the back."

CHAPTER 9

"You told me there shouldn't be anybody else coming around asking for her," the administrator, Mrs. Anchorman said, handing me release papers to sign. "I made a sketch of him." She handed me a detailed sketch of Laughton, including the mole on the right corner of his bottom lip and the swatch of white hair on the right side of his head. "I like to draw."

Dr. Altman, Nareece's psychiatrist, came into the administrator's office as I finished signing the papers. We went down the hall to his office. He shut the door and gestured to a chair in front of his cube-sized desk.

Nareece spent the last three days at the hospital with Rose, during which time she almost seemed like her old self. Now that Rose was being discharged from the hospital, Nareece insisted on coming home too.

"She's not well," Dr. Altman said. He sat down at his desk, then rolled his chair forward until his watermelon-sized belly squeezed against the desk. He leaned way forward and let his forearms take his weight. "She needs support and should come to sessions. Miss Mabley, Nareece experienced deep depression and has been in severe shock. While she is physically healthy, she still has some deep psychological trauma that she hasn't dealt with. I know you and I discussed her son, who is your son." He shook his head back and forth. "Anyway, she has been focused on him, Travis, right?" I nodded. "Concerned that he'll hate her because she gave him up."

"Travis is over all that."

"Apparently, she's not. She could display some negative emotions around that, and depending on how she processes the home situation, it is possible that she could slip back into her unresponsive state. Nevertheless, I believe taking her home so she can be with her children is an excellent idea. As I said, she is physically healthy and has no restrictions there. I strongly recommend that she continue to come to the private and group sessions here until she is stable."

"Sometimes she sounds like she's fine, and other times she's in another world, talking about things that make no sense, like nothing ever happened. Like her saying she's taking her daughters back to Boston to live in their house that is no longer theirs because we sold it."

"And that may be the best she can do. Only with a lot of support and time can she heal."

I stood in the doorway of Nareece's room and watched Travis help her pack. He jumped to her every request. Nareece beamed. I had feared she would stay distant and silent for the rest of her life. Now we were packing her up to come home and make the rehab center a distant memory.

She stooped down in the closet and pulled out some clothes and shoes. Then she stood on her tiptoes to reach something on a shelf over her head, but she couldn't.

"Travis, baby, can you reach up there for that box?" she crooned, pointing over her head and smiling back at Travis, who stood behind her. He reached the sweaters with little effort.

Twice, he stole a look at me with his mouth turned up on one side and his brow down on the opposite side: annoyance. Another time, he framed his hand as though choking Nareece, behind her back, of course. Nareece, loving his attention, did not attend to any of his antics.

It occurred to me that this was the first interaction he'd had with her since he was a toddler. It had to be difficult sharing space with me and his aunt, who he had learned only a few months ago was his real mother, and Jesse Boone, his father. A twenty-year-old secret revealed.

It took way longer than anticipated to pack Nareece's things. Then we went to Children's Hospital to rescue Rose.

When we entered her room, Rose tossed aside the book she had been reading, slid down from the bed, and rushed to her mother with one outstretched arm. Her other arm, tightly bound in a sling, made her movement awkward and unsteady.

Travis picked up the book she had been reading and flipped it over, opening the pages. "Where'd this come from?"

Rose shrugged. "This handsome man gave it to me. He also gave me that teddy bear." She pointed to the windowsill, to a scraggly brown teddy bear with a crisscross white bandage over its heart and a red-and-white-striped ribbon tied around its neck. "He said I was probably too old for stuffed animals, but I took it."

"What handsome man?" I said, an inner smile taking hold. There was no way Calvin's guys would let just any man get past them. No one except Laughton.

She shrugged again. "I don't know," she said. "He came in and gave me the stuff and left. Mr. Calvin's man stuck his head in and gave me the thumbs-up. Said the guy was a friend. I didn't feel much like interrogatin' him."

"How you doing, baby?" Nareece asked. Before Rose could

answer, she said, "C'mon, let me help you put your clothes on so we can take you and me home." Instead of helping Rose dress, Nareece moved around the room gathering Rose's things and packing them in the overnight bag she brought, seemingly oblivious to the conversation.

I sat in a chair, thumbing through the book and squeezing the stuffed animal as though a bomb or some other kind of destructive device awaited. "What did this man look like, Rose?"

"He was tall and he looked nice. He had a mustache and a white patch on his head." Rose hesitated, then said, "Auntie, I think the man would have been upset if I didn't take it."

"It's okay, baby," I said, giving her back the bear. "I'm sure you made the man happy by accepting his gift."

Nareece picked up a jersey from the bed and put it over Rose's head, jabbering on about the things they were going to do after Rose was completely healed. Doctor's orders had her on bed rest for the next week, as if that were possible.

When we got to the house, Helen ran out and was at the car before I turned the engine off. Rose put her arm around Helen and let her half walk, half carried her inside and up the stairs to their bedroom. Nareece followed. I stopped her at the stairs as I heard the twins' bedroom door close.

"Give them some time, Mama," I said.

She looked from me to Travis, who gave her the nod. She spun around and stomped down the stairs. "I guess you're right." When she hit the bottom step, she called to Travis, who had ducked into the den, "Travis, please help me take these bags up to my room so I can unpack."

"Sure, Auntie," he said, coming out of hiding.

Nareece stopped in her tracks. I caught her gaze and sucked in my breath, waiting for it—her rant about him calling her *auntie* rather than *ma*. Travis grabbed all her bags at once and trudged up the stairs and was back down in one swoop. Nareece stood on the stairs, motionless, all puffed out and holding her breath.

Travis moved past us and went to the kitchen. I could hear Dulcey yapping to him about how she had cooked the twins' favorite foods: enchiladas, beans and rice, and pulled pork. Without taking a breath, Dulcey asked, "Where's that baby girl?" It was quiet for a few seconds before she appeared in the hallway, filling the empty space between me and Nareece with a resounding, "Hey, girl, what's wrong with you? Come here and give me a hug." Nareece stayed put, so Dulcey made the move. Nareece's head near disappeared in Dulcey's bosom. When Dulcey released her, Nareece stormed upstairs and slammed her bedroom door.

"Go on up there to that girl, Muriel. You need to talk to her."

"Dulcey, I can't deal with her mess now. She's already back to thinking the world has to revolve around her without giving any thought to how other folk might feel. How Travis feels about her. Hell, how I feel. The road's been rough for her, for everybody. We need to deal with the situation, not sulk around. I thought she would change when she came home, just be happy that we're all together. Doesn't look like that's happening. Not yet anyway. You'd think she'd just be happy she's out of that place, if nothing else. You'd think she'd at least want to talk about it before going through changes."

"Just say a prayer and take your butt up there."

Like a child being given direction from a parent, I went upstairs and knocked on her door. She did not answer. "God, help me out here, please," I said to myself. I cracked the door open, expecting a shoe thrown at me. Instead she waved me in. I sat beside her on the bed and embraced her.

"What's wrong, Reecy?"

"You know what's wrong." She snorted. "He's my son. He knows he's my son and he calls me Auntie, like he still doesn't know."

"Look, baby girl. I have been his mother for his whole life. You have been his aunt. He just found out you're his biological mother. Give him some time to adjust."

She frowned at me. I suspected it was about the biological mother part. I continued to dive in.

"You can't expect everything's going to change because he knows a new truth. He loves you." I waited for her to say something, but all I got was a sickening, whiney sound and a sniffle. "After some time, you, me, and Travis will talk things out. This is a beginning, Reecy. Don't let anything come between you and him or you and me. We're all here as a family again. Let's be thankful for our family."

Nareece pushed back and glared at me. "You're right," she said, getting up and moving around the room—a room I had decorated for her with a sitting area, a king-size bed for sharing with the twins, and a full bathroom. It had been our parents' room.

She picked up the suitcases and laid them on the bed, forcing me to get up. "We're a family." I watched her shuffle between the closet and the dresser and stuff clothes in drawers.

It seemed forever ago that Nareece and I talked on the phone every day, sharing every piece of our lives, being there for each other no matter what—best sister-friends. As I watched her plow through the motions of settling in, my feelings of annoyance and doubt that she would adjust, eventually anyway, melted away. I got the message—her lips were stilled for the time—so I left.

I peeked in on the twins before going downstairs. They lay in one of the beds; Helen held Rose to her chest as they both slept. I pulled the cover over them and tiptoed out.

"You act more like an adult than those of us who have years of practice," Dulcey was saying to Travis when I entered the dining room.

"Who acts more like an adult, this kid here? I'm not buying it," I said, taking a seat at the table with them.

"Get you some short ribs," Dulcey urged me.

"I'm not hungry." Egging Travis on, I continued. "So, who acts more like an adult?"

"We were talking about Aunt Nareece."

"Oh." I backed down and shifted to serious mode.

"I don't know how to act around her. One minute she's all happy and the next minute she's acting like she doesn't like me. I know it's been hard for her and she needs time. Just know I'm good with it. I can handle it."

"I guess you are the adult in all this."

"Patience, Moms. I know that's not your strong suit, so I'll help you along with that."

"I bet I'll smack you, boy." I flicked his head.

"Hold that action," he said, running to answer the doorbell. Sam followed him in. Sam and Travis had been friends since kindergarten—my other child. His mother and father were doctors, the kind that used their talents to help people in Third World countries. They were Ugandan. Sam had spent more time in my home than his own. This was the first summer he would be home alone while his parents traveled.

Sam wore a long-sleeve button-down shirt stained with sweat and worn jeans that rested below his backside, revealing multi-colored undershorts. Tiny white bumps spread across his thick cheekbones and chin. His appearance triggered my concern.

As soon as she saw him, Dulcey made a plate of food and directed him to sit and eat.

When the banter quieted, I said, "So how you doing on your own in that big house?"

"Good. I'm good, Miss Mabley."

"And your parents? Are they in Uganda?"

He set his fork down next to his plate. His eyes watered.

"What's going on, man?" Travis said.

"I've been trying to reach my parents for the past three days. We Skype every other night. They missed our last call and now I can't reach them."

"Have you called the embassy?"

"Yes. I'm waiting for them to call back. I was told there have been no terrorist attacks, but there have been some demonstrations and protests that have left a few people dead, which I don't think would have anything to do with where my parents are, out in the country.

"My uncle is making further inquiries, though he tells me not to worry, that my father knows the region and the people too well and is too ornery for anyone to mess with him." He smiled, the burden of worry planted on his lips.

"That boy is different," Dulcey said, after Sam and Travis left to go out. "He ain't never been that raggedy. Something is wrong with him more than not hearing from his parents. He's been through this before and they always turn up."

She spoke the words that were in my head.

CHAPTER 10

I pulled around the back on Haverford and parked beside Calvin's black Mercedes, the only car in the lot at the rear of the old four-story warehouse that housed Calvin's Place, a nightclub that catered to the locals for drinking, dancing, and dining. Calvin's Place was noted for Philly's most succulent crab legs and fried chicken. Calvin lived above the club on the third and fourth floors. The second floor was used for private parties.

I had my finger on the buzzer when the door snapped open and Calvin reached out and pulled me inside, hanging me all up in his embrace. He rocked me back and forth and crooned some of Luther's "Never Too Much." Mmm.

He smothered my mouth with his, forcing my lips apart with his tongue. I fought for position and gave it back to him as hungrily and hard as he did.

When we managed to pull apart, Calvin held me by the shoulders and moved his fingers in a massaging motion. I moaned.

"What's wrong, babe? You're tense."

I lowered my neck and let him work through the mangled muscles that had knotted there. Each time he pressed on one, the good pain it caused forced a moan.

"Talk to me, darling," he said, guiding me to a stool. He went behind the bar and poured two glasses of sauvignon blanc.

"I love my family more than anything. Travis is my life. Nareece and the twins, I love them . . . I do." A twinge of guilt came over me.

"I know you love your family, and have and will do anything it takes to protect them."

"Everything's changed. No more me and Travis going and coming without a thought. Knowing each other's way and not having to worry about stepping on each other's toes, or which way to turn to make sure you don't offend, say too much, say too little. No more me and Nareece talking about anything. She's hung up because Travis doesn't call her Ma. What kind of sense does that make? But then I know it's her way of dealing with or not dealing with all that happened to her. Better be focused on Travis calling her Ma than talking about the aftermath of Jesse Boone. But Travis is twenty years old and just found out his auntie is really his mother and his mother is really his auntie and she expects him to call her Ma, no problem. This shit has got to be worthy of a TV series, for crying out loud."

"Patience, my dear."

"You sound like Travis."

"You can handle it. You're a strong woman, one of the many things I love so much about you."

I let his words penetrate my doubting spirit and took a sip of wine to seal it.

Then I told him about Mr. Kim's daughter disappearing and how he asked me to check into it. "I got a call from a detective friend, Zoila Burgan, who runs the Mobile Street Crimes Unit. You must have worked with her at some point." Calvin nodded he did. "She called me about an Asian woman's body in the morgue, so I went and checked it out. Turned out not to be Mr. Kim's daughter, thank God." I pulled a picture of the dead girl out of my pocket. "It was this girl." I showed him the picture and the business card. "She had your card in her belongings with my name scribbled on the back."

Calvin examined them, then came from behind the bar and grabbed my hand. "C'mon, let's go upstairs."

Calvin's residence on floors three and four spanned the length and width of the building, with loft-sized wall-to-wall windows. The third floor was mapped out into a kitchen, dining room, living room, and gym. Two bedrooms and an office took up the fourth floor, where we got off the elevator.

"Her name is Thu Trang Pham," Calvin said, as he crossed the floor to his office. He walked around and sat down in front of his monstrosity of a desk, pulled open the top drawer and took out a manila folder. I sat down in a captain's chair in front of the desk. He flipped open the folder and pushed some photos toward me.

"She's one of the workers at the center, an intern you could say. Her mother died recently of a heroin overdose and her father is this guy." He pointed to a photo of a black man that I recognized from photographs that the DEA detectives had shown me. "She hasn't been around for a few weeks now. Her cell phone was turned off and none of the other participants knew where she was or had seen her."

I recognized another man in the photo. "DEA agents showed me this guy. Said he's Berg Nation."

"He's a hit man." He pushed back in his seat. "How did Thu die?"

"Hayes, the medical examiner, said she overdosed."

"Bullshit. She didn't do drugs. She was a good kid. Man!" He slammed the folder down on his desk. "You know the story. She wanted out of here to chase a real life."

"You're saying you think she was murdered?"

"I'm saying there's no way Thu Trang overdosed."

I walked behind his chair. It was my turn to massage his

shoulders. He reached up and grabbed my hand and looped me around to sit on his lap.

"She has a little baby girl that her grandmother was helping her raise. I think she was a year or two."

"Why would somebody want to kill her?"

"Why do these gangs kill anybody? They rule by terrifying people so they don't talk, or killing them if they do. I don't think Thu Trang talked to anyone, but I do think she knew some things. She never came out and said anything, but she was very protective of some of the younger kids that come through the center."

I twisted around to pick up his hand from my shoulder and wrap it around me tighter. He tensed.

I gripped his hand, uncertain what I was looking at, or certain but not believing. Calvin never wore any jewelry, at least not as long as we had been together.

"Is that a wedding ring?" I surprised myself with the calm I exhibited.

He pulled his hand away.

Still calm. "Is it? Is that a wedding ring?" He didn't answer. He didn't even look at me.

I jumped up from his lap. "That's a wedding ring," I screeched. "You can't be serious. You are fucking married? What? You were rushing and forgot to take it off or something?"

He bowed his head in defeat or sorrow that his secret had been found out. My face burned. My heart tried to force its way from my chest. My head spun and I puked on his shiny, blond wood floor.

Did I mention I have always sucked at relationships for whatever reason? My job, my own insecurities that maybe I'm not good enough, the idea that he would leave me first, that at damn near fifty years old I have never been married, never loved anyone except of course my old partner, Laughton McNair, and the man who stood before me, a lying bastard.

"Muriel. Calm down. I can explain."

"You can explain! What's to explain? You're married! How do you do that? Make love to me and then go home to a wife. What were we doing? What? We were having an affair and fucking, is that it?"

"Not even close."

"You're wearing a wedding ring. What the hell does that mean, *not even close*?"

He came to me and grabbed my arms. I tried to pull away. He held firm.

"Listen to me. I'm sorry. Yes, I'm married. I wanted to tell you but . . . I was afraid you wouldn't see me anymore." He turned me loose.

"That's all you got? *I'm sorry I didn't tell you I was married because I wanted to have my wife and you too*," I mimicked him. I was off and running again, my arms flailing like a lunatic. *After all, I'm a man's man and one woman is just not enough for what I have to offer*. I grabbed my crotch and did a Michael Jackson. Childish. Out of control.

I stopped and fell in the chair. "That was my decision to make."

"You're right, it was your decision. I was wrong. Please, just let me explain."

All I could think was how stupid love is. So why not hear him out? It couldn't be any crazier if it were happening in a movie.

"I've been married for twenty-five years. Five years ago she had a massive stroke. She's been bedridden ever since. She can't move, can't talk, she just stares. She's not brain dead. Doctor says her brain waves show activity, but something keeps her from reacting. So she's brain dead but she's not."

I was stunned.

He sat on the edge of his desk in front of me.

"She's terminally ill but hanging on . . . It took a long time for me to go on with my life, knowing she would never come back. I thought . . . When I met you I didn't intend to fall in love with you, it was about working the case for the feds. You know how it goes. In all my years of working with law enforcement . . . that was a first."

I looked up at him with more surprise. "A first what? You mean when we sang duets all night and I thought we were falling in love, it was all about working a case for the FBI? You were trying to get next to me for information?"

"Only for a minute. Then I couldn't get enough of you. It's the first time I've felt anything for a woman other than my wife."

"So you just brush your wife aside and pretend she's not there anymore?"

"No. I love my wife. But she isn't there anymore. It's a hard reality, but it's real." He got up and came to me. He took my hand and kissed it. "Yes, circumstance brought us together." He kissed my other hand. "And I never want us to be apart. I love you, Muriel Mabley."

He swooped me up and carried me to his bed. The heat of his kisses over my body, between my legs, him inside me, filled my brain long after I left him.

Driving down I-95, my heart pounded, making breathing difficult; my heart ached with love for him. But he lied. He looked me in the eye with heartfelt sincerity and told me he loved me and wanted us to be together for the rest of our lives, a vow already spoken for.

CHAPTER 11

Fran was on the phone when I arrived at my desk forty minutes late to work. He grunted at my greeting.

Parker chided me. "Nice of you to show up."

I crumpled a piece of paper and tossed it over the cubicle wall that separated our spaces.

After Fran hung up, Parker said, "We need to talk. You too, Riley."

We followed him to the archive room, where about twelve hundred rifles, handguns, and other weapons are kept. The archive room is used as a reference room, for training, and when a firearm comes in broken and needs to be test fired. An examiner will take a part from a working gun to replace a part in a broken gun so it can be test fired to obtain evidence.

Parker held the door open for me and Fran and followed us inside.

"So what's with all the secrecy?" Fran asked.

"I was doing some digging, like you asked, trying to figure how many cases our fellow officers completed and all that; and, well, I stumbled upon evidence of a cover-up."

Fran perked up. "What kind of cover-up?"

"It looks like a few years back the son of retired Chief Inspector Bentley Norris confessed to stealing gun parts from two automatic weapons from evidence. Son's name is Officer Bentley Jr.—that is, officer until he shot himself and claimed someone else shot him."

"I remember," I said. "Happened about a year ago. He'd only been on the force a few months, said he was patrolling in Germantown and his car was fired on. He chased the suspect, they exchanged gunfire, and he sustained a gunshot wound, in the arm, I think."

"Resulted in a major manhunt for the guy, the schools were closed, folks in the neighborhood were panicked. Turned out to be a lie. Bentley is in the nut house as we speak and his daddy died about six months after the incident," Parker said.

"So why are we talking about this now?" I said.

"The gun parts he stole, and by the way were never recovered, were taken from this gun"—Parker held up a Ruger— "found at the scene of the DePalma murder a few years back. It disappeared from evidence and the guy who killed De-Palma, Joseph Bonanno, who you just testified against, got off, partially because of it. Turns out someone shipped it directly to the evidence storage room without its being examined."

"How did you get it?"

"I can't give away my secrets. Let's just say I got lucky."

"Wow. So it's possible that Chief Norris was into the Bonanno family for something? Maybe the chief was clueless until his son confessed, or maybe they were both dirty."

My phone buzzed on my hip for the fifth time. Each time it had been Hampton.

"Fact is, none of this may have ever been discovered if Internal Affairs wasn't investigating the backlog of cases," Parker said.

"You still haven't answered my question. What is the deal with the backlog?"

"This is not the only gun shipped without being examined

first. Good news is, it looks like only a few hundred got shipped. Bad news, it could still affect a number of convictions."

"You need to update the lieutenant."

Parker squinted his eyes at me like I was demented. He turned to Fran, who only shrugged.

Parker shook his head in denial. "I do all the work around here," he mumbled on our way out.

When I got back to my desk, I called Hamp. "Finally. Hampton Dangervil. I'm about two minutes from kicking your behind back to Haiti, never to return," I halfway kidded. Silence on the other end. "Hamp. What's going on?" More silence. "You're pushing it now."

"I'm sorry, Muriel. I'm just so disgusted with myself and afraid for my love, Dulcey."

"I'll tell you this, you need to be afraid that you don't end up dead and buried by the time your love gets through with you."

"This's serious, M."

"You think I'm not?"

"Can you please meet me at the dock later on? I cannot talk about this over the phone."

I agreed to meet him after work.

I was almost at the marina, rounding the corner from the exit to Columbus Boulevard, when Bertha decided she'd had enough, sputtered a stream of protests, then cut off. Bertha has served me faithfully for more than fifteen years. For years my to-do list has included buying a new car. I guess I finally needed to act on it. "Please, please, please don't fail me now." I turned the key and pumped the gas pedal in hopes of her making it another half mile to the parking lot. She revved right up. About a quarter mile down from Penn's Landing marina where the *Dulcey Maria* is moored, Bertha died again. I got out and checked for any signs that prohibited parking. Finding none, I locked her up and went on my way.

Penn's Landing is a waterfront area that runs along the Delaware River, where there are concerts, festivals, fireworks, and restaurants. It is named to commemorate the landing of Philly's founder, William Penn. During the summer months, tourists fill the stores and restaurants along the way. Now, the car traffic clogged the streets but foot traffic was minimal.

I first stopped in the boathouse, where folks who housed their boats used the shower and bathroom facilities. Dulcey had given me a key some years ago, prompted by a Travis mishap. He was ten when Dulcey and Hamp invited us on our first boating excursion. Before we got to the marina, Travis said he had to go to the bathroom, bad. After we parked, I rushed him into the boathouse, but we could not get into the bathroom area without a key, and no attendant on duty or anyone else was there. By the time we ran down the walkway to the boat, Travis had crapped his pants. We did not go on a boat trip that day. He refused. After I got him home, he spent three hours in the bathtub and the rest of the day hiding in his room. He made me promise that I would never speak of the mishap again for the rest of our lives, and that I would make Dulcey and Hampton make the same promise. He said if anyone ever talked about it, he would kill himself by jumping off the Benjamin Franklin Bridge.

So Dulcey gave me a key, just in case.

I chuckled at the memory as I clopped down the last length of walkway to the boat. Most days, other boat owners would be lounging on their boats, cleaning them, having cocktails and such. This night, only Mr. Lowry, who lived year round on the *Family Sanctum*, had his relaxation mode on, stretched out on a lounge chair on the deck, reading. Mr. Lowry's boat was almost twice the size of Hamp and Dulcey's twenty-eight-foot cabin cruiser. Yacht size, in my book. He and his wife had bought the boat for family vacations with their children and grandchildren. His wife died not long after their first family vacation when they cruised to the Bahamas. Cancer, I think Dulcey said. Anyway, Mr. Lowry vowed he would spend the rest of his life living there in memory of his wife, even though the children didn't care to go on any more trips.

I approached the *Dulcey Maria,* moored in the farthest spot on the dock, set to nail Hamp for whatever stupidness he had gotten himself into but mostly for upsetting Dulcey. As soon as I stepped onto the back deck, I heard glass break. I pushed open the sliding door. "Hamp? What the hell is all the racket about?"

A tank of a man rammed me, pushing me backwards and over the side of the boat into the water.

My aquaphobia had me thrashing around, my brain fixed on drowning before settling on how ridiculous that would be since I now knew how to swim. I allowed myself to sink before pushing my way up and breaking the surface before my lungs burst. I thrashed around, trying to reach the dock to grab ahold of it. When I made it there, Mr. Lowry was kneeling down, reaching out to me. He pulled me up.

"Did . . . did . . . did you see the guy?" I said, through chattering teeth and breathlessness.

"Naw, I'd gone in the cabin. I heard someone running down the pier and heard splashing, so I come out to see what was goin' on. We've had quite a few break-ins lately. Ain't like it used to be when you didn't have to worry. Folks are losing they minds, I swear."

"Thanks, Mr. Lowry."

"Let me get you a towel, young lady."

"No thanks, Mr. Lowry. I'll get one inside." I sat on the back railing of the boat and took my boots off, then swung my legs over the railing. "You seen Hampton today?"

"Naw. Just been enjoying the day. Heat and humidity, I love

it. But he usually comes around 'bout this time. You just wait a minute, he'll be here. He ain't gonna be too happy with that mess inside there."

I twisted around to look at the mess.

"Glad I was here to pull you outta that water," he said, walking away. "Tell Hampton to knock on my door later, if I can do anything to help him out."

I crossed the back deck and went inside. Every cabinet drawer and storage bin was open and emptied until there was no room to walk or stand even, unless you kicked cans, towels, utensils, paper plates, and other contents that covered the entire floor area. I unhooked my gun holster and set it down. I picked up a towel from the floor and dried off the best I could before sitting down to tackle drying out my gun before rust took hold.

I disassembled my gun and wiped the parts dry with a pillow case I picked up from the floor. The next step would be to douse the parts in oil, but all I could find was WD-40, which may turn to goo and restrict the movement of the parts. Oiling the parts would have to wait.

I was reassembling the gun when Hampton arrived. "What? You decided to go for a swim this time of day?" he joked half-heartedly, checking his watch. His expression switched to surprise after his eyes adjusted to the mess.

"You're a half hour late," I snarled at him. "When I got here, I surprised an intruder."

He set his bag on the table and fell onto the bench seat across from me.

"The guy surprised me more, though," I continued. "Pushed my ass over the side on his way out."

"Are you all right?"

"Don't I look all right?" I continued working on putting my gun together to avoid looking at him. I wanted to claw his eyes out of his head and feed them to the fishes. "How you gonna ask me to meet you here and then leave to buy some . . ." I stopped and checked the bag. "Some whatever the hell this is."

I finished putting together my weapon and snapped the magazine in place. Hamp slid out of the seat and began pacing, as much as he was able in the amount of available floor space. One step, two steps, turn—anything but fessing up to whatever it was he was into—using heroin again, I figured.

"Sit down," I said.

"I think we should leave here now," he countered. "We can go elsewhere and talk. If someone was here, they know about this place."

"Sit down, Hamp. Mr. Lowry said a few of the boats have been broken into, druggies looking for cash. The man I saw was not a professional; he definitely looked strung out. And look at this place."

Hamp sat down and took a six-pack of Prestige, a Haitian beer, out of the bag. He offered me one. I declined. I'm repulsed by the skunky smell and bitter taste of beer.

He opened a bottle and took a long slug. "I got myself in a mess. And even before you ask, I'm not using again. I would never do that to Dulcey—or myself, for that matter. No, though I might be better off if that was what was goin' on." He shifted in his seat and took another swig of beer. "I gambled, trying to get enough money so Dulcey wouldn't have to work at the shop so much. Maybe she could sell the shop to one of the ladies there. Retire. She's so sick, my Dulcey. An age-old story. I was doing good for a while, before a losing streak hammered me. I knew I was going to win it all back and make things right."

"How much, Hamp?"

"Fifty."

"Thousand?" I shrieked. "Just tell me it isn't the Berg Nation gang." He looked at me, then away. "Damn. I don't know much about gambling and the Berg gang, except they kill people who don't pay their gambling debts. Shoot 'em, execution style."

"They don't know about Dulcey, I mean that she's my wife or anything else about me, where I live. That's why I've been staying here. Nobody knows about the boat but us. They gave me a week to come up with the money, and when I couldn't, they gave me an ultimatum, said they would be calling on me soon and I would have to do what they ask or they'd kill me."

"I can give you the money, put these guys off your ass."

"They will not take the money anymore."

"What do you mean, they won't take the money?"

"That is what they said. I must do a deed for them, end of story."

"What the hell were you thinking? Are you out of your mind? Your wife is fighting for her life and you're out here being stupid." I leaned back on the bench seat. Hamp stayed silent. "What if they told you to kill someone? You really think killing someone would be worth it, even if it meant saving Dulcey's life or your own?"

"I will do whatever I have to do to save my Dulcey." He finished his beer and pulled another from the bag. "I just wanted you to know what is going on; in case something happens to me, you can tell Dulcey."

"Nothing's going to happen to you that you can't tell Dulcey about yourself."

"I do not have a choice but to do whatever they ask."

"You have a choice. Don't even go there. You wouldn't have called me if you seriously were considering doing this thing, so shut the hell up." I got up, straightened my clothes, and pushed down my hair, which I imagine was swirling about my head, making me a mirror image of Medusa by now. "You got food and drink here. Stay here. I mean *stay here*, Hamp. Don't go to the store, don't go anywhere off this boat until you hear from me."

He nodded.

As angry and disgusted with him as I was at that moment, my other side felt his pain. He stood when I moved to leave. We hugged. When I moved away, tears streamed down Hamp's face.

"I got you," I said.

It was still light when I got to Bertha. Lost in thought about Hamp's situation and Dulcey being sick, I forgot that Bertha had died right where she was parked. I got in and turned the key. Did I mention that Bertha had never failed me? She sputtered and went into chug mode. A mile or so down the road, she switched into purring mode, smooth as the day I bought her.

Hamp's situation needed the kind of help Calvin offered. When I called, he answered on the first ring.

"I was worried I might not hear from you again."

Strictly business, I thought. I explained Hamp's situation and the ultimatum they put before him. When I was finished, Calvin was silent.

Then he said, "He should stay hidden for a while. Somewhere they can't get to him to even put their demands on him."

"That could make it worse. They could put a hit out on him or some mess."

"Yes, and they could kill him anyway after he does whatever it is they order, which is probably executing somebody. Trust me on this."

"Thanks, Calvin."

"Anything for you, my love."

"Really? You're going to put these love-actually lines to me like that? It's not all right, Calvin. So I appreciate your helping me out in this situation but don't expect—"

"You don't have to finish. I understand and I'm here no matter what," he said.

CHAPTER 12

I did not need a mirror to know a frizzy-haired water buffalo would garner less attention than me in my state. I crept into the house hoping to bypass inspection and interrogation by the twins and Nareece. The open floor plan made invisibility impossible. I could see the twins in their usual positions, stretched out on the floor in the den, drawing and watching a cop show. I closed the front door and made it to the first step before they sang out, in unison, "Hi, Auntie."

"Hey, girls. I'll see you in a minute. Gotta use the bathroom," I said, hauling butt, two steps at a time. At the top, I fell on my ass and slid the rest of the way into my room. I closed my bedroom door and leaned against it to catch my breath. I kicked my wet boots off, the cause of my fall. A knock made me jump up.

"Muriel, you in there? Muriel?" Nareece snarled.

I cracked the door. "What is it?"

"Is something wrong? The girls said you came in real quiet and ran up here like someone was chasing you."

"I had to pee. I'm fine."

"Well, dinner will be ready in about an hour."

"I'll be down."

"Why you holding the door?" She bumped against it.

"I'm trying to shower and change. Go on now, I'll be down when I'm done." I locked the door and listened until her footsteps faded.

My new life sprawled out before me—sneaking around in my own house so that the people who live in it wouldn't be exposed to unsavory situations. Mostly, I feared Nareece's escape to zombiehood again if upset by something even remotely traumatic. At least that is how I interpreted the doctor's summation of her condition. Nareece had ensconced herself in the confines of the house, its upkeep and that of its inhabitants.

The flowery odor of potpourri mixed with disinfectant and furniture polish tickled my nose and boasted the pristine state of my room, not its usual state or my preference. Lived-in, cozy, warm, reflective, would be me.

I appreciated the way I left my room that morning. Boxes that had not yet been unpacked lined the side wall, at least a few days' worth of shoes littered the floor, a box of Kellogg's Mini-Wheats, a bottle of water, and a dish of Hershey's Kisses covered my night table, and for sure, the bedcovers were strategically bunched into a mountain in the center of my most prized possession, a king-size, waveless, soft-side, deep-fill water bed. I swear, though, as I viewed the space now, I second-guessed my recollection. Clearly boundaries needed to be established.

I stripped off my damp uniform, dove on the bed and tore up the covers until I was buried in them, and did the five-minute power-nap thing. That's all I could control or I would have been out for the night, and I still had to check on Dulcey. Maybe I slept for more like a half hour. It took a few minutes for me to shake off the foggy-brain syndrome, then I went for the shower.

By the time I had finished showering and pulled my hair back in a braided bun, Nareece was yelling for Travis, Elijah, and me to come down to eat. I slipped on some jeans and an orange-and-navy Lincoln University sweatshirt with matching sneakers, compliments of my son, and went downstairs.

Everyone else sat around the center aisle, jabbering and stuffing their mouths with spaghetti and meatballs. I made a plate and slid in between Travis and Elijah.

Travis leaned toward me and said in a muted tone, "You look much better." He straightened up and took a mouthful of food, a smug expression on his face. After he swallowed, he moved toward me again. I stopped my hand shy of filling my mouth with a meatball, anticipating his words.

"You think you can sneak in this house without anybody noticing? You can't fool me."

I nudged him and stuffed the meatball in my mouth.

"I know. Police business. Saving us from all the bad things in the world. Ooooooh."

I nodded and smiled.

⁂

I pulled to the curb behind Dulcey's Jaguar—a gift from Hampton on their sixteenth wedding anniversary a year ago. White on white and loaded. She called it Pearl.

The house was dark. Even the outside light that came on automatically after dark was off. The tapping of my tennis shoes up the walkway seemed loud in the quiet. A broken bell had the button stuck inward, so I knocked, waited, banged, and banged some more. She still did not answer. I used my key. The door creaked when I opened it, sending chills up my back. I called for her. The only response, the small whiny meow of Sam, the cat, who brushed up against my legs, welcoming me. Sam waltzed to the stairway and shot up.

I flicked the light switches inside the door, which illuminated the entryway and the foyer. The air smelled stale, like the house had been closed up for a long time. The foyer opened into the living room on the left and the dining room on the right, which led to the kitchen. Across from the door, between the living room and dining room, a stairway spiraled upward.

In the living room, the drapes were closed, blocking off the bay window that faced the street. I walked through to the kitchen. It was spotless except for the stale smell of old food and grease. I called out for Dulcey again.

I walked back to the foyer and climbed the stairs. My heart pounded. I could not breathe. Her bedroom door loomed before me. I knocked and whispered her name. No answer. I turned the doorknob and slowly inched it open. Dulcey lay on the bed in a fetal position. I sucked in my breath and crept up to her. I touched her shoulder. She turned toward me and groaned. I jumped back and yelped.

"Damn, D, you scared me half to death."

She ogled me with eyes glazed over, as though she didn't know me. I wasn't sure if she had just woken up, or if her lack of awareness indicated a problem. I shook her shoulder lightly and called her name a few more times before she nodded and acknowledged me in a lucid manner.

She smiled up at me. "Oh, girl, I guess I passed out. Long day at the shop, and this medicine makes me so I don't know whether I'm dead or alive. Got me wishin' for death sometimes."

I took off my sneakers and climbed on the bed facing her. "You ain't dead and ain't gonna be dead anytime soon, so stop talking that mess." I wrapped my arms around her as much as I could and massaged the sides of her neck.

She lay quiet for a few minutes with her eyes closed. They opened and searched around to regain her bearings. Her gaze settled on me. "Hey, Miss M. How you doing, girl? You kill anybody yet behind those hot flashes?" She cackled and snorted like a sick pig.

"I'm glad you find going through the change, a woman's right of passage, so amusing. Just because yours has passed does not give you license to crack on the rest of us poor souls who are trudging down this path, struggling to maintain a sound mind."

"Oh, girl, please, you ain't never been, nor will you ever be of sound mind." We laughed. Dulcey choked on her weak titter. I ran to the bathroom for a glass of water. She sat up and swung her legs over the side of the bed. She sipped the water I offered, then waved it away. It took a few for her to catch her breath.

"I didn't mean to wake you," I said, wanting her to rest some more. "I wanted to make sure you have everything you need."

She smiled up at me. "The way you looking all pale and wide-eyed, you probably thought death sure nuff found me." She gave me a double take. "What is up with your head, Miss Mabley? It looks like you just got out of the shower and brushed it back outta the way."

I nodded. "Yep, that would be about it. Can't you just once say I did a good job fixing my hair? Just once."

"You need help, chile," she said, attempting to stand.

I put my hand on her shoulder. "You don't have to move. Go on back to sleep."

"Nice. You come into my house, wake me up, and tell me to go back to sleep so you can go home." She brushed my hand from her shoulder and pushed herself to a standing position. "I'm hungry. You can make me food." She sighed and gave me a strained look. "I'm not the least bit hungry, but I need to try eating something."

I got up beside her and took her arm, gentleman fashion.

She patted my hand. "Hmm. You're going to tell me what my husband has gotten hisself into," she said.

I smiled up at her. "Yes, I am."

Dulcey sat at the kitchen counter while I warmed a can of

Progresso chicken noodle soup on the stove. I filled a large bowl and set it in front of her; cut a slice of pumpernickel bread and spread it with butter and put it on a napkin beside her bowl. She pretended to eat some soup, moving it back and forth and around with a spoon. I watched her play with it for a bit before confiscating the spoon and hand-feeding her.

"Eat or I'll be forced to pour it down your throat."

"Yeah? I'd like to see you try that." She opened her mouth and ate all that I offered.

"What 'bout that tree-athlon you been training for, how's that goin'?"

"I'll be ready. I'm supposed to do my first swim in the river Monday. The thought of it really scares me. There isn't any side of the pool to grab ahold of if I get tired or feel like I'm not going to make it."

"You mean as in quit? Girl, please, you ain't never been nor will you ever be a quitter." This time Dulcey squawked loud and clear and long, sounding like a goose, but nevertheless, music to my ears.

I told her everything about Hamp's situation.

"I'll crucify them misguided, good-for-nothing, nose-picking, ass-hanging Negroes my damn self. They be done wished Mr. Calvin came for their butts when I finish with 'em." Dulcey slammed her first into the table, upsetting the bowl of soup and the glass of water I was drinking. I went for a dishcloth.

I heard the crack of a gunshot and dove for Dulcey, crashing us both to the floor. A few more pops followed by a deadened silence.

"Dulce, you all right?" I said, jumping up to see what happened. From the side window I could see folks gathering in the street.

"It'll take more than you throwing me to the floor to mess with all this flesh."

I helped her up. We hurried to the door.

"Oh, Lord," Dulcey said, grabbing hold of the railing and limping down the steps, old-woman style. People were gathered on the lawn of the duplex across the street from Dulcey's house. Dulcey and I parted the crowd, making our way to the center. Billy Teal lay spread-eagled, shot three times in the chest. Billy was Dulcey's godson. His mother, Cora, knelt over him, holding his hand. She opened her mouth but no sound came out, then she took a deep breath and the air filled with her guttural wail, long and low. Dulcey caught Cora's arm, pulled her up and embraced her.

"I told that boy time and time again to stay away from them damn gangs," Cora said. She cried into Dulcey's chest. "Told him he shouldn't oughta be selling them drugs that kill people." Cora pulled away from Dulcey's embrace. Before Dulcey or I could catch her, she turned in a fury, looking through the crowd that had gathered, found her target, and bolted up to a giant of a guy, muscle-bound to the point that his arms stuck out because they had to. He had a black bandanna wrapped about his head, pulled low over one eye.

"You bastards killed my boy. You and your damn stupid gangs that don't know nothing but killing. You go to hell! She spit at him, then stumbled back over to where Dulcey stood over the body. "He never listened to me, and now our baby is gone." She wailed some more. Dulcey held her.

Muscle man pushed his way through the crowd and disappeared. At least I lost sight of him for a moment. I scanned the crowd, filtering through the faces and listening to conversations. Police behavior. I meandered my way to the edge of the lawn and surveyed the neighborhood. Ward Griffin was sitting on the porch railing two houses down, watching. Muscle man stood at his side.

Police cars crammed the street and officers from the Mobile Street Crimes Unit scurried across the grounds, led by Zoila, rounding up known gang members. Zoila and another officer were on Griffin and muscle man. The officer handcuffed them and led them to a police car. Once in the car, Griffin turned his head and caught my eye with a contemptuous smile before turning away. I wondered if he recognized me from his visit to the house to get Elijah.

"They'll be back on the street by morning," Zoila said, walking back across the lawn to where I stood. "That is, unless someone steps forward and gives us something." She looked around at the fifty or so people gawking and whispering amongst themselves. "Someone called it in, which is how we got here so fast. Nobody is owning up to it now. The caller identified Griffin and his sidearm, Magnum. That's his name, the big guy. The caller said someone was about to die."

"Why? What's it about?"

"What else? Heroin."

"And the kid?"

"I'll get back to you," she said as she walked away, waving her hands in the air. "He's not one we know."

CHAPTER 13

Two nights after the shooting of Dulcey's godson, Billy Teal, we got called to another shooting in Fairmount Park.

I parked and walked in to the small clearing along the riverbank below Strawberry Mansion Bridge, where lights blazed around the activity.

Philly's Fairmount Park is said to be the largest landscaped urban park in the United States. There are those who argued Fairmount was only the third largest park in the US, beaten out by two parks in Phoenix, Arizona—South Mountain Park and Phoenix Mountains Preserve.

The Strawberry Mansion Bridge goes across the Schuylkill River. Divers were going into the water, the clattering of helicopters overhead that were mapping out the area to find the murder weapon. In a case like this, it was all about the current.

"Mabley." Zoila walked up behind me.

"I don't see you or talk to you for years, and now we're hooking up every other day," I said.

"Yeah, the talk is either about guns or drugs." She held up a baggie that contained a powdery substance. "Probably heroin mixed with fentanyl." She turned to the officer at her side. "Make sure the chem lab lets me know the results as soon as possible." The officer moved away. Zoila gestured toward the body. "We let him off. Devon Taylor, street name "D". We busted him a few days ago along with three other men. He got out last night. He's a minor and we couldn't hold him any longer. That's the way it worked out. My bet is his friends thought he snitched. Fact is, boy would be dead soon anyway from an overdose. Stone addict."

I was struck by how handsome and innocent-looking he was. I stepped back as Hayes stepped in, nudging Fran aside, and crouched over the body. "I'll have the particulars after an autopsy, though it would appear this young man died from a bullet to the heart," he said, seemingly putting his pointer finger through the bullet holes in the boy's chest.

Zoila backed away. I followed her. Fran walked off in another direction.

"Officers Barry Holden and Michael Aubry were parked across from the tennis courts, waiting for the sergeant to come sign their logs about nine p.m. when they heard a gunshot from the far end of Chamounix Drive. They radioed the location and reported shots fired. Aubry and Holden drove toward the direction of the shots. Aubry exited his car, his flashlight and gun in hand. They heard a car start and saw headlights come toward them. As the vehicle approached, two shots rang out and Officer Aubry fell to the ground just as the sergeant was approaching from Ford Road." Zoila pointed toward where the dead officer lay. "Officer Holden rushed to Aubry's side. The vehicle, a dark-colored SUV thought to be a BMW X5, made a left and headed the wrong way down Greenland Drive with the sergeant in pursuit. As the vehicle approached the Strawberry Mansion Bridge, one of the occupants leaned halfway out of the passenger window and tossed an object out of the vehicle. The sergeant continued pursuit across the bridge onto Woodford Drive then onto Ridge Avenue, where he lost them around Dauphin and Ridge."

I watched Fran searching the bridge where the sergeant indicated the object was thrown from the vehicle. Then I couldn't see him for a few minutes when he stooped behind the railings, a few feet out on the iron girder. I hoped he had found something.

I walked the area around the body, checking the ground to a distance of twenty to twenty-five feet, even though the victim was shot at close range. Maybe they picked up after themselves or shot him somewhere else and dumped the body here, or they tossed the shell casings, thinking we would only go but so far after recognizing that the victim was shot at close range. Also, pistols can eject shell casings a surprising distance in some instances.

The rotting, sweet smells of hundreds of varieties of flowers and trees wafted into my nostrils, too much for my nose to handle, and threw me into a sneezing frenzy. By the time I had finished, I was dizzy, spent, and my eyes were swollen. The blurry scene had stilled as I had become the point of attention. After about a minute and no sneezing, the buzz began again. I leaned against a tree to regain my composure, looked down, and there it was at my feet—a shell casing. I bent over to pick it up and noticed an oval-shaped object the color of moldy bread. I called Fran over and pointed it out to him. He examined it for about five seconds and said, "Definitely human."

"Just like that, you know for a fact that this is a human bone?"

"Maybe a clavicle bone."

"A clavicle bone?"

"Yep. The clavicle is the last bone to complete growth. Happens when a person is about twenty-five. Human bones differ from animals' in density and shape. The internal structure is different as well. Few animals have bones, something like four or five percent." Fran took a few steps away from where I found it and bent to examine the ground.

"Another bone?" I asked in a kind of screechy tone, a bit disturbed by our findings.

"This place could be some kind of dumping ground," he said.

"How do you go from two bones to a dumping ground? Stay here while I get Hayes."

By the time Hayes and I got back, Fran had found three more small bones or pieces of bones. Hayes made a quick examination and confirmed the objects were human bones.

Thirty minutes later, a half dozen examiners clad in Tyvek suits and rubber gloves, armed with shovels, handheld rakes, and trowels were digging around where the bones were found. The electric company sent PECO trucks to light up the search area. Four hours later, holes containing bones covered the area. The bones were photographed and documented before being packaged for transport—enough bones for two people, by Hayes's estimation.

Police established a large perimeter that blocked off Chamounix Drive, Ford Road, Greenland Road, Strawberry Mansion Bridge, and the two roads that go from the bridge to Martin Luther King Jr Drive north- and southbound.

At the sixth hour, Fran and I left, having found no more shell casings or other firearms evidence. I had just pulled onto our street when I received a call that the divers had found a weapon. Fran beat me back.

A Smith & Wesson semiautomatic had been found a short distance downriver from the bridge and twenty feet down. The gun was put in a container the size of four shoe boxes, with river water added to slow rusting. The slightest bit of rust could render the evidence useless because rust alters the individual characteristics that are necessary to identify which gun fired which bullets.

We wouldn't know for sure if the gun from the river was the

gun used to kill our victims until we tested it and matched the bullets from the victims and the casings we found to the gun. There might even be fingerprints on the weapon to identify the shooter. It could take months to solve, but Officer Aubry's murder put all cases on the back burner until we ran out of evidence to follow.

When we got to the lab, detectives from the scene had already submitted the gun and other evidence to the Evidence Intake Unit. I signed the transfer of custody while Fran retrieved the evidence bin. I asked the evidence supervisor to buzz me if any other evidence was turned in, then followed him downstairs.

Fran set the container with the gun in it on my desk. He took a couple of large envelopes that contained four small bags, each containing a single fired cartridge case, to do a microscopic examination.

First thing to do was a visual inspection, even before taking the gun out of the water.

When I removed the top from the case I noticed the serial number had been obliterated by an abrasive method. I snapped on a pair of plastic gloves and flipped the firearm over, keeping it in the water to prevent rusting. When I took it out, I would have to dry and lubricate it, which would destroy any microscopic markings. I had to keep it submerged throughout the examination. The right side appeared intact, with normal wear. From the left side I noted that the clip was still inserted well into the magazine. On the top of the slide, near the rear sight, was a deep indentation in the metal. Another mark caught my eye.

I grabbed a magnifying glass and made out a fingerprint on the surface of the frame. "I never thought I'd see this," I mumbled.

"What was that? Talking to yourself again?"

"I think we got a fingerprint. Take a look."

Fran rolled over in his chair to look through the magnifier

while I set up a video camera. He raised the firearm near the surface of the water for a clear shot. I also took a few digital shots, then took the case to the crime scene guys, who took more pictures with more sophisticated equipment. If they could lift a good enough print, the Fingerprint and Identification Unit could do a search of the national data base.

When I returned to the lab with the case, I took the gun from the water, disassembled it, dried all the parts with compressed air, then lubricated them.

Fran's examination of the cartridge cases established they were all the same caliber, fired in two different guns, one with a conventional type firing pin impression, the other with a clock-type impression.

We finished just after 2:00 a.m. My neck, taut with muscle knots, cracked with each move right, left, back, forward. My shoulders ached from hunching over. I reached behind my neck and pressed on the knots that refused to surrender.

"We may have stumbled on something really big," Fran said. "There are a few Mafia cases where the bodies were never found. Other members of the DePalma family."

"You really think the Mafia would use Fairmount Park as a dumping ground?"

"No matter who they are, they were killed and dumped, and whoever is responsible, well, we're much closer to finding out who it is and putting them away."

"You're right. I didn't mean to sound like I don't care or no big deal. Just thinking about that officer's family. Zoila said he has a wife and four boys. He didn't have a damn thing to do with any bones. Wrong place, wrong time is all."

"He was doing his job."

"Yeah . . . Like the two other officers killed so far this year who were just doing their jobs."

Fran scooched up to me in his chair, using his feet as the engine. He stopped short of ramming my knees.

"What's going on with you, Miss M? You sound like a disgruntled employee."

"Nothing. I'm just saying." I attempted to turn my chair back around to my desk, not wanting to get into a conversation about my personal issues right then.

Fran pulled it back and sighed like a beast. "This has got to be one of the hardest jobs I've ever had."

"Being a police officer can be that way sometimes."

"It's not being a police officer I'm talking about. It's about being your partner."

I stopped what I was doing, grabbed my bag, and headed out. "C'mon, let's get some coffee. You drive."

Fran drove down to Sixth and Market Streets to the Dunkin' Donuts and went through the drive-up, then pulled to the rear far corner of the parking lot.

"Before you pound on me, I didn't take this job because of stories about Jesse Boone or Laughton McNair or you being undercover back in the day. That stuff didn't matter when I requested to work with you."

"Too bad. You might have changed your mind."

"So, are you going to tell me or not? I'd much rather you told me than listen to what's going around the department."

"You listen to that crap, right?"

"Doesn't mean I believe it all. I like the stories about your previous partner, Laughton McNair. Seems like he was some kind of secret agent man, suave and mysterious."

"None of that matters. You're right, I have not been a very good partner these past few months since you signed on. For that, I apologize. So, let's move on from here."

"I'm game for that. I would like to hear the real story though, from you."

"Sometime, maybe. What about you? How do you know so much about bones? Better yet, why?"

"In the beginning I wanted to be an archeologist, then switched to humans and wanted to be a doctor, a bone doctor of sorts. Things didn't work out. My parents split and I had to drop out of school."

"From doctor to police . . . does not sound like a logical path from my viewpoint."

"My father and four brothers, all older, are all police officers in Richmond, where I'm from."

"What? You're from some kind of blue blood family?"

We laughed. Fran nodded. "Something like that."

"Twenty years ago, Jesse Boone was my sister's boyfriend. He was twenty-five, she was seventeen, about to graduate high school. He was the son of a hit man for the Black Mafia. She was Carmella. That's her real name. He abused her and, Nareece being Nareece, she got tired of the abuse and decided to do something about it. So she stole some drugs and money from him. Stupid. Boone caught up with her and . . . he left her for dead. If I hadn't come home . . . she would be. She ended up pregnant, with Travis."

"So Jesse Boone—"

"Is Travis's father."

"Nareece, I mean Carmella, changed her name and relocated to Massachusetts. Fast-forward twenty years, Boone gets out of prison after serving fifteen years for killing his father. He finds out about Nareece and goes after her again, this time for the two million dollars she stole. I didn't know about the money. Hell, I didn't know Jesse Boone was her boyfriend back then and I sure didn't know that my partner, Laughton McNair, was Boone's half brother, until about nine months ago. You know the rest. May the devil burn Jesse Boone alive."

"I heard you were undercover before you got into firearms."

"When I first got on the force, they needed a sucker and I was it. My job was to get certain information needed to bring down key Black Mafia figures. My cover got blown. They turned me into a heroin addict and dumped me in an alley to die. I guess God had other plans for me and my sister."

My phone buzzed. It was Calvin. At two thirty in the morning, alarm set in. "I gotta take this," I said and got out of the car.

"Is Hampton in a safe place?" Calvin asked.

"He's at the marina. Nobody knows about the boat but us."

"I have a few more cards to deal, but for now he needs to stay there or at least stay hidden. Griffin is not playing nice."

"Griffin? Ward Griffin?"

"That would be him. He runs Berg Nation, which is ultimately who Hamp borrowed the money from, though I don't think he knew who he was dealing with. Ward Griffin, street name War. He is head honcho in the Nation. Ruthless brother. You don't pay up when it comes due, you die. No extensions. No negotiating. No exceptions. No apologies. Just dead."

"Shit." I knew Griffin was a member of the Berg Nation gang, but the leader?

"Yes, that sums it up nicely."

CHAPTER 14

We stood on the banks of the Schuylkill River about a quarter mile down from the Strawberry Mansion Bridge, the very place two men, one a police officer, died a week ago. I eased my way into the water, shuddering at the feel of the mushy sand and stringy weeds that attacked my feet and legs. I pushed off, away from the shoreline.

"You ready?" Marybeth, my swim trainer asked, with all the concern of a catfish.

I nodded. I was in twenty-feet-deep open water with nothing to grab ahold of if I panicked. Swim or drown. I had to believe Marybeth's vow not to let me drown.

This was my first time in the river or any body of water for that matter, other than the swimming pool at the Kroc Center. Not being able to swim to the side and grab ahold of anything or to the shallow end and stand caused my heart to race, cutting off my ability to breathe. Marybeth held one elbow, which allowed me to keep my head above the water.

"Muriel, calm down."

Calm down, she said. Six thirty in the damn morning and I was in the freakin' Schuylkill River acting like I could swim, with a human fish telling me to calm the hell down.

"I'm right here. I will not let anything happen to you. You can do this. You have swum the distance fifty times. This is a different body of water is all. Breathe, girl. We'll stay close to the shore so you're more comfortable. Not too close though, because of the weeds." She pointed off to the distance. "That parking lot is where we want to get, where the transition area will be."

The other four women I trained with swam ahead of us with a trainer, in a line, as though synchronized. I claimed the noto-riety of being the only one who'd had to learn how to swim, which earned me a designated trainer all to myself.

I nodded confirmation to make the move. The current moved slowly this time of year, though I wished differently so it could push me along. I settled into a steady rhythm, with Marybeth keeping pace on my left. The black water made it difficult to identify anything beneath the surface. Sometimes I could see things. My imagination ran wild about those things coming to eat me alive. I closed my eyes. Still, thinking about it forced panic and shortness of breath, so I opened them. I stopped again and dropped like a rock. Marybeth rescued me and held me above the water again, supporting my elbow while I kicked my legs.

"We're almost halfway there. You're doing good."

"Right."

"I admire what you're doing. Not many people your age would go through what you're going through to do a triathlon to support a friend."

Your age? I almost puked. I nodded, then made the move to finish the half mile. *Your age* be damned.

We rounded the slight curve in the river. I felt stronger, more confident. Each time I turned my head sideways to take a breath, I could see the other swimmers sitting on the banks now, watching me. One of them pointed toward us. I imagined they had bets on whether I would make the distance or not as I glided down the final few feet.

What I first thought was a floating tree branch struck me. I reached out to push it away. It wasn't a tree branch. I sunk, panic-filled. I opened my eyes and screamed, taking in a mouthful of water, choking. Weeds wrapped around my leg. I fought with what strength I had left and pushed through to the surface, sucking for air. Marybeth grabbed my arm and pulled me to the riverbank. We were about three hundred feet from the group, who ran toward us as we climbed to shore and collapsed.

"You saw that, right?"

"Yeah," I said. "A body."

I took a quick shower and washed my hair, then soaked in the tub. I rested my head back and closed my eyes. I couldn't squash the visions of bodies under the water, bodies in the park, Jennifer Humphries's brains blown out. I lifted my hand from the water. I couldn't hold it steady. I sunk down into the water and held my breath until I couldn't anymore and pushed myself back up, sucking air.

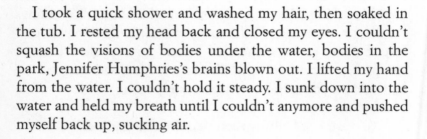

Nareece stood at the stove cooking bacon and eggs. I looked over her shoulder to nab a morsel, a move that earned me a slap on the hand. She blocked my view and pushed me away.

I grabbed a banana from the counter and sat at the island. "I was not aware you could cook," I teased. "Never heard tell that you cooked, cleaned, or any of those lowly duties. It was always John . . ." Damn. Silence followed for what seemed like forever before Nareece shut the burner off, turned from the stove, and came and sat down at the counter across from me.

"I'm aware of what's going on, Muriel. I'm present, here, in the real world. Jesse Boone killed John, my husband, the father of my children, and you sold our house in Boston. The girls and I live here now. You killed Jesse. Travis is my son but you raised him as his mother, and I'm grateful for that." She took my hand and put it against her cheek. "Without you I would be dead." She let go of my hand and got up. "I wish we could still have our daily conversations."

For the past ten years, Nareece and I talked every day by phone. During the last nine months, when she was in the hospital and nonresponsive, we had not talked, though I had gone to the hospital every day.

"I know you have to work and all, but maybe we can talk by phone while you're working, like we used to."

"Sounds good to me. Let's make it happen," I said.

Nareece filled a plate with food and set it in front of me. She may have seemed fine to other folk, but I knew there was something off. This person, who walked and acted out like Reecy, definitely was not.

"Hey, Moms, Auntie," Travis said, interrupting my thought.

"Travis, call the twins down for breakfast, please," Nareece ordered.

"I already told them to c'mon or they're going to be late."

"Call them again, like I asked," Nareece demanded.

"Auntie, they're coming."

Nareece slammed the frying pan down on the stove. "Travis, when your mother asks you to do something, you do it."

My stomach growled. I opened my mouth to speak, then shut it. This was Travis's to settle.

"Auntie, I already did what you asked me to," Travis said in an even tone that surprised me. The sweet sound of the twins running and jumping down the stairs came at the end of his last word.

Nareece did not respond to Travis's remark. She just kept messing with the frying pan, and cleaning up the food she spilled.

The twins raced into the kitchen, a challenge to be the first to climb on a stool. The narrow margin had both declaring it a tie.

"Elijah and I are 'bout to bounce and go over to Kenyetta's place to catch up with her. She's been absent for the past few days. Not answering her phone. I'ma make her pay for makin' me worry about her dumb ass . . . I mean behind." He gave me an apologetic look for cursing, chuckled and got up to leave.

"Where's Elijah?"

"Boy is taking way too long to get ready, that's where he is."

"Things been good? I mean with his brother."

"He's been cool. Elijah's keeping his distance. Got a job working nights at the Wawa round the corner on Cleveland."

"You need to be following suit," I said.

"Ma. I got this. Be patient. Hey, Auntie, could you please fill Mom in 'bout the job thang?"

"I will, baby, I will," Nareece called after him in a tone sculpted in joyfulness.

Nareece and Travis were communicating in a somewhat civil manner. Yeah. At the very least they shared information, information I was not yet privy to. I was pleased, or at least, I think I was pleased. Stupid. Of course, I was pleased. Travis kissed Nareece on the cheek and then did the same to me. He lifted my chin and winked at me before leaving. I was pleased.

Nareece explained Travis's plan to work at the center with Calvin. It was the most animated I had seen her since she came home.

Calvin hadn't mentioned anything about it. I supposed he never had the chance.

"He's just like his mother," she said. "I mean me, Muriel.

He's a lot like you too. You probably don't remember this, but I always wanted to work with young children."

"I remember. You worked every summer at camps for kids and babysat a lot. I anguished over the thought that you would pop up pregnant. All you talked about was having babies." I bit my tongue trying to shove the words back down my throat.

"Muriel, you have to stop acting like you can't talk around me, like you're afraid of saying something wrong. It happened. I'm well aware that I gave Travis up and you took him and have been his mother all his life, but I gave him life." Nareece sucked back tears, then plowed ahead. "He doesn't call me Ma, and I'm trying to live with that." She got up and went to the stove.

My cell phone rang. It was Hayes.

⁂

Travis's words echoed in my ears as Hayes opened the door, slid the drawer out, and unzipped the black bag that hugged a lifeless figure. *Going over to Kenyetta's . . . She's been missing for the past week . . . I'm going to make her pay . . .* I was anchored a few feet away. Hayes spread the body bag from Kenyetta's face. I prayed he would not say anything that would warrant a response, a movement; that he would not re-cover Kenyetta Mae Jones before I looked.

I twitched at the sight of the long slender body, the sculpted features that were no longer sculpted but bloated, dark, and shapeless.

"The cause of death was a heroin overdose. She was dead when she went into the water. The other two victims, Percy Morris and Sam Gunther, both nineteen, were also dead before going in the water. Heroin overdoses as well."

"Sam Gunther?"

"Yes. You know him?" Hayes pulled the sheet over Kenyetta's face and pushed the drawer in, then moved down two drawers and pulled out another drawer. I followed, holding my breath. He pulled the sheet away from Sam's bloated, bruised face. I backed away.

"Sam and Kenyetta did not use drugs. They were both good kids." The words sounded hollow in my ears. There was no way that could be going on and I would miss it, I thought. I bowed my head and let the tears come.

"Loving eyes oftentimes cannot or rather do not, see," Hayes whispered in a tender way, tender for him anyway. I appreciated the attempt and had no reply. I recognized that it was the second time in as many weeks I'd heard those words.

Fran came into the chamber as Hayes was closing the door on Sam's body. "The gang unit had these pictures showing the three victims at the Blumberg housing project with the head honcho over there, Ward Griffin, street name War. They also had this photo."

I ignored Fran, stuck on Kenyetta and Sam's death.

"I'm sorry, Muriel. I know these kids meant a lot to you," Fran said. "You have to look at these."

I took the pictures he held out to me. The first two showed Kenyetta and Sam entering a four-story apartment building. Fran said the photos were taken two weeks prior to finding the bodies. The second one, taken a few days earlier, showed Elijah and Travis entering the same building.

I called Travis's cell. No answer. I called the house and Nareece answered. Travis had not returned since leaving earlier. I called his cell again and left a message. He called right back. We agreed to meet at the house.

I pulled into the driveway just as Travis and Elijah pulled up curbside. I sat in my car and listened to their banter and watched them playfully push and shove each other up the walkway and into the house. After they went into the house, I sat for a long while, gathering my thoughts and words. I said a prayer and went in.

The house was quiet except for the voice of the television news anchor coming from the den. Travis was sitting on the couch helping Helen make a Scrabble word. Elijah was stretched out in the recliner next to the couch.

"... *Police are not yet commenting on what happened or releasing the names of the victims* ..."

I walked into the room and sat on the couch next to Travis.

"What's happening, Moms? You sounded all serious on the phone, like somebody died or something."

"Something's happened to Kenyetta and Sam, baby. They're gone."

Travis looked at me with the same blankness Nareece did before she snapped out of it. I reached out to him. He pulled away.

"What . . . what do you mean, they're gone?"

"They're dead."

Elijah popped up out of his reclined position. "How?"

"The police are investigating."

Travis turned to me, anguished. I embraced him. "I have to ask you something, son."

Travis pushed back to look at me.

"Did Kenyetta and Sam use drugs?" The words forced their way past my lips.

Neither of them responded right away. Travis's face turned red. The wrinkles in his brow flattened as he calmed.

"No. Kenyetta and Sam didn't use drugs. I would know if my girlfriend and my best friend since kindergarten used heroin. You might as well ask me if I'm using."

"Well, are you?" I regretted the words as soon as they came out.

Travis slammed his fists into the seat of the couch.

I took the photos of Kenyetta and Sam with Ward Griffin out of my bag and spread them across the coffee table. "Tell me about these."

Travis leaned forward and handled each photo carefully. Elijah got up and strode over to the table and did the same. Elijah's air of confidence chipped away until his shoulders slumped forward and he crumpled to the floor, cross-legged.

Elijah spoke first. "I am so sorry I got anybody involved in my mess with WG. I just wanted to get right. I thought because I was his brother he wouldn't . . . He'd just let me be." He lay back on the floor.

"Do you think your brother had something to do with Kenyetta and Sam's death?"

Elijah sat up and turned his attention to Travis. Neither spoke for a few moments.

Then Travis said, "A few days ago we went to get Elijah's things. He called his brother first, so we went and picked up his clothes and a few other things. I don't know what Kenyetta and Sam . . . I don't know what these pictures are about. I told you she's been acting trifling, disappearing and not answering her phone." He started crying. "She wasn't using. She said she had some crazy stuff going on and would tell me about it when we got together, which we were supposed to do yesterday, but she never showed and never answered my calls. I've been trying to catch up with her ever since. I even went to her place today."

"I'm sorry, son."

"Miss Mabley. That guy, Mr. Kim."

"What about him?"

"You're looking for his daughter, right?"

I nodded.

"I saw her at the apartment while we were there. I mean, it didn't seem like she wanted to leave or anything. She was pretty messed up . . . high."

"In your brother's apartment?"

"Yeah. He introduced her as his girl."

"Was she all right?"

"Yeah, I guess so. Like I said, she was cooked."

"Why didn't you tell me this before?"

"Travis didn't see her and I didn't think of it until just now. I mean, I didn't want to snitch on her or anything. She acted like she wanted to be where she was and all."

"Nobody wants to be messed up on heroin," I said.

CHAPTER 15

Calvin was waiting outside when I pulled into the parking lot behind Calvin's Place. BJ and two other men were sitting in a black Cadillac with the engine idling. Calvin opened my car door and offered me a hand. After we got in his Mercedes, he handed me a notebook.

"We have visitors sign in to keep track of the comings and goings of folks who come to the center. Monroe mans the entrance and makes sure that everyone signs in. The log shows that Mr. Kim's daughter was at the center the day before you said she went missing. My guys say she's been hanging out with members of Berg Nation, or rather young dudes who claim to want out of the nation. I'll tell you, she didn't get mixed up with them for love."

I had the notebook open on my lap. He pointed to her signature, flipped a page and pointed again. "She signed in twice a week for the past month or more. If she's on that junk, my bet would be that Griffin's holding her in one of the crash pads at Blumberg. He controls several apartments. A few of them are flop houses for users. He keeps girls hepped up on that shit, just enough, and rents them out by the half hour."

"Elijah said Griffin called her his girl."

"Yeah, right. His girl that he pimps out for cash."

"How the hell do these kids even get it in their heads to use drugs? How does anyone get that thought moving through their brain? I mean, I know what happened to me . . ."

"Don't be naïve, Miss M. This stuff hits little black children and executives, doctors, lawyers, mothers, fathers, sisters, brothers alike. No boundaries this go-round."

"I got guys doing surveillance to confirm what apartment in which building before we go storming in. Your police com- padres would not be very happy if things got out of hand. Ward Griffin is a pretty shrewd young man. He controls eyes everywhere. Blumberg is a fortress. His own little city, if you will."

"So what you're saying is we can't walk in there friendly- like, and take her out?"

"Let's find out where she is first."

"Waiting . . . we could be too late. She could end up like Kenyetta."

"Always the pessimist." His phone buzzed. After a few curt grunts, he clicked off and shifted into drive. I got out and got back in my car to follow them.

Calvin waited at the entrance to the Norman Blumberg Apartments while I parked. Across the street from the entry- way to the projects was a vacant lot, overgrown with weeds, covered in cracked cement and trash. The rancid odor of decay floated on the hot air.

"We must stop meeting like this, my darling Miss M," he halfheartedly joked, when I got in his car. "She's not being held against her will, right?"

"According to Elijah, she's not there against her will."

"So we can't go busting in. Well, we'll have to go in proper- like, and knock. If she doesn't want to come, you'll have to leave her?"

"That is not an option."

The Cadillac followed us into the Norman Blumberg housing complex that stretches between Jefferson and Oxford and Twenty-Second and Twenty-Fourth Streets in North Philly, dodging between the two high-rise buildings and fifteen barracks-style buildings. He knew the area well and filled me in on the history. Blumberg was one of the most dangerous housing complexes in Philly. He called it a forgotten city. It was surrounded by a few hundred acres of vacant lots resulting from abandoned housing and other housing complexes that endured a more humane demise.

The area was in the beginnings of a revitalization project that would include new affordable housing units on some of the lots in hopes of bringing it back to its once vibrant and productive state, a time I could not remember. It seemed clear from the transactions going on at every corner within the complex that certain factions denied the upgrade.

Calvin stopped in front of building 1B on the Jefferson Street side of the complex, one of the two high-rise buildings.

"You and me," Calvin said. "Fifth floor."

When we entered, the smell of funk, mold, piss, and weed made me gag. I held my breath, squeaking it out a little at a time, until I had to breathe in again. Calvin breezed through as though he did not have a nose.

The metal door clanged behind us. The elevator had "out of service" written on the door in black marker. We took the stairs rather than take the chance, even if it was working. My training for the triathlon paid off, allowing me to keep up with Calvin. Almost. I had to make a stop on floor three.

When we entered the fifth floor, three armed men blocked our path.

"Got a call to pick up someone on this floor," Calvin said.

"Who called?"

"A young lady, Karin Kim."

"Wait here."

"We're not going anywhere without her. You can tell who-ever it is you grovel to. It ain't happening."

The guy was gone for about two minutes. He came back and directed us two floors up to another apartment.

We continued up the two flights. Calvin opened the door to the inside hallway, which reeked of the burnt-vinegar smell of cooked heroin. My eyes watered. My stomach lurched. I backed out and ran down a flight of stairs with Calvin on my heels. I puked in the stairwell, barely missing his shoes.

"You good? C'mon." Calvin gently took my arm and went to guide me down the stairs. I shook my head and leaned over. More puke. I took a breath and wiped my mouth with the back of my hand. I took a deep breath and moved to go back up-stairs. I looked up to see Ward Griffin standing above us on the landing.

"You treat someone else's home like this. You shit and just move on, huh?" Griffin said.

Calvin responded with cool reserve. "Hey, man, we're here for a pickup."

"So my man here told me."

"Look, man, we don't want any trouble." Calvin turned to me. "Move."

I continued up the stairs behind Calvin. Griffin stepped aside for Calvin when he reached the landing. He backed up inside to the hallway.

Karin came out of apartment 725 and froze when she saw Griffin. She turned to go back inside, but stopped when she saw me. Griffin grabbed her arm. Calvin stepped forward.

"Where you goin', you sexy thang, you?" Griffin pulled her close to him like he was going to kiss her but shoved her away instead. "She's a damn junkie. Take the bitch."

I moved past Calvin, grabbed Karin, and double-timed down the steps. Two men were coming up, each anchored with a young girl. A flash of recognition of one of the girls registered before my focus returned to taking Karin out of the building.

"You think you can come in here and take anything you want, you're wrong. Next time you come up in here, don't plan on visiting long. I got plenty for your fine ass. Tell my brother the next time he even thinks he wants to come up in here, he won't be leavin' either, along with his new brother, cuz they ain't gonna wanna leave. What's that nigga's name? Travis, ain't it?" He snarled, baring his teeth.

I moved down the stairs, pulling Karin by the arm behind me.

When we got outside the building, Calvin's men were there holding ground, two against at least ten. I pushed Karin into the backseat and slid in the front passenger seat as Calvin exited the building. He jumped in the driver's side and pulled away.

"What the hell kind of place is that? Why hasn't the gang unit or the DEA been able to shut them down?"

Calvin gave me a sideways look.

"Yeah, yeah, no evidence, no witnesses, I know the drill."

I twisted around to Karin. Her face was smudged with dirt except for white circles around her eyes, making her look like a raccoon. The black halter-dress that hugged her body like a girdle accentuated her boniness, not a word I would have thought of to describe the Karin I remembered. "How you doing?"

She nodded. Calvin dropped us at my car. I drove down Jefferson and made a right on Girard Avenue.

"I just went . . . the guy I was with said we were going to a party . . . I got messed up and couldn't leave . . . I don't know, but then I didn't want to leave."

"So they didn't force you to stay."

"No."

She was quiet for a bit, sniffling and looking out the window, anything to avoid facing me, or anyone for that matter. I remember well. I decided not to press, leaning on the hope that daughter and father would win out.

"I'm sorry, Miss Mabley. I didn't realize so much time had passed. I couldn't call my father." She turned toward the window. "My daughter."

"Your daughter and your father are fine, just worried sick about you. I haven't called them."

"It was my own fault, Miss Mabley. I went with the guy for drugs."

"How long have you been using?" I glanced over at her when she didn't answer. "You know you'll have to go into rehab for any hope of stopping—that is, before you overdose and die. And you still might kill yourself, because getting clean messes you up. You get so sick you want to kill yourself. Cold hugs your bones with pure hatred, makes the devil retreat, and drags you every which way but right, toward the warmth of another fix." I slammed on my brakes to keep from ramming the car in front of me. I realized I had been yelling. "I'm sorry, Karin. Hana and Kim are going to be so happy to see you. That's all that matters now."

"I'm not so sure my father will want to see me, until I get clean, I mean."

"He will. We'll get you freshened up before we call him and take you home."

"Miss Mabley, you talk like . . . I mean, I know you couldn't have been . . . I was just wondering . . ."

"Yes, I'm a recovering heroin addict. I've been where you're at and then I got clean. I've been clean almost twenty years now. There's not a day goes by that I don't think about it. Maybe a day here and there. But I've come to where I can brush it off and keep going. One day at a time."

Karin was quiet for the rest of the ride to Dulcey's shop.

Dulcey's other business was taking care of women in need. Homeless women, women running from men, drug addicts. In the basement of her shop was a shower, clean clothes, and food.

Dulcey said, "The doors are open to those passing through to the next opportunity."

After Karin was showered, Dulcey did her hair.

"You might be feeling like some poor thing right now, feeling like you been beaten and bruised in more ways than you could shake a stick at. For sure you need a lot more than a shower and some clean clothes to set you right for the long haul, but right now it's what you got," Dulcey said, putting the last touches on Karin's hair. "The rest is up to you, young lady."

"You a pretty little thing," Marsha, one of the hairdressers, said. "Don't you worry, young lady, there's a man out there just for you. One who'll treat you like his queen, the way you're supposed to be treated."

"Yes, ma'am. And when you find that right guy, you won't even remember the foolishness you been through till now. A good man, with good loving, makes you forget your own name," Tracy said.

The woman whose hair Tracy was doing said, "Amen to that."

Karin smiled, the first since I picked her up.

When we pulled up to the top of the block on Longshore, Karin asked me to pull over. Sweat slicked her bangs to her forehead. Her chest heaved as she rocked back and forth, shaking her hands in the air.

"Deep breaths, baby. Take deep breaths. You're going to be fine." I looked down the street and saw Mr. Kim standing outside the door. "Your father doesn't care about anything else but that you're okay. He loves you, Karin. Now you have to love yourself enough to get the help you need."

She took a deep breath and nodded.

As we pulled to the curb, Mr. Kim strode down the walkway. Karin looked at me with shame in her eyes. I patted her hand. "You got a long road ahead, but you'll make it."

I got out and walked around to open her door. Mr. Kim stood with his arms folded across his chest, waiting. His arms opened when she jumped out and ran to him. Kim scooped her up like he was six feet tall. Hana ran out of the house and leaped into her mother's arms.

I leaned against the car and watched until they went inside and closed the door. While my heart was warmed, I knew that it was not a happy ending. Not yet.

CHAPTER 16

I wish I could say the chilly air motivated me to move my lard butt faster, but the only breeze making headway was the one my butt made swinging through the experience of jogging. Jogging three miles proved to be the second biggest challenge. It would be the first behind swimming, except I can't drown jogging. Die from a heart attack, maybe, but not drown.

At 5:30 a.m., the sidewalks were all mine to conquer. I went twenty blocks one way for a mile and a half, then a block over and kept the pace, jogging Rocky-style to the beat of Pharrell's "Happy." The car moved slowly about a half block behind me. I turned my head left, choreographed to go with my boxer moves. A gray coupe with tinted windows inched along. I got to the corner and sprinted to the right. The car sped off, keeping straight. Maybe I was being paranoid. Maybe not. I slowed and checked my watch. The good news, I did the three miles without stopping. The bad news, it took me forty-five minutes. I had a month to cut my time down to thirty minutes.

Two blocks from the house, I picked up the pace and arrived home, as Travis hustled the twins out the door to take them to day camp at the Kroc Center. Elijah was the last to scoot by me, going to work. Travis reminded me that Sam's funeral service was tomorrow and Kenyetta's the day after. I had already requested the time off from work.

Nareece was in the kitchen nursing a cup of coffee and reading and tearing pages out of *Philadelphia Style* magazine. Recipes to satisfy her newfound obsession with cooking. Other than her bedroom, she stayed in the kitchen, cooking or not cooking. I'm a tea drinker, so I filled a mug with water, put it in the microwave, then got a tea bag from the canister and put it in the hot water, and took a seat.

"I'm thinking about getting my own place," she said in a sober tone. I choked on a sip of tea. I sucked for air, raised my arms, sucked for air some more. Nareece flipped a page of the magazine without looking up. I sucked for air some more, sounding like a donkey in pain.

"You gonna make it?" She ogled at me until my airway cleared enough for me to take a breath.

"I think it would be better for the twins if we got our own place. I'm fine now and I can certainly afford it."

Before I answered, she was bent over the magazine again. I wanted to reach over and smack her, but what would be the sense? One minute she seems good because her and Travis are talking and the twins are happy, and the next minute, she's angry at me or Travis for God only knows what. I took a deep breath and reveled in my ability to do so.

"Do you think moving is what's best for the twins? They're settling in and love being around Travis. Those girls will be heartbroken if you take them away now."

"They'll be fine. Travis will be going back to school soon, so it won't matter. I suppose we can stay until then."

"Yeah, I think that'll be good." I downed the last of my tea and got up to put my cup in the dishwasher.

"Leave it, I'll clean up."

I set the cup back on the counter. "Reecy, I'm right here

when you decide you want to talk. We should be able to talk about anything at this point in our lives."

She moved the magazine to the side and poked her lips out at me. "We'll talk some more, but I don't think I'll change my mind."

"Fine, as long as we talk first."

I was about cross-eyed from staring into a comparison microscope for most of the day, when Fran came in. I welcomed the interruption.

"What's it looking like?"

"I'm still working on it."

"What about the fingerprint?"

"No such luck. It was in the water too long, wasn't good enough."

"How's your son doing?"

"He's messed up. He usually talks to me about everything. Or at least he used to. Not this time, and it's making me a little crazy. If Kenyetta and Sam were murdered and he is somehow privy to this or mixed up in some stuff . . ."

Fran sat on the desk next to the microscope. "I'm not that well acquainted with him, but from the way you talk about him, he sounds like he's smart enough to come to you if he needs to. I think you're more worried about his friend. What's his name?"

"Elijah. Yes. And the idea is that they come to me before things get bad."

"Mabley, in my office," Pacini bellowed, sounding like he was standing right next to me and blowing my eardrums up rather than on the other side of the door down the hallway. I gave Fran the thumbs-down and went to the lieutenant's office.

"I'm told you visited Blumberg." He pushed a photograph of me coming out of the building with Calvin and Karin.

"A friend's daughter got jammed up in there and called me for help. Asked me to pick her up."

"That friend's daughter wouldn't be affiliated with any gang?"

"No, Lieutenant. She got lost for a minute. How'd you find out?" I said, tossing the photograph across his desk.

"You might want to talk with your friend in the gang unit and or DEA before you decide to rescue any more of your friend's children."

"Thanks for the warning."

"You're scheduled to report to Internal Affairs this after-noon at three. Tell them what they want to know, Mabley. Don't make a big deal about it. They're going to do what they're going to do."

"Well, what they aren't going to do is make a point by dis-crediting all the work we put in, not if I have anything to say about it."

"Which you do and will, I'm sure, and they will experience the Mabley wrath. I'm sure about that as well," Pacini snarled with a hint of playful sarcasm.

During the ride over to Internal Affairs, I called Dulcey to vent about Reecy.

"She could be right," Dulcey said. "Those girls may be bet-ter off having to deal with her one-on-one, and you going back to being their auntie and Travis . . ."

"Yeah, what about Travis? They don't even have a clue that he is their brother. I'm thinking that might be the way it should stay too."

"Well, Travis doesn't leave for a few more months. A lot can happen before then, like you two talking this thing out, whatever this thing is."

"Tell her that, because I'm clueless. I mean, I can't control Travis's feelings and actions toward her. That's something for them to work out. I feel like she wants me all up in it, like I should be *making* Travis call her mom. She isn't going anywhere. She's being an ass, but she's not moving." Dulcey stayed silent. "Enough about all that. What is going on with you?"

"M, Hampton didn't call last night or the night before. I'm not one to worry so much, but he calls every night. I'm thinking of taking a trip down to the boat."

"You stay put. I'll go down there this afternoon and see what's going on."

"Right."

"Dulcey, you hear me? You're going to stay put."

"Yes, Miss M, I do."

I called Calvin and left a message when he didn't answer. I wanted to talk to him before meeting with Hampton.

The Internal Affairs Bureau was a two-story, redbrick office building on Dungan Road in Northeast. I pulled into the parking lot on the side of the building and walked around to the front entrance. The receptionist showed me to a conference room across from where she sat. She offered me coffee or tea. I declined. She told me to help myself to the water and candies that were in the center of the conference table and that the inspector would be with me right away.

I always thought of Inspector Slater as a nice enough guy. I only met him in passing, like at holiday gatherings of police officers. I have never been on the receiving end of questions, suspicions, or anything else that had to do with the workings of

Internal Affairs. I've been told but could not believe the description of Inspector Slater as a bastard. Then again, he's getting paid to dig up the dirt on his fellow officers, justified as that may be. So I could understand the attitudes of some officers, but I couldn't condone them.

Today I believed it, as he attacked. "Did you and Laughton McNair have an affair while he was in the unit? Why did Laughton McNair leave the department? Did you and Laughton McNair do favors for the mob for money? Did you and Laughton McNair send firearms to evidence without being tested? Did you ever lie while testifying under oath?"

"Yes, Laughton and I had an affair. We stopped it as soon as it began, because both of us valued our positions in the department and neither of us was willing to leave. You'll have to ask Laughton why he left the department. He and I did not do favors for the mob, nor did we send any cases to evidence before testing was completed. And no, I have never lied under oath."

As soon as I got in my car, Calvin called.

"Hampton is into more than he is saying. They want more from him than he said. There is a contract out on him. I think your guy witnessed a murder or did the job himself."

"Hamp couldn't kill anybody. It's not in his nature."

"You'd be surprised what's in a person's nature when they are being threatened with the right consequences. Look, they're going to find out about the boat. He needs to leave the city. First, he needs to tell you what's really going on."

That almost explained why he hadn't contacted Dulcey the past two nights. If he was . . . If something had happened to him . . . I floored the gas pedal.

CHAPTER 17

I pulled curbside a block from the entrance gate to the docks. I cut off the engine and sat in the car and watched the thick tourist traffic, typical for the summer months. I got out and meandered my way through the throngs of folks before I broke into a sprint. Halfway down the block, I nearly tripped over a little girl who ran into my path. I hurdled over her to keep from knocking her to the pavement.

I entered the marina from the front side, bypassing the bathhouse. The gate required a key to enter. As I closed it behind me, Dulcey called.

"Well, what'd he say for himself?"

"I'm still en route. I'll call you back shortly."

"Oh. Girl, I can go myself."

Dulcey's voice quivered as she continued. "I just want him to be all right. You tell him I just want him to come home."

"Dulce, I'll call you back. I'm almost there," I said, as easy as I could, given the emotional stress she exhibited. A big guy bumped against me, almost knocking the phone from my hand. He mumbled some kind of apology and kept stepping. I tucked my irritability under my immediate concern for Hampton and moved on.

I hustled down the walkway toward the *Dulcey Maria*. The noise of the busy surroundings dulled in the quiet of the boat area. All the boats I passed were closed up, I supposed because of the dinner hour or an art or music festival happening. All except for the *Family Sanctum*. Mr. Lowry stuck his head out and greeted me as I passed.

I slowed my pace, remembering my last stroll on the dock. I cringed at the thought of swimming again. As I approached the *Dulcey Maria*, I heard a banging noise. I decided to be safe this time. I tiptoed over the back of the boat and edged up to the doorway, staying hidden. I stuck my head out and did a quick peek around the corner, once, twice. A man in a dark-colored hoodie hunched over a storage container. My first thought said to wait for him to exit rather than announce myself and tempt a scuffle in the tight confines of the boat. My second thought argued the tight confines would work to my advantage.

I slid the door open and drew my Glock. "PPD."

He froze, cocked his head to the side and turned around, his face wrinkled with an annoyed expression. His five ten, two-hundred-pound stature filled the small cabin. He rushed me as soon as he turned toward me. I clocked him as hard as I could in the head with the butt of my gun before he rose up and spun me around, causing the gun to fly out of my hand. He stumbled forward, pressing me against the cabin wall. My chest caved. No air escaped. I kneed him in the groin. He bent over and stumbled backwards. I anchored a sideways stance to lessen the blow as he lunged at me again. He slammed me back into the cabin wall again. I elbowed him in the jaw, which knocked him back a step before he lunged forward again. I sidestepped and pushed him backward out the cabin door. He lay spread-eagled, faceup on the deck, a bullet hole in the middle of his forehead.

I ducked inside the cabin and checked the tiny windows on

both sides of the boat, staying below the line of sight. I stepped outside the door far enough to bait another shot, the whirring sound of the bullet skimming my ear.

I pulled my cell from my hip. "Officer needs assistance at Penn's Landing. Shots fired."

I stayed low and inside the cabin door, peeking up a few times to see where the shooter might be. The dock was empty. I prayed Mr. Lowry had not heard the gunshots and stayed inside his boat. Five minutes felt like an eternity before I heard police clomping down the walkway. Still I was unsure I wanted to stick my head out the door, before a detective knocked and slid it aside.

I recounted the happenings as Zoila milled through the throng of officers.

"I'll take it from here," she told the homicide detective. "She's one of mine."

"One of yours, huh," I said after we moved down the walkway. "Why are you here, stepping over homicide?"

"Not stepping over, working with. The dead guy is Edgardo Ramos, a petty thief. So, I ask you, what's going on, Muriel?"

"I came to help out a friend."

"Your friends seem to be very needy lately."

I ignored her sarcasm. "When I got here, the guy ransacking the place had his back to me. I announced myself as police and we got into a struggle inside the cabin. I pushed him out and . . . he went down. Sounded like sniper fire, fast and furious."

"Fast and furious, huh?"

"Yeah. I stuck my head out and almost got dead too."

"And you can't say why someone would want to kill this guy, or your friend, or maybe you?"

"I know, you think I'm putting you off, Zoila, but I'm not. Just give me a little leeway and I swear I will find out what's going on and fill you in."

She did not respond. Rather she surveyed the scene, checked

out the crowd gathered on the bridge overlooking the dock area, and then back at me.

"I never messed over you," I said in earnest.

"Never been a time such as this."

"But I mean, I would never mess you up."

When I got back to my car, I called Dulcey. No answer. Hamp didn't answer his phone either. Travis answered before the first ring stopped.

"Ma, where you been? I been banging your number. Go to the hospital. They took Aunt Dulcey to Mercy. Aunt Nareece took a cab there."

"What do you mean? I just talked to Dulcey about a half hour ago."

"Just go to the hospital, Ma. I'll meet you there."

I called Nareece. She yelled into the phone as soon as she answered.

"Where the hell are you? Dulcey is fighting for her life and you're nowhere to be found and she's asking me where you are and where her husband is and I can't tell her anything because I don't know, and you call after we've been trying to reach you but you don't answer your cell, like you never answer your cell, especially when I'm calling and—"

"Nareece, stop!" I yelled to gain her attention. I gave her a second before I asked about Dulcey.

She said in a nasty tone, "Dulcey is in a bad way."

When I walked into the waiting area at Mercy Hospital, Nareece and Hamp, the lone occupants, sat on opposite sides of the room—Nareece with her head in a magazine on one couch, and Hamp with his head hung, a pitiful vibe surrounding him, on another couch. He popped up and confronted me the minute I walked through the door. I should be focused on Dulcey, I kept telling myself. I was focused on Dulcey, and only on Dulcey, which is why, when I saw Hamp, all self-control was lost. I socked him.

He fell backwards, crashing down on an end table and bringing down the lamp and some magazines with him. Two nurses came running to investigate the commotion and assist him, one telling the other to call the police.

"I am the police," I said, flashing my badge.

Hamp pushed away attempts by the nurses to examine him, finally raising his voice to make them leave.

Surprisingly, Nareece kept her seat and her mouth locked shut for a change. After the nurses left the room, she approached Hampton and offered him a hand up. He accepted. She helped him sit on the couch and moved the broken pieces of the table off to the side of the room.

A maintenance man came into the room as Nareece pushed aside the last piece of broken lamp with her foot. He picked up the pieces, swept up the remnants, and left. We were all quiet through the process. Until the door closed.

"What are you doing? You not only put yourself in danger, but everybody around you just by your being here. And for what, Hamp? So you can play your games and get stupid? You don't need my help, you need to be locked up and the key lost." I plopped down on the other end of the couch from Nareece. I leaned back and rested my head on the back of the couch and tried to take deep breaths to slow my heartbeat and regain control of my faculties.

"Muriel, it's not what you think," Hampton said in a low, grumbly voice.

I sat up and bore into him with my most disheartened gaze.

He glanced at Nareece, then back to me, wondering if he should talk in front of her, I supposed. When I did not flinch, he continued.

"I was there the other night when they killed the kid and the cop."

"In Fairmount Park?" I squeaked.

"Yeah. They wanted me to kill the kid." He ran his fingers through his hair. "They said a snitch deserves death. The kid claimed he didn't talk to the police, that they let him go because they lacked evidence against him, but they wouldn't hear the boy. The one, War, he beat the boy near to death. Made him kneel. When I refused to do the deed, he made me kneel beside the boy. I thought my life ended right there, that God judged all I've done and decided killing me was the best course of action."

"Who shot the kid and the cop?"

"War shot the kid. He's the boss of the . . ."

"Berg Nation." I finished his sentence.

"Yes. We heard the cops call out and everybody ran. They went for the car and took off. I took off in the opposite direction, thankful that my life had been spared. When I heard more shots, I stopped running and turned around. That's when I saw the police officer fall. A big man come out of the shadows, but I could not see his face. I called it in to the police and kept on running until I got to the street and hitched a ride."

"So you haven't called Dulcey or been back to the boat because you're afraid they'll find out about her? How the hell did you know she was here?"

"I was talking with Dulcey on the phone when she started feeling bad. I called the ambulance and came right here. I tried to call you, but it went straight to voicemail." He hesitated before continuing. "I figured they knew about the boat after you told me about the break-in. I figured it best to stay different places, hotels, motels, rooming houses."

"So the dead guy who destroyed your place yet again, is off your radar?" I pulled out my phone and showed him a picture of the dead guy.

Hamp scanned the picture and put it aside way too fast for me to think he'd tell the truth and nothing but the truth. "Dammit, Hampton, if you lie to me again, I swear I'll . . ."

"I don't know who he is, Muriel. There have been many break-ins in the past weeks, kids looking for valuables, cash, for a fix. Nowadays, nothing is off-limits. Nothing at all."

"Yeah, except someone shot this intruder in the head." His startled expression said the news sank in. "Word is there's a contract out on you."

A surprised expression flashed across his face.

"I'm considering somebody thought your intruder was you."

He got up and paced back and forth from the couch to the door. "Something else. When little Rose got hurt, they wanted me. They were sending a message." He hesitated, I supposed waiting for me to respond. "I only tried to make a few dollars. But I'm not using. I borrowed some money is all." He stopped in front of me. "It's years since I been mixed up in the game. I would never hurt Dulcey or put her or any of you in danger." He walked back to the door and looked out the vertical strip of glass embedded in the door facing the hallway, then came back to the couch and sat down. "And now she is fighting for her life. I should be fighting."

"I agree. Apparently God has other plans for your black ass."

"Muriel, you should cut Hampton some slack. He made a mistake. We all make mistakes." Nareece was speaking.

The doctor came in and saved us. He said Dulcey's low white blood cell count resulted in her contracting a serious infection. They were keeping her a few days and treating her intravenously with antibiotics. She was sleeping and a nurse would retrieve us after settling her in a room.

After the doctor left, Hamp crumpled to the floor. I let him blubber for a moment.

"So you're not sure whether they know about the boat or where you live, or about Dulcey?"

"I know they want me dead. I witnessed the murder. I'm pretty sure if they find me, I'm dead."

"You'll have to testify," I said. "It may be the only way out of this. Witness protection."

He nodded.

I went out to the hallway to call Travis, who I knew would be worried about Dulcey's condition. I stood off to the side and pulled my cell from the clip on my hip. I punched in the code to open the phone and pressed Travis's name. When I put the phone to my ear and looked up, Ward Griffin and two other men crowded the hallway.

CHAPTER 18

I clicked off as Travis answered.

Griffin, flanked by two of his soldiers keeping pace in a military-like march, stopped at the nurses' station before he sauntered down the hall. He stopped when he noticed me, and took a menacing stance, like a bull. A smirk darkened his face. He held my gaze for a few seconds before letting his eyes roam over my body, licking his lips and shifting his stance from one foot to another.

As cocky as he was, I blinked, and his mockery stopped. A scowl replaced his crooked smile. He reached his arm out and pushed open the stairway door, turned on his heels and left, his soldiers on his tail.

Calvin's hand on my shoulder explained his action.

I turned around and hugged Calvin until my nerves settled. Then I hugged him just because . . . because I couldn't get enough of the feeling I experienced every time he wrapped his arms around me. It stormed my heart, leaving me breathless and wanting him . . . again. I released my hold and took a step back.

Calvin stepped to the window and looked out. "I knew my man Hamp would make an appearance to see his woman. I also know that Griffin and his gang of idiots would be on his ass if they even got a whiff of him. Knowing how broken up he is, I had to figure in a carelessness quotient." He came back to me and pulled me in for another hug. I relented.

I looked up at him. "A carelessness quotient, huh? Thank God for that."

"We need to get my man in some protective custody. They may not know why he's here; they may even think there's something wrong with him. But it's for sure they will not be leaving the vicinity without putting eyes on this place. This is probably the safest place for him right now. I'm going to get a room change and we'll keep watch for the night."

I was in Zoila's office first thing the next morning. She hung up her phone and leaned forward on her desk. "Girl, what's the big urgency?"

"Suppose I can present a witness to the killings in Fairmount Park."

"This person witnessed the shooting of the kid and the officer?"

"He witnessed the shooting of the kid. He cannot say with certainty who shot the officer, but he can say who the occupants of the car on the bridge were when the officer got shot."

"And he's willing to testify in open court?"

"Yes. But would need protection until testifying and possibly witness protection after. I'm not sure the witness wants protection."

"I'm guessing here, but will it take down Ward Griffin?"

I nodded.

"I'll listen. Who's the witness and where is he or she now?"

"A friend, Hampton Dangervil."

"Bring Mr. Dangervil in to make a statement about his involvement. We'll talk protection after he makes a statement."

"Look, Zoila, he's a good guy. He wants his life back. His wife is sick and he wants to care for her without being hassled or killed for some gambling debts."

"Why didn't he just pay the money back?"

"At first he couldn't raise the fifty K. And when he could, they wouldn't take it because they wanted to hold him by the throat."

"Don't worry, I got you covered," she said with an offhanded smile. She got up and put out her hand. "I owe you. Remember?"

No, I did not. It must have showed on my face.

"I wouldn't have made it through the academy without you," she said.

"Oh please," I said, brushing off her comment. "We wouldn't have made it through without each other."

When I left Zoila's office and got in my car, I called the hospital to check on Dulcey and fill Hamp in about the meeting. Hamp said they had given Dulcey something to make her sleep because she'd had a bad night.

"She's weak but doing better than the doctor expected. I'm not sure how much longer we can stay here," he said. "I mean I appreciate Calvin and his guys guarding the room and all, but I am not sure it will be enough to keep the crazy sonofabitch away."

"Look, Hamp. The hospital is the safest place you can be for right now. Calvin will be back with BJ to take you out of there and get you to Burgan's office to give your statement."

"I'm not feeling it, Muriel."

Muriel. Nobody ever calls me by my name. Makes alarms go off.

"You having doubts about testifying?"

"Not because I'm worried about me, but I'm worried about Dulcey. If they find out she's connected to me, they'll go after her. I witnessed a murder, M. They almost killed me that night too. Maybe I should be dead."

"Nothing is going to happen to Dulcey or you. Trust me." I told Hamp about Kenyetta's funeral that afternoon and that I would return to the hospital after.

When we hung up, I dialed Calvin's number.

He picked up on the first ring. "I was about to call you. Where are you?"

"I came from talking to Burgan about Hamp testifying and getting protection."

"I need a minute, so let me call you back. I'll call you as soon as I can."

When I got to my desk, neither Parker nor Fran were there. I snuck past the lieutenant's office and slipped into the microscope room, praying he would not decide to come out of his office at the wrong time. Fran and Parker were bent over microscopes.

Parker looked up from his when I entered. "You do still work here, right?" he chided with a hint of sarcasm.

"I covered for your behind so many times, Parker."

"Well, don't get all huffy. Making light here," he said.

Parker was such a white boy, and a nerdy one. "Who says 'get all huffy' or 'making light'? How many times must I tell you to take a lesson in how to talk? I am not the least bit huffy."

Parker snickered. "You're pissed because they made Fran your partner instead of me."

"Well, it won't happen again, my pet. Next time—" I cleared my throat and mumbled to myself loud enough for him to hear, "Please, Lord, do not let a next time come." In a louder voice I continued. "I will make sure they do not make the same mistake."

"I accept," he said and went back to peering into his microscope.

I took a seat at the desk to the right of where Fran worked. He looked up at me, then went back to looking into the microscope. I waited.

Finally, he looked up and pushed his chair back from the desk. "The semiautomatic they found in the Schuylkill River is the gun that killed that kid and the officer in Fairmount Park. And, it is also the same gun used on your niece."

"We find the owner of that gun and we find the shooter."

"Yes, but it has no numbers, so without any fingerprints we are not going to find the owner. And even if we suspect someone to be the owner, nothing connects that someone to the gun. So, we got nothing."

"There's a witness."

I told Fran about Hampton being the witness and my talk with Zoila to get him and Dulcey into witness protection.

"My only concern is that Hamp might be exaggerating or somehow not telling the whole truth. I don't think he'd play his usual games, with Dulcey sick and all. But there is that possibility that he's lying. It wouldn't be the first time he lied to save his ass. I don't think that's the case this time, though. No reason for it. I don't think."

Parker looked up from the microscope again. "When are you going to learn to let folks deal with what they got coming, especially if they messed their own self up?"

"Their own self, huh, Parker?" I chuckled. "C'mon, Parker, if one of your siblings or other member of your family or a good friend was in a mess, you're going to tell me you would let them flounder on their own? I don't think so. Not sweet, loving Parker. Maybe not so sweet or loving." We laughed.

"Not so sweet is right. Depends on what they did and how deep in they are. I'm not about to put my ass on the line for someone who is in the wrong."

"You're telling me you never skirted the law a wee bit for someone you care about when they were in the wrong?"

"I didn't say that. But it did not require me putting my behind out there."

"If you skirted the law, you put your ass out there, whether you see it or not."

"This guy is not your family."

"Trust me, he is more my family than many a blood relative of mine."

"Boys and girls, can we get some work done up in here?" Fran said.

CHAPTER 19

Travis chose a white casket with pink shading and pink crepe interior for Kenyetta. It didn't matter, since she was going to be cremated. No family member claimed her body, so we took on the task of laying her to rest. Travis planned to spread her ashes on the beach at Sea Girt in New Jersey, where they went on their first getaway.

Flowers, enough for ten funerals, surrounded the casket. Lilies, roses, mums, carnations, snapdragons. One arrangement said *Loving Daughter*. Another said *Loving Aunt* and still another said *Loving Sister*. Travis and I bought them.

He said Kenyetta's eight siblings were scattered who knows where. Kenyetta was the youngest. She had learned through the Department of Human Services that some of her siblings were married with children. She had initiated the process to locate them. She also discovered her father and mother were alive, though homeless, and she had made plans to bring them all together for a reunion.

The largest arrangement, in the shape of a heart, placed on the far side of the casket, was from Calvin. He was not at the service. He had texted and apologized but said he was still tied up.

Nareece and the twins, Travis, Elijah, Fran, a few of Travis's basketball buddies, and three people from the Department of Human Services who worked Kenyetta's case during her ten years in the system, occupied the first two rows of pews. I did not want the twins to come, but Nareece insisted and Travis supported her. They sat quietly on either side of Nareece with their heads resting on her shoulders.

Travis and Kenyetta had stuck together since their first meeting in high school. Kenyetta stayed with a foster family. She graduated high school, turned eighteen, and was kicked out of the system and left to fend for herself. Travis helped her find a job and a place of her own in a rooming house. He also helped her get into the Community College of Philadelphia's nursing program, where she completed her first year.

The good Reverend Thomas droned on. "Death is not the end of the story for those who love the Lord. Young Kenyetta loved the Lord. The Bible tells us what lies ahead for those who love Jesus. As we come to Second Corinthians, chapter five, we discover wonderful truths that give us hope as we face death with all its dark fears . . ."

Only three days prior, we attended Sam's funeral at African Methodist Episcopal Church on Sixth Street. Rev. Kasonga preached Sam's eulogy to a packed sanctuary about how Sam was taken away like so many other young people by the demon heroin. "So is the case for so many young people struck down way too soon, by the beast, drugs."

Sam's family and friends gave remarks. A full choir sang praises to the Lord, a major contrast from the few of us who sang praises for Kenyetta—the sound hurtful to the ears but as heartfelt as the magnitude of a full choir.

After Kenyetta's service, refreshments were served in the community room located in the basement of the church. It was the first time I saw Travis eat since learning about Kenyetta and Sam's deaths. Now he was laughing and exchanging banter with his friends, as though this were a recovery session after basketball. When Reverend Thomas approached, the boys quieted for a moment before breaking out in laughter over something the Rev said.

"Seems like he'll be fine," Fran said.

"Yes, he's finding his way." We both watched the interaction among the boys and Reverend Thomas. "What about all the other young people whose lives are getting mangled and lost behind heroin? Nothing new, and the battle continues. The stuff being distributed now is deadly."

"Your son's friends were not heroin users. Someone drugged them and dumped them."

"Someone murdered them just like the other two hundred or more people who have died in the city so far this year because of that junk." I felt my body temperature rising and pulled off my suit jacket.

"Yes, and the DEA and the gang unit are doing their thing to get the junk off the streets and put the drug dealers behind bars." He bumped me with his hip. "It is not our job to go after drug dealers, Miss M."

"No, but it is my job to protect my family by any means necessary. A job I have not been doing well and neither have the police. That boy over there, Elijah, he's trying to make something of himself, and it is not his fault his big brother, his only family, is one of the biggest drug dealers in the city. A murderer. The police, the DEA, and the gang unit can't do anything about it, at least that's how it appears, with no witnesses and missing evidence."

"They are planning a big bust."

"Hmm. And the dying continues."

CHAPTER 20

A week passed since I last swam in the Schuylkill River and the bodies of Kenyetta and Sam surfaced. I almost gave up the idea of completing the triathlon, given everything that had happened. But the running, biking, and swimming workouts gave me calm.

The tepid temperature did not encourage easy entry into the dark water that matched the murkiness of the drizzly day. The only saving grace was the eighty-degree temperature at six thirty in the a.m. Thank you, Lord.

My trainer, Marybeth, relegated herself to the rear, since my confidence had elevated and my swimming technique had improved, from flailing my arms to long, even strokes. Her swimming behind rather than alongside me simulated my being a confident swimmer. Not. Still, her being there made me feel more secure. I picked up the pace, keeping a decent distance from the rest of my training group—decent because I could still see them in front of me. When I got out of the water, all my training mates clapped and whooped and hollered. It felt good.

When I got home, I pulled into the driveway and shut the

car off. I sat in the car, thinking about the feat I had accomplished. Who would think at fifty years old I would learn how to swim, and not only in a swimming pool but in a damn river? The Schuylkill, nonetheless. That was death for sure when I was a kid. I shook my head and smiled to myself. Not to be cocky—still, the event loomed. I grabbed my gym bag from the passenger seat, put my Black Dog cap on my head, picked up my teacup from the cup holder, and got out.

I fumbled with the keys at the door, unable to isolate the house key with my available hand. I put my gym bag down and pushed the door open. I pushed my gym bag inside and pulled the door closed with my foot, hoping not to wake anyone on this Saturday morning. Some quiet time before the ruckus. I stood with my back against the door and listened to make sure the silence was still golden. I leaned forward to pick up my gym bag.

The force of the door opening sent me tumbling forward, stopped by the wall jutting out next to the staircase. I flipped over and rolled to a standing position.

"Police. Freeze," a young, rookyish-looking police officer yelled, his arms stretched out and pointing a gun at me.

"Really?" I said weakly, relieved. Dizzy from the tumble, I leaned against the wall for support.

The pitter-patter of bare feet across the floor and Rose, Helen, Travis, and Nareece were at the top of the stairs, gawking at about a dozen police officers aiming guns up at them.

I raised my arms to stop everyone's action. "What the hell is going on here?" I said.

One of the officers grabbed my arms and pushed me to the floor. I did not struggle. Too many fingers on too many guns when it only takes one who thinks it will be their claim to fame, or worse, initiation into the mightier-than-thou club; this from a fellow officer, even.

"Someone please explain why you broke into my house," I

said loud enough for the neighborhood to hear. "Where is the warrant?"

"Let her up and take the cuffs off," Zoila said, strolling in with an outstretched hand holding a paper.

When my wrists were freed, I got up and took the paper from her. I looked to the top of the stairs to see Nareece, the twins, and Travis standing like statues, with their eyes popping out and mouths hanging open. I assured them the police made a mistake and sent them back to bed.

"You live here?"

"What do you mean, do I live here? Yeah, I live here."

She almost registered embarrassment, then her demeanor changed. "We had a tip Elijah Griffin entered this residence. He is the brother of Ward Griffin, who runs Berg Nation." She cocked her head to the side and smiled.

I cocked my head to the left and didn't smile. "Being the brother of a drug dealer and murderer doesn't make Elijah a criminal."

"His brother is wanted for the murder of Officer Michael Aubry and Devon Taylor. He was seen with his brother a few days ago. We want him for questioning." She stepped farther in and stretched her neck to look around. "Muriel. This is your home?"

"This is my home? This is my home? Yes, this is my home." I took a deep breath to smooth my ruffled feathers.

"Pretty nice place," she said, brushing past me, strolling through the den to the kitchen. I followed on her heels. "This is not listed as your home address, rather Esther and Elliot Washington's residence. I thought you lived in Northeast." She pulled out a stool and sat at the island counter.

I took a seat across from her. With every ounce of will I could muster to control my temper, I said, "You bust through my front door without even the courtesy of a phone call and you want to sit at my kitchen counter and question me?"

"Like I said, I received incorrect information." She perused the kitchen and settled on me. "I'm doing my job, Muriel. The intense emotions are soaring when one of our own is murdered. I'm sorry I didn't inquire further. Who are Esther and Elliot Washington?"

"My parents."

"I see. Is Elijah Griffin here?"

"No."

"Where is he? Has he been here or stayed here recently?"

"Yes."

"Under what circumstances?"

"He's a friend of my son's. He was homeless and needed a place to stay until he got his act together. He's trying to break away from his brother, find a new life. We talked about this already."

"I'd like to talk to your son."

"I'll call him."

"Officer Petro will call him, so we can continue our conversation," she said, nodding toward the officer to leave his position at the kitchen entrance.

"What is going on here, exactly? You're treating me like I'm a suspect or someone harboring a fugitive or something. I'm law enforcement, remember?"

"And I truly am sorry that we barged into your house, like I said. If I had known, none of this would be happening this way, but since we're here, we might as well straighten it all out now rather than make your family come down to headquarters to answer questions."

Travis entered the kitchen in front of Officer Petro. He took a seat beside me.

"Travis, I'm Detective Burgan of the Mobile Street Crimes Unit. I understand that you are friends with Elijah Griffin, is that right?"

Travis nodded, focusing on me.

"Son. Your mother is here only as a courtesy."

He kept his gaze on me.

"Zoila. If neither I nor my son is under arrest, I would like you to leave. Elijah's whereabouts are unknown. If you would like to ask us more questions, we'd be happy to come down to headquarters at some point and answer them." I looked at the clock on the wall above the sink. "I'm going to be late for work so, if you please." I stood. Travis stood with me.

Zoila stayed seated for longer than I would have thought, maybe trying to make some kind of point that she controlled the situation.

"Muriel, I thought we could put this all away now, friendly-like, since we are fellow workers and share the same desire to catch the bad guy."

"We do, but apparently we prefer different methods."

She stood and stared. I stared back, in an exaggerated kind of way.

As soon as the house cleared of police, I was on Travis. "Where is Elijah?"

"He didn't come back last night. Went to hang out with some friends, he said, and then didn't come back."

"Do you know if he's been in contact with his brother at all?"

"Why would he, after Ward said he'd kill Elijah if he came back around?"

"Yeah, but that doesn't make it so," I mumbled to myself.

On the drive to the lab, I called Dulcey. She was being discharged today.

Hamp answered her phone. Before I could say anything he said, "Hold on."

Calvin got on.

"I'm moving Dulcey and Hampton to a place in Fort Washington. They'll be comfortable and safe there. You and your partner . . . You trust him, right?"

"Yes."

"Meet me at my place tonight after work. There's some things going on you and your partner should know about."

"Things like what?"

"Now's not the time. Please come to the club later."

A few seconds passed while we listened to the hum of silence in the receiver. I heard footsteps, and other hospital noises—muted voices, phones ringing, doctors being paged.

"Muriel, I never meant to hurt you. This might not be the time, but I would give anything to begin again. I am so sorry that the situation . . ."

"We'll stop by after work. I gotta go," I said, and hung up.

"Good morning, Officer Mabley," Parker chirped as I rushed by his cubicle. "Fran's in the lieutenant's office. They're waiting on you."

"Thanks, Parker," I said, then rushed down the hallway to the lieutenant's office.

"I understand you had uninvited guests this morning," Pacini said.

"Uninvited is right. I wasn't given a clear explanation about why, either."

"It seems you have a houseguest that the narcotics and gang units have had under surveillance. Your guest was in direct contact with Ward Griffin and a member of a Mexican cartel—this guy, Montero Reyes." He pushed a photograph across his desk, of Griffin, Reyes, and Elijah. "We have more than our share of work. There were 280 murders in the city last year, of which eighty-five percent involved firearms. Corruption in the narcotics division has resulted in 167 overturned convictions so far. I am not looking for any overturned convictions because we did not do our jobs."

I was not feeling listening to the lieutenant's rantings.

"Lieutenant, Elijah is a good kid. He's staying with me because he wants to stay away from his brother and Berg Nation and the whole damn scene. His brother threatened to kill him if he ever went back."

"Well, it looks like he went back. That picture was taken two days ago. All I'm saying is that you need to question this. Cut the boy loose if he's involved and just do your job. Don't get caught up in this damn war. The DEA, FBI, all are out for blood to take this junk off the streets and avenge the death of one of our own."

It was almost 5:30 by the time Fran and I left the lab to go to Calvin's Place. The traffic was at the height of rush hour, so moving was slow on Interstate 76.

We turned left on Haverford and into the back parking area at 6:38; more than an hour to make a twenty-minute drive. Calvin's Mercedes was the only other car in the lot, though usually at this hour the dinner crowd would be here opting for the best fried chicken wings in Philly.

As I stepped out of the car to the other side where Fran waited for me, I said, "I'm saying that what's going on in the department now is only because it has gone unchecked for so long. I don't even want to think about all these kids and adults dying, and it doesn't matter whether you're rich or poor, the heroin mixed with fentanyl does not discriminate."

Fran walked a few steps ahead of me. "It's never going to end. I mean, folks are going to use illegal drugs until the end of time. That said, if sellers can make more money from cutting the goods with whatever, it's going to happen. Always has, always will."

"So what are you saying? We can't just stop . . ."

The explosion sent us both flying. I lifted my head to see the building engulfed in flames and Fran unconscious a few feet away before I passed out.

CHAPTER 21

My eyes burned with the heat from the flames pouring out of the first-floor windows. I raised my arm to block the heat from my face. When I lifted my head and tried to move, a spinning sensation forced me to lie back and cover my ears to lessen the ringing. I looked to both sides of the lot, trying to remember what happened. Elijah appeared at the street end of the lot. Panic surged when I located Fran, who was motionless, his face pressed into the gravel. I sat up, and using my heels and arms, pulled myself over to him. I reached out to him. Fran rolled over and began coughing.

Another smaller explosion. "Calvin." The word scorched my throat and drowned in the noise of firetrucks arriving. Then Elijah was there helping me and Fran up.

"Is anybody else in the building?" a fireman asked.

"Calvin Bernard," I said.

The fireman yelled to four other firemen, who put on their oxygen masks and charged up the stairs and into the building, defying the flames. Two of the firemen emerged a few minutes later. A few more minutes passed before the other two emerged carrying Calvin.

"He's barely breathing," one of the firemen said.

They laid him on a gurney. An EMT climbed on top of him and began chest compressions. Another attendant wheeled the gurney to the back of an ambulance and pushed it inside. I climbed in with them.

The siren sounded far away and dreamlike. One attendant put pressure on a gunshot wound in Calvin's left chest while the other covered his face with an oxygen mask and gave him a shot.

Calvin's face, charred from the fire, appeared ghoulish. The color matched his forearms below the fold of his rolled-up sleeves. He wore a white shirt, sooty and bloodied, and creased Levis. One shoeless foot bobbled each time the EMT pressed his chest. The other foot had a two-tone loafer on it, stuck in the gurney's frame, which kept it stationary.

I sat on the other gurney beside him, willing him to wake up again. I swear he squeezed my hand. My imagination. I squeezed back. The irregular beep of the heart monitor became a constant whine. The attendant shut the heart monitor down and removed the clip from Calvin's forefinger. The siren went silent as we pulled into the hospital emergency entrance.

The attendants lowered the gurney with Calvin's body and rolled it away. One attendant said, "He didn't make it," to the doctor at the door when it opened. "Gunshot wound to the chest, severe burns and smoke inhalation."

I jumped down from the ambulance where Fran and Elijah waited.

We sat in Fran's car outside the hospital of the University of Pennsylvania in silence. A thousand questions clogged my brain. My emotions would not allow me to ask them out loud.

"Miss Mabley."

I put my hand up to stop Elijah from speaking. He got the message.

My phone vibrated. Dulcey. I ignored it. She called again.

"I'm watching the news and they're talking about Calvin's Place burning down."

"Where are you guys?" I asked.

"At Calvin's place out in Fort Washington. He's not answering his cell."

"He's dead, Dulcey. He's gone," I cried.

"They didn't say any of that on the news. They said everyone got out safe."

I sneezed. Fran handed me a tissue. I put the phone down and blew my nose. I picked it back up to hear Dulcey still talking about the news report. I waited until she quieted.

"Calvin asked Fran and me to meet him at the club. We almost reached the door when the blast happened. They carried Calvin out. I went in the ambulance . . . we didn't make it to the hospital in time . . . I don't think time mattered. He died."

"Oh Muriel, girl, I am so sorry. I want to be with you. Where are you?"

"We're at the hospital. Getting ready to leave," I said, nodding to Fran to drive off. "You two need to stay put until I call you back. Calvin's men still standing guard?"

"Yes. BJ, Calvin's main man, he said they're going to take Hamp to make his statement tomorrow, orders from Calvin. I think Calvin knew something might go down because all his men are acting like something was expected so everyone was, is, on guard. Now, the major thing is getting Hampton to the place Friday as Calvin instructed."

"I'll call you later. Stay put."

"I love you, girl," Dulcey said in a weepy tone.

"I love you too."

I turned around to face Elijah sitting in the backseat. "Elijah. How did you happen to be at Calvin's Place?"

He looked away out the side window.

"Elijah, look at me."

He turned his head to face me. "I had met with Mr. Bernard about working at the center. I stopped in the sub shop at the corner and then the explosion happened. I ran back and saw you and Mr. Fran. Scared the hell outta me."

"Does your brother run Berg Nation?"

"Well, he's the one that everybody goes to, listens to, takes orders from."

"So there's somebody else? I mean like somebody he answers to?"

"I think so. I mean, I'm not sure. I used to hear him talking on the phone to someone, like answering to a boss man, the way everybody else talks to him."

"You can't tell us anything else?"

"One time I saw WG talking to someone in a car on the side of the road, but I couldn't see who it was."

"What kind of car?"

"A black Town Car."

"How come you didn't meet with Calvin at the center?"

"He said he had an appointment and he needed to be at the club in case his appointment arrived early, so he asked me to come to Calvin's Place."

"Did his appointment show up before you left?"

"No, but I did see a guy going in when I left."

"What guy? What did he look like?"

"Big, like Mr. C. I think he works for him, because he's been to the center a few times."

"How long before the explosion?"

"About twenty minutes."

"You didn't notice anything unusual, or anybody who looked suspicious?"

"I freaked out with the fire. I recognized your car and freaked out even more." He whimpered. "I can't believe Mr. Bernard is gone. Those young dudes from the center will go back to the Berg and War will beat them down."

"One more question. Where do you go at night? Where'd you go last night?"

"My girl lives over in North Philly with her parents."

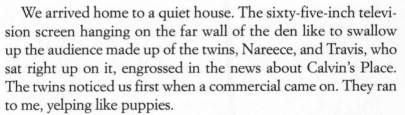

We arrived home to a quiet house. The sixty-five-inch television screen hanging on the far wall of the den like to swallow up the audience made up of the twins, Nareece, and Travis, who sat right up on it, engrossed in the news about Calvin's Place. The twins noticed us first when a commercial came on. They ran to me, yelping like puppies.

"Auntie, you look like you need a drink," Helen offered as her and Rose each took a hand and led me to the couch. I fell into the seat.

"A glass of water, please," I said. Helen ran off.

Elijah moved to the loveseat where Travis sat engrossed in the news report. Elijah leaned in close and whispered something to him.

"Is Mr. Calvin all right, Auntie?" Rose said, sliding in beside me. "The news didn't say anything about him."

Travis and Nareece's attention was on me.

Helen returned with a glass half filled with water. She handed it to me and took her place on my other side. I set the glass on the coffee table and put an arm around each one.

"No, Mr. Calvin is not all right."

"Is he dead?" Helen asked.

"Yes, baby."

Nareece popped up. "Let's leave Auntie alone for a little while. C'mon, go upstairs and watch television in your room."

"You call us if you need us, Auntie."

I nodded, unable to hold back the flow of tears any longer.

First thing in the morning I drove to Fort Washington where Dulcey and Hamp were holed up. Two cars accompanied us from Fort Washington to FBI headquarters: BJ and another man in front and two other men in back. Dulcey and Hamp rode with me.

"Girl, Calvin opened that center for young folk to help them," Dulcey said. "His niece died from an overdose of heroin. She got caught up with them gangs too. Her mom found her in the bathroom. So many young people dying from that stuff. Whoever killed Calvin is going to burn in hell."

Dulcey sat in the front with me. She turned around to face Hamp. "Yeah, and I'm worried, Hampton, you and me could be added to the list of dead folk."

"Don't you worry about a thing, my sweet," Hamp cooed.

"Don't you 'my sweet' me. If it weren't for your ass being out there doing things you ain't supposed to be doing . . ."

"Dulcey, stop! Please," I said, sounding harsher than I intended.

We rode in silence the rest of the way to FBI headquarters. Calvin's men pulled curbside when I made a left into the parking garage below the building. A guard directed me to a parking space toward the back of the garage directly in front of an entrance door.

I turned the car off and took a breath, relieved we had made it without any problems. "Hamp, tell them what happened and who pulled the trigger, like you told me. They will put you both up in a safe house until the trial."

"I don't want Dulcey messed up in all this any further. I'll go to the safe house by myself. You take Dulcey with you."

Dulcey huffed and rose up in her seat. "I'm going with you," she said in her deepest baritone voice.

Hamp leaned forward and pressed her shoulder down. "Dulcey, I seldom lay into you. I always let you do what you want to do. Now, you are going to do what I say, and I say you are going to go with Muriel and stay with her while I do this."

Dulcey put her hand atop Hamp's. She sucked back tears. "I want to be where you are."

"Everything's going to work out fine, baby. Taking care of my mess is my responsibility and I need you to be safe while I'm doing it."

Dulcey sniffed, backhand-wiped her tears away and nodded. Hampton settled back in his seat again.

This was only the second time I'd witnessed Hamp command Dulcey in any way. The first time, Dulcey said she would not go through chemotherapy or any other treatments for her cancer. She said she put her life in God's hands. Hampton rose up with another reasoning—that it did not matter what her God said, his God said she was going to have the treatments and come out on the other end more beautiful and stronger than ever. No more argument.

Zoila sat across the table from Hamp. She pushed a microphone closer to him and said, "Please state your name for the record."

"Hampton Dangervil."

"Mr. Dangervil . . ."

"Hamp."

"Hamp, please tell us what happened on the night in question and the events leading up to the night in question."

Hamp glanced over at me. I nodded.

"I will tell you everything, but I only want to say it with Mabley and you in the room."

There were two other people in the room—Zoila's partner, Enrique Santiago, and an FBI investigator, name of Holstrom. Zoila raised a doubting eyebrow at me. I shrugged and gave a nod. She gestured for the two to leave.

"Now, Mr. Dangervil, I have done what you asked."

"I been clean for going on fourteen years. Have to stay clean or the woman who I love most in the world, I might lose her and I couldn't live if that happened.

"I came here many years ago and got messed up with drugs. I bought from the father of the man who wants me dead now. I didn't remember the son, but he couldn't have been more than ten or twelve back then.

"I did not recognize him when I borrowed the money. I knew from the git-go it was a mistake borrowing money for gambling. Gambling, period. I'd borrowed a small amount before and won big, and paid it back. So I figured I could do the same thing for . . . it doesn't matter. I lost and could not pay up when the due date rolled up. The amount I owed got to be too much. They said, interest. I asked for another try. So he . . ."

"Who is 'he,' Mr. Dangervil? Please use his name."

"Ward, 'War,' Griffin. He told me my debt would be paid in full once I did a favor for him. I been in the streets for a long time. I been off them for a long time too. I guess the disconnect came in when he didn't tell me right away what kind of payment he expected."

Hamp reached to the center of the table where a pitcher of water and glasses sat. He poured a glass of water and drank it down in one motion.

"So he, War, picks me up and says we are going for a ride. I get in the car with two of his foot soldiers and the kid sitting in the back."

"By the kid, do you mean Devon Taylor, street name 'D'?"

"Yes. I remember thinking what a shame to see this young blood messed up by these guys. I felt ashamed of myself for even being there, letting myself get in such a situation.

"We parked the car in the lot and walked into Fairmount Park. I asked War where we were going. I thought for sure my time to die had come, right in the park. At first my whole body shook. War goes on talking nonstop about what happens when someone's mouth gets to flapping. I did not get his meaning, so I didn't pay much attention to his words. I stopped being so anxious about dying. Sadness took hold because I would never see my Dulcey again. Next thing I know he hands me a gun and says, 'Kill him.' He meant the kid.

"I have committed many acts I'm not proud of, but killing someone is not one of them. I am not proud of the killing I did in the war. I had a reason then, a purpose, to keep my friends and my country safe. I had no reason to kill the boy, so I asked War why. War said it didn't matter why, he said so. He says, 'Danger, just because you're such an honorable dude, I'll tell you. This boy here let his lips flap to the po po.'

"The kid, D, 'bout had a fit. He said he did not say anything to the police and the only reason he got out of jail was because he's a minor and they couldn't hold him without any evidence of his involvement.

"I said it did not matter what he did, I had no intention of shooting him. I said I did not care if War killed me. War snatched the gun from me and told me to get on my knees, then shot that boy in the head. I thought he'd shoot me too, except we heard the police yell and everybody took off running. I ran in the opposite direction from them, then stopped and hid behind a tree. Two police got to where that boy lay dead then took off running after the others. The police officers shot at the car as it went over the bridge. Then one of the guys in the car got out and shot back, hitting one of the officers. The guy threw the gun in the river, got back in the car, and they drove away."

Zoila leaned over the table. "Mr. Dangervil, Hamp, will you testify in open court?"

"Yes. As long as you give me some protection until it is done."

"Hearing first, then open court."

"Put it in writing," I added.

CHAPTER 22

The breeze whirled across the gaping hole waiting to receive the gold casket that uniformed soldiers carried from the hearse. The heavy silence was disturbed only by the squeak from a soldier's boots, accented by a sniffle every few squeaks.

Seemed all the mourners who attended the church service made the trek to Calvin's gravesite—vets, gang members, local business owners, politicians, law enforcement, and Calvin's men.

I stood between Fran and Dulcey in the front, anguishing over the thought that the killer might be among us. I looked around as far as I could see with my head raised halfway. Mine seemed the only eyes not closed, the only head not bowed, until my gaze met Zoila's. She nodded and directed her attention back to the preacher's prayer.

To my right, Calvin's sister, Shea, her husband, and two teenage daughters sat huddled together. I'd only met Shea once before when Calvin was in the hospital from a car accident. He stayed in a coma for almost two weeks.

Calvin never spoke about his family. I assumed now, because he was married. In my work, my intuition is spot-on and reliable. Matters of the heart bring on a different characteristic—I become a sniveling fool.

BJ met my gaze. He smiled. My thoughts raced. *Big like Mr. C*, Elijah had said. I closed my eyes, trying to concentrate on the pastor's words. Calvin trusted BJ with everything. BJ, his closest friend.

I jumped when the rifles sounded the first of three volleys. Dulcey squeezed my hand. The soldiers finished folding the flag that had draped the casket and presented it to his sister. A bugle began playing taps and I ducked away, unable to maintain control. I rushed down the path, away from the service, sobbing like a lost two-year-old and hard enough to suck the breath from me. I stumbled forward. A hand reached out and steadied me. I looked up to see Laughton. I let myself fall into his embrace.

My body trembled as though a chilled breeze swooped over me on this eighty-five-degree day. Laughton squeezed me tighter. I let him for a minute, before I pulled away.

"Where have you been?" I sputtered, a morsel of spit flying out of my mouth onto his shirt.

"Shh."

"Shh hell. You disappeared. You dropped out. No explanation. No nothing." I turned away. "Never mind. This is not the time or place."

"I'm sorry I haven't been here for you."

"Been here for me. What the hell does that mean? Been here for me?"

"Muriel."

"Oh, so now I'm Muriel. Seventeen years and you never called me Muriel. Now I'm Muriel, and you're an asshole."

He grabbed my arms and pulled me to him. I tried to pull away, but he held me tight to his chest as an indescribable pain erupted inside me. He released me, pulled a handkerchief from his back pocket, and handed it to me.

"Well, if it ain't Mr. Laughton, showing up at the right time, I might add," Dulcey said as she approached. "I am glad you decided to grace us with your presence."

"Miss Dulcey." Laughton reached out to hug Dulcey. He pushed her an arm's length away to check her out.

"Looking good, Miss Dulcey. A little peaked around the edges."

"A bit, Mr. Laughton, but nothing that can keep me down for long." She took both of Laughton's hands and lifted his arms up slightly to check him out. She shook her head side to side. "You still all up in tall, dark, and handsome, Mr. McNair." She nodded toward me. "We got the help we need now, girl." She let go of Laughton's hands and stepped away. "I'ma wait for you at the car, Miss M."

When she moved out of earshot, I told Laughton about her breast cancer.

I leaned my back against the tree we were standing under.

"Calvin called me two days ago. Left a message saying he had some trouble and needed help. I got in this morning."

I froze. Calvin had known Laughton's whereabouts and how to reach him all this time—and I hadn't.

"We've known each other since we were kids," Laughton said, sensing my hurt feelings. He reached his arm above my head and leaned in against his palm. "His message said trouble."

"Nothing I can't handle."

"Yeah, my first reaction exactly. Not now."

"Officer Mabley. Muriel."

Laughton straightened up and stepped back. Shea looked like Calvin with hair and curves.

I stepped forward with outstretched arms. "Shea. I am so sorry," I murmured. We embraced.

She turned to Laughton. "Well, well. Laughton McNair. It's been a while."

"Shea." He reeled her in for a hug. "I am so sorry about my man. There are no words."

Shea stepped back and bowed her head. "He . . ." She shook her head side to side in slow motion. "He was a good man." She faced me, wiping tears away. "Can we talk for a minute?"

We moved down the path, away from Laughton.

"Calvin really did love you, Muriel. He couldn't find the words or the courage to tell you about Brenda. She's unaware that he's gone. Nothing. She exists, period."

"Thank you for telling me."

She moved closer to me, angling her body away from the passersby. She reached in her bag and pulled out a letter-size white envelope and gave it to me. I put it in my bag. "Calvin gave it to me a few days ago. He said if anything happened to him, I should give it to you. He was good, into a lot of things, privy to a lot of things about all different kinds of people. Whatever is in that envelope, please be careful. Nothing is worth losing your life too." She hugged me and continued down the path to where her family waited.

As soon as Shea walked away, Zoila stepped up.

"Have you heard from Mr. Dangervil?"

"Zoila, this is not the time."

"I need reassurance that he will be at the hearing on Friday."

"He'll be at the hearing."

Laughton walked up to us.

"Laughton McNair, isn't it?" Zoila asked.

"It is. Detective Burgan, isn't it?"

She nodded and smiled. "I was sorry to hear you quit the department." She waited, giving Laughton a chance to respond. He did not. "You take care now."

She walked away with her head tilted skyward. If she looked back, she was hiding something, I thought. I considered she could be just doing her job, except that my stomach was acting up again, something that only happened when things weren't right. My stomach never led me astray.

She made it to the parking lot.

Laughton laced my arm through his and escorted me back up the path to the gravesite. Only the attendants remained, removing flowers. They stopped when we approached. Laughton gestured for them to continue.

The scratchy sound of the shovel against the pile of dirt. The thud of the dirt hitting the casket.

"Calvin calls, I come without question. This isn't over," Laughton said as though talking out loud to himself.

"I'd say whoever killed Calvin knew him, because there is no way he would let his guard down, let someone into the club and turn his back unless he trusted them."

We stood at the gravesite in silence until the hole was covered.

Dulcey and Fran leaned against the car, watching our approach. Dulcey bent sideways and said something to Fran. Fran stepped up with his hand stuck out to Laughton.

"The famed Laughton McNair. Fran Riley, Muriel's new partner in crime."

Laughton accepted his handshake.

"It is definitely a pleasure to finally meet you," Fran said, jerking Laughton's arm up and down. Laughton reached his other hand out and put it over Fran's to calm the motion.

"Famed, huh? What's that about, young man? Fran?"

"You're talked about as the best firearms examiner on the planet, for starters," Fran said, sounding like a starstruck fan.

Laughton winked at me.

Fran countered. "I wouldn't know a damn thing if it was all up to Muriel. No sir, you are talked about throughout the department."

Dulcey smiled and nodded her head in agreement as she opened the back door to get in.

"Nice to meet you, Fran," Laughton said, then turned to me. "Your place." He walked away. He didn't get very far before Pacini came upon us.

"Laughton, that you?" Laughton stopped and turned around. Pacini motioned him back. Laughton hesitated.

"Man, don't even play that. C'mon back or I'll chase you down."

"Funny." Laughton chuckled, walking back.

"Listen, if the two of you have your heads together, something's up. Frankly, McNair, you're wanted for questioning about some missing gun parts."

Laughton searched my face with a quizzical expression. I nodded.

"I can make it all go away, but I need you both in my office within the hour. And don't bother telling me about your friend and how his protection is up to you because the FBI, DEA, and the Mobile Street Crimes Unit can't do the job." He stuck his neck out turkey-style, so I could feel his breath on my face, and smell it. I sniffed and wrinkled my nose. "Be there," Pacini said and stormed off. "Riley, you be there too," he called back over his shoulder.

"I'll meet you at the house," Laughton said.

"I moved. We don't live in the same . . ."

"I know your address." He smiled and walked away.

As soon as we got going, I took the manila envelope out of my purse and opened it. Inside was a plain piece of white paper tri-folded with a key and a flash drive taped inside the folds.

CHAPTER 23

When Fran pulled into the driveway, Laughton pulled to the curb. Travis and Elijah ran out of the house to Fran's car. Elijah opened the rear door for Dulcey and helped her out, while Travis opened the front passenger door for me and offered me a hand.

"You straight?" he inquired, as I rose from the car.

"I'm straight."

"You don't look like you're straight."

"You don't look like you're straight either," I said, brushing at his hair. He swatted my hand away.

"Oh snap, my man, Laughton!" Travis glided down the driveway toward Laughton, who sported a broad smile as they came together and did the man-hug thing. They exchanged some banter I could not hear except for the outbursts of laughter. They horseplayed their way to Fran's car. Travis introduced Laughton to Elijah, who offered his hand, though Laughton pulled him in for a man-hug.

Then the twins raced out the door. Nareece stood in the doorway watching the action for a minute, then moved back inside.

"And who are these beautiful young ladies?"

"I'm Rose. She's Helen."

Laughton shook their hands. "The pleasure is mine, I'm sure." They giggled like high school girls and ran off, back into the house.

Dulcey started a slow stroll to the door, with Elijah and Travis at her sides, their arms interlocked with hers. "You-all go ahead and do what you gotta do. Me and Reece will cook dinner for you when you get back."

Twenty minutes later we were in Pacini's office.

"Damn, McNair, I thought you were dead," Pacini said, gesturing to us to take a seat. He pushed back in his chair, rested his elbows on the arms of the chair, and interlaced his fingers. "Seems like things are out of hand."

Parker, Fran, Laughton, and I sat in silence.

Pacini glanced at each of us in turn. "Somebody is going to tell me what the hell is going on or nobody is getting out of here."

Laughton started. "I had just left here a few weeks ago. Then Calvin called me a few days ago, said he needed my help. I arrived this morning. I was on the other side of the world."

"He didn't tell you the trouble?"

"Said he couldn't talk about it over the phone."

"So he didn't say why someone would want to kill him?"

I nudged Fran, who said, "I think Hamp's testimony has a great deal to do with all this. I think the guy at the park who Hamp can't identify, Mr. Big, is the key, the boss behind Berg Nation operations. Ward Griffin is a punk. He's not smart enough to be pulling all this off without a hitch."

"I also think Detective Burgan of Mobile Crimes has much more to share," I said. "I'm not sure how yet, but Sam and Kenyetta—and the Taylor kid, Calvin—they're all connected."

"This isn't even in our purview," Pacini said. "So all this speculation doesn't mean a damn thing unless it is directly connected to you doing your job, matching the weapon used in the shootings to the shooter. From what you said, that is not the case. End of our responsibility."

"Lieutenant, I can't sit around and wait for Street Crimes . . ."

"Mabley, this is not about what you can or cannot do. Last I checked this is my command and I say you need to leave it be. That goes for you two as well," he said to Parker and Fran. "Laughton, I don't care what you do, you're no longer part of this department."

I pushed back. "But Lieutenant, hear me out, please. Zoila thinks that Hamp's testimony is going to solve everything, but this all isn't about Ward Griffin. There's somebody behind him pulling his strings. Somebody who stays in the shadows and is not afraid of being identified or can't be identified for some reason. I think Calvin found out who that someone is. Someone he trusts got past him. Only someone he trusted could move in close enough to kill him."

"Are you saying someone in law enforcement killed him?"

"Calvin worked with law enforcement, but he didn't trust the police, the FBI, DEA, none of them."

"Where is Dangervil now?" the lieutenant asked.

I thought he sounded perturbed, maybe because he was not privy to the situation before now.

"He's safe."

"What? I'm not trusted?"

"If you were privy to that information and asked about it, you'd be required to tell it or be in violation . . ."

"Well, I'm also responsible for the people who work in my unit. You go ahead with this little investigation of yours, but I want to be kept informed. No one else outside of this room. What about this kid Elijah, Griffin's brother?"

I responded with raised eyebrows, surprised Pacini had knowledge of Elijah.

"I may spend a lot of time in the basement, but I do keep my head and ears in the world."

"He's been staying with us for a few months. Travis said he was homeless and spending a lot of time at the basketball courts, trying to get away from his brother and the gang. So Travis asked if he could stay with us for a while, until he got his act together. I got a visit from Ward Griffin, who threatened to kill Elijah if he ever showed his face in Blumberg again."

"What about revenge for you harboring his brother?" Pacini said.

"Then why not go after me or Travis?"

"Or members of your family. An eye for an eye."

"Lieutenant, five people are dead, and the FBI, the DEA, the Mobile Street Crimes Unit, it seems like their hands are tied. The only person they have hooks into is Ward Griffin, and there is no way he could pull off five murders without a trace of evidence or witnesses willing to testify."

The lieutenant's phone rang. He listened for a few seconds, then hung up.

"Mabley and Riley, your presence is requested at FBI headquarters for questioning."

A receptionist escorted Fran and me into Zoila's office.

"Are there developments in the investigation into Calvin's death?" I asked as we took our seats around a small conference table at the far end of her office.

Zoila did not answer. Instead she took a seat at the head of the conference table. Her partner, Santiago, and Holstrom, the FBI agent who was at Hamp's deposition, and another man I wasn't acquainted with, came in and sat around the table.

"Muriel and Fran, you've met Santiago and Holstrom."

I nodded.

"This is DEA agent, Dalton McKay," Zoila said. "Officers Muriel Mabley and Fran Riley of Firearms Identification."

Fran and I exchanged looks.

"So we're clear, neither of you are being charged with any crime. This is an information-gathering session."

Zoila opened her mouth to go on, but McKay jumped in and cut her off.

McKay gave a wide smile, revealing yellow teeth behind the thin cracked lines that were his lips. His reddish-brown hair covered his forehead and his sideburns extended below his ears. The hairdo emphasized his big ears.

"Officer Mabley, were you romantically involved with Calvin Bernard?" His pleasant facial expression did not match his grim, no-nonsense tone.

"My private life is nobody's business."

"Muriel, if you answer the questions, we can move past all this," Zoila said.

"Move past all what? We don't even know why we're here. Why don't you fill us in? Then I'll be more than happy to answer your questions."

"Muriel, could you trust me, please? Answer the questions."

No way I trusted Zoila. "Yes, I was involved with Calvin Bernard."

"How long have you been in a relationship with Mr. Bernard?"

"About a year."

"Did you know he was married?"

"What is this about? What difference does it make whether or not I was involved with Calvin or whether or not I knew he was married?"

"Officer Mabley, answer the question."

Fran had gotten up and was standing behind my chair. I felt his finger poke into my right shoulder blade.

"I learned of Calvin's married status a few days ago."

"Mr. Bernard being married really pissed you off. He lied to you."

"Is there a question?"

"Where were you the night before Calvin was killed?"

"Are you suggesting that I killed Calvin because the news that he was married pissed me off?" I shrieked.

"Are you aware that Calvin's center is a neutral ground for gang members, and your son and Elijah Griffin, brother of Ward Griffin, who is the head of the Berg Nation, are seen at the center on a regular basis, talking and socializing? Ward Griffin is a drug dealer and murderer. He is a suspect in at least twelve murders in the last three months."

"My son plays basketball and works at the center."

"Is it true that Elijah Griffin lives with you?"

"Yes."

"That's all, yes?"

"Yes."

"Officer Riley, are you aware that your partner harbors a felon?"

"I am aware that Elijah Griffin lives with her. I'm not aware he's a felon."

"He isn't," I said.

"We have been watching Calvin Bernard and his whole operation—the center, his connection with gang members. We believe he was working with Ward Griffin to receive and distribute heroin from a cartel in Mexico."

"Calvin worked with the FBI, the DEA, the gang unit, the police, for over thirty years, helping catch bad guys, make the neighborhoods safer, keep drugs off the streets. I . . . I . . . I can't believe . . . You know what, this doesn't even make any sense. Why would Calvin be involved in any of this except if he was working to shut it down?"

"Money, Officer Mabley. Ten million dollars' worth."

"Not enough. I don't know an amount large enough that would sway Calvin."

"How about the threat of death to his loved ones?"

"No way Calvin would let anyone come anywhere even close to his family. He would protect them with his life."

"And so it may be done."

CHAPTER 24

After suffering through questioning at FBI headquarters, Fran and I drove to the Rittenhouse Hotel, where Laughton was staying. I called Laughton. It went right to voicemail. I swear the man never answers his phone. I left a message for him to call. I went to his room and knocked anyway. On my way out, the front desk clerk said I had missed him by minutes. He left in a Freedom Taxi.

Fran said he wasn't feeling well. He took me to the lab and went home. It was six o'clock, after work hours. Pacini's car was still in the lot. I wasn't feeling rehashing the FBI interrogation with him, so I went home too. I tried Laughton again on the way. He still did not pick up, so I left another message. Normal circumstances warranted irritation rather than the concern rippling through my gut now.

Crying while driving is dangerous. The tears cause blurred vision and can sometimes block your view completely, depending on how hard you're bawling. I wiped at my eyes and went for a tissue in my bag. I looked up to see a man crossing in front of the car. I slammed on the brakes, nicking his toes, no doubt. My purse fell, dumping its contents on the floor. I pulled over to regain my composure. The first thing I picked up was the envelope Calvin's sister had given me with the flash drive and a key in it. With everything going on, I had not thought about the envelope since the funeral. My tears dried. I finished picking up the contents of my pocketbook and headed for home.

Dulcey and Nareece had dinner ready and ushered everyone to the table. I told them to go ahead without me and went upstairs to my bedroom. Dulcey knocked and came in behind me.

"The flash drive, Dulcey," I said, powering up my laptop. "With everything going on I forgot all about it."

"What flash drive? What are you talking about?"

"Calvin's sister Shea gave me an envelope at the funeral. She said Calvin told her to give it to me if anything happened to him. A flash drive was inside."

Technology is a wonderful thing, most of the time. Except when it doesn't work, the screen goes blue when you've been hacked, or it takes more than two seconds for it to power up. My laptop was older than my nieces. Slow was its first name. I plugged the flash drive in and waited for the files to load.

There were three files: Routes, Berg Nation, and Schedules. I clicked on the Routes file. A map popped up on the screen with a route from Mexico to Philly outlined in red. Along the route, black marks noted exchange points. The final destination in Philly was Blumberg.

The Berg Nation file contained an organizational chart with Ward Griffin's name second to the top. The top two positions indicated by boxes, side-by-side, were blank. Lines drawn out like tentacles connected to names of Berg Nation members and their positions and responsibilities within the gang.

The Schedules file listed Dates, Weights, Dollars, and Destinations as headings of four columns. Destinations listed Philly, Brooklyn, Jersey City.

"This is the kind of information can get you killed," Dulcey said.

"Somewhere in Blumberg is a stash house, receiving and distributing heroin not only to street-level heroin operations here, but in New York and Jersey too. Check this, Dulce." I traced the red line up the map from the Mexican border to Philly. "This is Mexican cartel stuff, a direct pipeline to the Berg." I disengaged the flash drive. "It still doesn't say who killed Calvin or why."

"Maybe he was working undercover and making a buy or something."

"He wouldn't conduct an undercover op at his place. Whoever knew he knew about the stuff on this drive could be who killed him." I tried Laughton again, then BJ. BJ answered on the first ring.

"Hi, BJ. Muriel."

"Miss Mabley. We need to meet and talk."

I was taken aback by his curt directness. "BJ, is there something you want to tell me? Something I need to do?" There was silence on the other end. "Why do we need to meet?"

"Calvin didn't talk to you before . . . well, before he was killed."

"He didn't have a chance. I was on my way to see him when it happened. We were almost at the door."

More silence.

"I'm going to find who did this and kill them. I'll have the other guys keep an eye on you and your family."

"Thanks, BJ. I was calling because . . ." He clicked off.

"Something about that man doesn't sit right with me," Dulcey said as soon as I hung up. "I don't trust him. I know he was Calvin's ace and he kept Hamp and me safe, but there is something about him with his big burly self."

"Calvin trusted BJ. He never said anything bad about him. I can't believe BJ would even think about killing Calvin. That sounds crazy to me."

Nareece called up the stairs like Old Mother Hubbard, for us to come to dinner before the food got cold. "That's why they made microwaves," I mumbled.

"Don't be so hard on her. She's trying to find herself and care for you-all too."

"I guess. I love her no matter what."

Travis and the twins were back in the den watching television. Nareece fixed us both plates of sausage and spaghetti, then sat at the counter across from us, her face stuffed into the crease of *Philadelphia Style* magazine, as usual.

"Reecy has something to tell you, don't you, Reecy?" Dulcey pushed.

Nareece kept her head down in the magazine. I kept eating. Dulcey coughed and scratched her throat.

Nareece sucked her teeth and said, "I think I found a place."

"What do you mean, you found a place? Travis goes back to school in September, remember?"

"I can't wait until September because I need to enroll the girls in school. I know you had the house fixed so we could all stay here. But I think things will be better if we move out on our own. We can sell this house and you can move back into your other place, or you can stay here. You'll be glad not to have to deal with me and the twins."

"Tell me that is not what this is about."

"I'm just saying. And you don't have to worry about paying for this place. I mean, you know John left me and the girls pretty well off with his investments and all."

"I'm not going to argue with you, Nareece. You want to move into your own place, fine, I'll support you in that effort."

"Good, because I signed the paperwork and our move-in date is August first."

I stopped chewing.

"What? You said you would support my decision, and my decision is to move." She closed the magazine and looked at me. "The girls don't know yet, but I'm sure they'll be fine."

"If they aren't?"

"They're my children, Muriel. They'll be happy with the place. I found a luxurious single-family in Chestnut Hill."

She put the magazine back up to her face. End of that story.

I arrived at the courthouse early the next day, hoping to have a cup of tea with Fran before going into the courtroom. He did not answer his phone before I left the house or after I arrived. I called the lab. Parker said no Fran.

Fran still had not arrived when I took the stand in a case dealing with a shooting death at Dirty Harry's Bar in South Philly.

Melrose, the prosecuting attorney, approached the witness box. "Officer Mabley, please tell the court your findings in this case."

"Exhibit one is a Smith and Wesson thirty-eight special, double action revolver." I flipped the gun so I could read the number. "Serial number 895742. This is the gun found at the defendant's home. Exhibit two is a fired, plain lead bullet. Exhibit three is the bullet taken from the victim's body, and exhibit four is a spent, centerfire cartridge case found at the scene.

"In this case, from our analysis, we determined that the bullet taken from the victim's body came from exhibit one, the weapon found at the defendant's place of residence."

"Officer Mabley, please tell the court how you arrived at those findings?"

"We analyze bullet casings by comparing a casing's grooves and scratches to match those on test bullets fired by a gun of the same make and model or in this case, the alleged murder weapon. When a weapon is fired, individual markings are transferred from the hard surface of a weapon to the softer surface of the bullet or cartridge case. Each barrel has its own identifiable markings unique to that gun. We use the ballistic comparison microscope to compare the markings to a particular weapon. "

I finished testifying and made a beeline for my car. I called Fran again. No answer. Parker said Fran had not been at the lab or called in. I decided to swing by Fran's house before going to the lab.

Fran lived in a duplex on Forty-Eighth Street across from the Calvary United Methodist Church.

I pulled curbside and perused the neighborhood before I got out. Fran's car was not in front of his house or in the driveway. The duplex was a white and redbrick-faced tri-level dwelling with high Victorian windows and a curved tower. A wide cement stairway led up to a large porch decorated with a farmhouse-style oak bench.

The door was ajar. I pulled my gun from its holster and gently kicked the door open. A large circular entryway gave way to a long, curved staircase straight ahead. I crept in and went left to the living room. Fran lay on the floor at the far end with his hands and feet bound. I went to him and crouched down. He was unconscious but breathing. Men's voices came from above. I moved back through the living room to the staircase and began the climb up, then stopped with the thought—there was more than one perpetrator. I backed down the stairs, retraced my steps through the living room, and hid behind the wall that connected the dining room, keeping Fran in my line of sight.

Fran groaned, waking from his unconscious state.

I heard the stairs squeak as the men came down. I waited, then peeked out from behind the wall. Two men stood over

Fran. One of them had their gun aimed at him. Fran squirmed on the floor.

"You don't want to do this, man. I'm a cop. You shoot me and you're done."

"I don't shoot you and we're done," one snarled.

I stepped out and yelled, "Police!"

They both turned with weapons pointed in my direction. One of the men turned his gun back on Fran. I got off one shot and hit him. The other guy fell on the floor next to him. Laughton crowded the entryway.

"Damn, about time you-all showed up," Fran mumbled. " 'Bout got my ass dead." Fran tried to get up. I held him down. Laughton called an ambulance. "I'm thinking we need to finish this before one of us gets killed. I don't know who these two were, but I do believe my death was going to be a message to you. They tried to beat out of me where Calvin stashed some heroin."

CHAPTER 25

Laughton parked curbside in front of Calvin's Place. There were two doors. The one to the club was boarded up. The other door led up to Calvin's living quarters on the third and fourth floors of the old warehouse. I had never accessed Calvin's apartment from the front, always by the elevator in the club.

The lock to the outside door was broken. Laughton pushed it open and we climbed the stairs with weapons aimed and ready. The air smelled of smoke and burnt wood. At the top of the stairs, the entry door, a reclaimed barn door on a track, was open. The first floor of Calvin's apartment was one large open area with vaulted ceilings and huge windows. The furniture had been tossed and turned over, along with broken lamps, shattered glass, splintered tables and chests.

The second floor was walled off into three bedrooms and an office. In his office, the desk was upside-down with the underside caved in. I holstered my gun and went back into the bedroom and opened the closet door. A pile of clothes sat on the floor; the pole they had hung on was broken in half and dangled from the wall on each side.

"Nice place. My man definitely had it together," Laughton said.

I pushed the pile of clothes out of the closet. I tapped the top left corner of the closet three times and twisted the hinge that held the pole on the left side of the closet. The back wall ground open to reveal a small room, big enough for a child's bedroom.

A faint smell of cleaning solvent made my nose run. The three walls were lined with different kinds of guns and rifles, top to bottom.

"Damn, this is like something out of a spy movie," Laughton said, as he took a rifle off the wall and inspected it. "Man, this is a Freund Boss Gun, said to be the finest weapon . . . how the hell . . . ain't but a few of these in the world." He replaced it and took another one down. "This baby is a Soviet AVS-36 automatic. This is some collection," Laughton marveled as he rehung the weapon.

"You never cease to amaze me when it comes to guns." I knelt to access a black footlocker set off to the side. From my pocket I got the key Calvin left me and tried it in the lock. It fit. I pulled out two backpacks filled with packages of what I suspected was heroin. Laughton did the taste test to confirm my suspicions.

Laughton picked up each backpack one at a time. "There has to be fifty to seventy-five pounds here. Damn. That's worth about twenty million."

I fell back on my butt, dumbfounded. "I can't believe Calvin played in this game." I thought about it for thirty seconds and dismissed it. "No way. I don't know where this came from, but I do know that Calvin was working an angle to keep this stuff out of circulation."

"How'd you know about this room?"

"Calvin showed me after we'd been dating awhile. It was all about his gun collection."

"Whoever tore this place apart didn't get in here. We need to leave before they come back. Leave the stuff here. We don't want to be seen leaving with it. This is the safest place for it until we figure this all out."

We went back to the Rittenhouse and parked the car, then walked around Rittenhouse Square to Fogo de Chão, a Brazilian steakhouse. The hostess sat us at a table in the rear corner of the restaurant.

"Here we are back in a situation that might get us both killed," Laughton said.

"What started out being about Hampton and his simple ass, turned into a major case, killed five people so far, three who are close to me, and put Fran in the hospital. The gang unit. Yeah right. FBI, DEA, police, can't do a damn thing about it. Or won't because there is some kind of conspiracy going on."

"No conspiracy. Not in the department anyway. Not this time."

"Laughton, I been checking into BJ. Calvin said he's known BJ most of his life. You know him too?"

"BJ's always been a stand-up guy. He's been with Calvin for a long time. They were in Special Forces together. I don't think he would turn on Calvin."

"Not even for twenty million?"

"So, say he is the man behind all this. Why would he protect Hamp and possibly get his main man Griffin put away? If BJ's involved and he is concerned about Griffin going down, he would have gotten rid of Hamp, not protected him."

I told Laughton about the guy at Hamp's boat who was killed. "I think Hamp got away because of circumstance and missed opportunities."

"Where's Hamp now?"

"He's in a hotel outside the city. How could Calvin have missed BJ?"

"I'd bet he didn't miss a damn thing."

"There is a way we can find out. We can call and tell him about the heroin, say we're going to turn it in to the police."

"Let's eat first," Laughton said, licking his lips as the waiter stopped at our table with beef on a skewer and put some on our plates. Another waiter came with chicken and another with pork. Laughton fed me from his plate. I took my shoes off and rested my feet in his lap, hidden by the length of table-cloth. He massaged my feet, my legs. I fed him caramelized bananas. We laughed at memories.

Two hours later, we had eaten every kind of meat—chicken, beef, pork, cooked every way possible, made two trips to the salad bar, and finished three healthy servings of caramelized bananas. We waddled back to the hotel. Laughton held my hand all the way. When we got to the hotel, we went to the bar. Laughton ordered a two-hundred-dollar bottle of champagne—Taittinger Comtes de Champagne Rose, to be exact. The semi-sweet bubbly went straight to my head. Or was I making excuses for being so easily lured from the bar to Laughton's suite?

Laughton scooped me up like a groom carrying his bride over the threshold for a radiant first night. Maybe not so radi-ant for the bride with her virginity to lose. No worries here.

It didn't feel right. "Let's not do this, Laughton. It's not the time for us to be . . ."

He stepped over the threshold, set me down, and pressed me against the wall.

"It is exactly the time," he whispered before kissing me so hard my head banged against the wall.

He reached behind me and in one move unhooked my gun holster, unclipped my phone, and undid my belt, letting them fall to the floor. I did the same to him. We tripped over a chair unbuttoning, kissing, unzipping, kissing long and hard, until we fell on the bed. More kissing on the lips, breasts, over and under soft folds, until we each got lost in the delicate flavors of each other's love. Trying to quench an undying thirst sent us crashing to the floor.

Uncontrollable laughter took hold, as though we were experiencing some neurologic condition or brain injury.

The laughter waned. We embraced, every body part intertwined with one another, on the floor, wrapped in the bedspread.

When we woke, the room was dark. Laughton lifted me on the bed and took me, with everything I had to give.

In the morning, I called into the lab and told Parker I wouldn't be in. He bitched but agreed to cover for me to the lieutenant.

We made the call to BJ, who said he couldn't believe that Calvin was dealing drugs and he didn't know about it. I thought he was putting us on. Laughton thought he was sincere. We decided to put it on hold and went to Mercy Hospital to see Fran.

From the outside, Mercy looks like an institution for the insane—an old brick monstrosity. The inside matched the depressing view of the outside. I made a mental note to let everyone know never to bring me to Mercy.

Fran was halfway sitting up watching television, or at least trying to watch television given the bandages on his face, swollen eyes, and stitches across his left cheek. He waved me away when we walked in. I stopped and turned like a soldier, and headed back out the door.

"No, no. Come back," he mumbled, because that was all he could do.

I did another turn. He waved me forward.

"Just messing with you."

"You're in no condition to mess with anybody, so ha-ha. They really did a number on you."

"They kept asking me where the drugs were. Hell, I didn't know what they were talking about, but I did figure whatever opens using that key you have, contains a lot of what they want."

"You figured correct." No sooner had I said the words than Zoila and Santiago came in with Laughton, who had stopped at the coffee shop on our way up.

"Hey, guy, they worked you over good. Son of a bitch." Laughton set a tall cup on the portable table that swung over Fran's bed. "Brought you a mocha latte with extra espresso, which I understand is your favorite."

"I don't mean to break up the party," Zoila said.

"Then don't. Can't you see this man is recovering from a brutal beating and needs to rest?" I said.

"I would say we'll come back, but we need to do this now, if you-all don't mind. I'm glad you're here, Muriel. Saves you a trip and me some time."

Laughton looked to Fran, who nodded his consent. Laughton and I sat down in the only two chairs in the room. Santiago stood by the door as though to stop anyone from entering. Zoila stood at the end of the bed. "The two dead guys were Berg Nation. Why'd they target you?"

Fran shook his head no.

"Ward Griffin's still in custody. His trial begins in two days. Did they say anything, threaten you, ask for something?"

Fran shook his head again.

She turned her attention to me. "Griffin's not going anywhere until after the trial, then he's going away for a very long time."

"You're that sure that Griffin will be convicted with Hamp's testimony, even though there is no way of connecting him to the murder weapon?" I asked.

"I'm that sure. He's gotten out of other cases, mostly because of witnesses changing their testimony or deciding not to testify, or turning up dead. That won't be the case this time." She bore into me with a hard stare. "Two days can be a long time."

"He'll be there."

"With Griffin locked up, the flow of heroin into the city should at least slow for a minute."

"All this and the flow slows, only to pick right up again with someone else."

"We can only do the best we can. It feels like a never-ending battle, but it's one we can't stop fighting."

"I didn't mean to sound righteous."

Zoila smiled and nodded. "No problem. By the way, I apologize again for busting into your house like we did. I really didn't know it was your residence. Elijah and his brother look so much alike, and I'm just not clear that Elijah is the good brother. I don't get how they can be so different."

Her phone buzzed. She excused herself and went out into the hallway to take the call. When she got back her face had paled.

"Ward Griffin hung himself in his cell last night."

CHAPTER 26

When we pulled up to his house, Hamp rushed down the walkway, Dulcey jumped out of the car, and they collided with each other and embraced, long-lost lovers reunited. Tears flowed, "I love you" spewed from their lips, and kisses and more kisses. Laughton and I leaned against the car, watching.

"This isn't over," I said. "We still have to find out who killed Calvin. A huge shipment of heroin and cocaine came into the city, and somehow Calvin confiscated it. Ward Griffin's death doesn't change anything, mainly because he's not the boss. Another thing? He didn't kill himself. Guys like him don't do suicide."

"Muriel, go home to your family. Let Burgan and her crew take it from here."

I pushed away from the car. Laughton walked around to the driver's side. Hamp and Dulcey moved up the walkway and into the house, a happy ending, in my book.

"You're right. Calvin's killer is still out there, but I guess you're right, we should give the drugs to Zoila, along with the flash drive, and be done with it. Let the detectives follow up and catch whoever it is."

"Indeed."

We got in the car and sat in silence for about two minutes.

"Let's pay a visit to Mr. BJ's place of residence," I said.

"We can't do that. If he's the head of Berg Nation, he's got a small army behind him. Berg Nation has a few hundred members. We can't fight them by ourselves and he won't hesitate to kill us. Besides, I don't know where he lives."

"I do."

An eerie darkness, the kind that brings out the wolf man, made for good cover by the time we pulled to the curb a half block down from BJ's residence on Chestnut Street in Center City. Laughton got out and entered the Commonwealth apartment building as someone exited.

"Biltmore Jones. What kind of name is Biltmore?" he said when he got back in the car. "He's on the sixth floor, 615A. Let's sit for a while and see what happens."

I called the house and told Nareece I wouldn't be home until late. She sounded agitated. Sounds of the twins clamoring for attention filtered through the receiver. She asked me where I was. I started down the path of a lie. She hung up three words in.

"How's your sister doing?"

"Physically, she's fine. Mentally, not so good. Half the time my own sister is a stranger to me. We were so close. At least I thought we were close."

"She's been through a lot."

"Yes, and those little girls have been through a lot too. Sometimes I think the only person she thinks about is herself."

"How is Travis handling knowing Jesse is his father?"

"Travis is Travis. He's a good kid, and knowing hasn't seemed to faze him. A bigger concern is how Nareece is always at him about being his mother and wanting him to call her Mom."

"How do you feel about that?" He reached over and took my hand and rubbed it between his.

"Honestly, apprehensive at first. Angry because she didn't want him when he was born, and now that he's a man, she wants to be his mother."

"Hmm." He put the hand he held in my lap, then took the other one.

"Now I'm good with whatever Travis wants. She is his mother too. I will always be his mother regardless of their relationship." I watched him caress my hand, then kiss it and place it on my lap.

"Where have you been?"

"After everything went down . . . you and Calvin were together . . . I felt like I needed to be out of here. I went over the water, Paris, London. Can't run away from what ails you."

"Tell me about it."

Two hours passed as we watched people enter and exit the building. We decided it was a waste of time to stay longer. Laughton started the car and turned the wheel to pull out, when a BMW pulled up and parked in front of the building. I told Laughton to wait. BJ got out of the passenger side. He walked around and opened the door. A woman got out. BJ pushed the car door shut. He stepped up on the curb and froze as the woman walked toward the building. He turned in our direction. I stopped breathing. He turned in the opposite direction from us, took a few steps forward, and froze again. I took a breath. Two minutes seemed like an eternity, before he followed the woman into the building.

"Travis said a woman picked Hamp up in a BMW."

"What are you talking about?"

"At the beginning of all this, Hamp called Travis for help. Travis picked him up somewhere and brought him home and kept Dulcey from kicking his butt. As Travis left Hamp's house, he saw Hamp come out of the house and get in a BMW with a woman."

Hamp's phone was turned off, so we went to the house. It was dark except for the television light that danced against the curtains. I tapped on the door. Hamp peeked out the curtain.

"What brings you two back here at this hour?"

Dulcey limped down the stairs as Hamp closed the door.

"What's going on? What are you two doing here this late?"

"Hey, girl. Didn't mean to wake you. I tried calling but both your phones are turned off. This couldn't wait."

"It's nothing, doll. You should go back to bed," Hamp said in his sweet voice.

"I'm not going anywhere." Dulcey stomped down the last steps. "C'mon in here and sit down." She switched on a light and ushered us into the den, then plopped down on the couch. Laughton and I sat in the loveseat. Hamp stayed at the door until everyone was seated. He came in and sat at the far end of the couch from Dulcey.

"Look, Hamp. I don't mean to bring you any more trouble, but something tells me this isn't over yet."

He moaned and pushed back on the couch. Dulcey glared at him but stayed silent.

"The night you called Travis. You left with a woman."

He sat forward and moaned.

"Who is she and what was that about?"

Dulcey's demeanor puffed up, like she was going to come out of her skin and pummel Hamp. "Relax, Dulce, he's not messing around," I said. "It wasn't about that."

Dulcey shrunk back down.

"Her name's Cat, Barry's daughter, the guy who owns the marina. She wanted to make a buy."

"Heroin?"

"Yeah. He's a stone addict. He called me and asked me to do him a favor. I owe him for some favors he's done for me over the years—loaned me money, made sure the boat was taken care of better than the usual. So I took her over to Norris Homes and showed her where to go so I wouldn't have to take her again."

"You took her to buy heroin?"

"Now Barry's dead!" Dulcey shrieked. "The man OD'd. You didn't say you had anything to do with it."

"I accept, I'm responsible. I did not intend to take her, I swear. I tried to say no, but he kept on, begged me and wouldn't let me say no. Called me out about how many times he's had my back when I needed something. He knows about using that shit. I think he wanted to die."

"Have you been in contact with her since then?" I asked.

"No. I only talked to her that once. What's that got to do with anything?"

"Man, what did you talk about while you were with her?" Laughton asked. "I mean, did she say anything that was unexpected or something that surprised you?"

Hamp pursed his lips. Sweat popped out on his forehead. He wiped it away with his forearm. "Nothing that I remember. I only saw her once or twice at the marina with Barry. Like I said, I owed him."

"You owed him, all right. Killed him is more what you did for him," Dulcey growled.

Hamp cringed at her words.

"Why is she important?"

"I don't know that she is, except we saw her with Calvin's man, BJ, tonight," Laughton said.

"Yeah, she's been dating him. I've seen them at the marina. Barry keeps a boat there. It's more like a yacht, at least compared to the *Dulcey Maria*. BJ doesn't speak to anyone much. Just comes and goes now and again."

"How long they been dating?"

"Three, four months maybe." He put his pointer finger and

thumb to his chin. "Let me think. Yes, I think it was just after the shooting at the church, where little Rose got hit. Cat said they met at the Dave and Buster's next to the marina. Tourists love that place. Cat began spending time on the boat. I believe she's going through a divorce. She dabbles a little herself. Her husband got custody of the two little boys because of an unfit mother charge."

"You know too much about other people's business," Dulcey chimed in.

Laughton and I got up to leave.

"You-all don't need to rush off," Dulcey said.

"You go back upstairs and get some rest." I gave her a hug.

"Everybody says the same thing. Get some rest. I'll rest when I'm dead."

"Dulcey, don't be so stubborn. Rest is what is going to help you heal."

"I got God for that."

I shook my head, gave her another hug, and moved toward the door.

"You can't move her once she's dug in," Hamp said.

"I'm gonna dig a hole for you and bury you deep when they gone," she threatened.

It was after eleven when I dropped Laughton at the hotel. Half hour later, I turned onto my street and my cell phone rang.

"Detective Burgan is dead," Fran said.

"What do you mean, she's dead?"

"They just pulled her from her burning car on Benjamin Franklin Parkway. It seems she drove off the road into a tree or was forced off the road. Where are you? Sounds like you're in a tunnel."

"How did you hear about this in the hospital and I'm out here and hadn't heard yet? What are you doing up this time of night?"

"Parker called me. I can't sleep in this place. I can't wait until tomorrow. I want out of here. Watch your back, partner. They are reporting Burgan's death as an accident, but I don't know, given everything that's happened in the past month."

"I can't believe it. I'm home now. I'm going to get some sleep. I'll call you in the morning, see what time they're going to let you out."

The house looked spooky with no lights on, inside or out. I pulled up into the driveway and looked around for Travis's car. It pissed me off that Nareece didn't leave a light on for me. With Travis still out, I was doubly pissed. Maybe it *would* be best for her to move, I thought.

"She wants me to say that," I said out loud. "I'm not going to. The twins want to stay right here with me and Travis." I reached in the back and searched around the floor for my bag, then grabbed my water bottle from the cupholder and got out.

"Makes no sense that she wouldn't leave a light on for us, at least on the outside," I mumbled. That angry itch inside my gut grew with every step. By the time I opened the front door and tried the switch to the entryway, I registered livid. The damn light didn't work. I walked in farther and clipped the switch for the stairway lights. The house remained dark.

I felt him before he spoke.

"Just put your things on the floor and turn around, real slow."

I did as he said. "Where's my family?"

"They're in the basement, alive. They'll stay that way, as long as you do what I say. You have to know I can get to you and your family anytime I want. Anytime at all. You keep that in mind and everything will turn out good for you and them."

"What do you want, BJ?"

"You know exactly what I want. I can't believe Calvin trusted you with his secret room and not me, after everything we've been through together and all that I've done for him. Even saved his life. More than once, I might add."

"And if I don't know what you're talking about?"

"Look, I know about the room. Heard you and him talking about it more than once, so don't play dumb with me. If you don't know what the hell I'm talking about I guess I'll just have to take care of your family now."

He yanked me by the arm and pulled me outside, leaving the front door wide open. His car was parked three houses down. I held my wrists slightly apart, as he tied them with a piece of nylon rope. He detached my phone from the clip on my waist and lifted me into the trunk and closed the lid. He started the car and we began to move.

I yanked my hands apart as hard as I could and gnawed on the rope until it loosened and I could pull my hands free. I felt around for a weapon and found a tire iron as the car slowed and stopped. I tensed. He shut the car off. His car door opened and closed. I listened as his footsteps moved around to the back of the car. I hugged my knees close, ready to kick at him when he opened the trunk. The trunk popped open and he was there with a gun pointed at me.

CHAPTER 27

"I can show you where the room is, but there's nothing there," I said as he pushed me toward the door to Calvin's building. Inside, he tied my hands again and pushed me toward the stairs.

"What did you do with it?"

"I'm telling you, I came here and there was nothing here."

"We'll see about that."

When we got to Calvin's apartment, BJ reached up and pushed back a section of the ceiling that revealed a small black box the size of a paperback. BJ removed something I thought must be an SD card. He pushed me inside the apartment and kept nudging me until we were in Calvin's bedroom. Then he pushed me down on the bed.

He inserted the card in his phone, made some adjustments, then turned the phone so that I could see the recording. It was me and Laughton coming out of the apartment.

"Looks like you left with nothing." He pulled me up. "Let's see what you left in there." He untied my hands and pushed me into the closet. I tapped the corner three times and twisted the hinge to make the wall slide back. He pushed me into the room in front of him. "Have a seat."

I sat on the floor. He tied my hands behind my back. I

watched him open the footlocker and inspect the contents. "Is this what you killed Calvin for?"

"You know Calvin has spent his whole life trying to save these stupid kids. No matter what he did, no matter how much he tried to help them, they just kept doing the same old stupid shit. The world is a fucked-up place. Everything has changed, and these young dudes think they are the king of the mountain. They don't have the slightest bit of what it takes to be the king of anybody's mountain."

"So you showed them that you were the king?"

"Calvin was a good guy. He just didn't want to make adjustments. We needed to change with what was going on in the world. Nobody cares about the neighborhood anymore. These kids would just as soon shoot him as look at him."

"What did it take for you to turn the corner? Money?"

"You're damn right, and lots of it. My man comes up here from Mexico and drops the shit, and I have those young bloods distribute it and we all get rich. I knew Calvin would never see it that way."

"That's because Calvin wasn't a murderer."

"You're right. He wasn't. But I am. I'm not going to kill you. The way I figure, your family means a lot to you. You go on about your business and I'll go on about mine and everybody stays happy." He pulled his Glock out of his belt, pulled me to my feet, and stuck it against my head. "You or any member of your family decide they don't like the arrangement and I'll kill you all. I'll be watching, so don't think I won't know everything that goes on. And don't think your girlfriend, Burgan, will be around to help you out because she has already taken a turn for the worse."

I was stung by his admission of killing Zoila. "Who you kiddin', BJ? Talking about you can kill us at any time so we'll be afraid. I'm not buying."

He backhanded me. I fell backwards. My head bounced off one of the guns hanging on the wall and I fell to the floor.

He let loose a sinister chuckle. "Calvin said you were a tough bitch. You won't be so tough when I kill your little nieces, and your sister, and your bastard son. We'll see how tough you are when I make you watch. I'll save you until last."

"Well then, let's get it done."

"Soon as I clean out this closet, that's exactly what's going to happen."

He pushed me out of the room, in front of him. I back-kicked him causing him to drop his gun. I ducked to the side as the wall slid back and almost closed BJ inside. Almost. He came barreling out and into Laughton's outstretched fist and crashed to the floor.

Laughton got one of my hands untied before BJ rolled over and jumped to his feet. Laughton jumped back and aimed his gun at BJ. Laughton was tall, but slight compared to BJ's bulk.

"BJ, man, how'd you get caught up in this shit? You were always the man to go to, always a stand-up guy. How could you kill my man, Calvin?"

BJ stepped toward Laughton.

"I will shoot you as sure as I'm standing here."

BJ stopped. "I told him to just give me the shit and leave it be, but Calvin and his self-righteous self . . ."

BJ barreled into Laughton before he could get a shot off and banged him against the wall, knocking the gun out of Laughton's hand. I scanned the floor for it. Laughton and BJ were rolling around on the floor. Laughton held on to BJ, to keep him close so BJ couldn't punch him. When he looked up and saw me with the gun, he turned BJ loose and pushed him away.

"Hold it, BJ. I'll shoot."

BJ did not hesitate. He punched Laughton straight in the temple and knocked him out, then moved toward me.

"Take another step and I'll shoot."

"You can't shoot me. I can't be killed."

"*I* can shoot you."

We turned to see Elijah at the top of the stairs, pointing a gun at BJ. "Oh yes, I can definitely kill your ass. Just like you killed my mother and father. Just like you killed my brother."

"I didn't kill your mommy and your daddy. They killed themselves, damn junkies."

"My brother didn't kill himself."

"Yes he did. He was too soft. You want a piece of the action, son?"

"Elijah, give me the gun. He's not worth it."

"You got that little peashooter. That thing can't stop a tank like me." BJ took a step toward Elijah and stopped. "I do believe you would empty that little thing into me. That would definitely hurt even me."

"C'mon, Elijah, give me the gun."

"If I don't kill him now, the police will come and take him away, he'll get out, and every day we'll be wondering if the twins are safe, if Travis is safe, if your Miss Nareece is safe, if you're safe. Every day."

BJ lunged toward Elijah and Elijah pulled the trigger. The bullet hit BJ center mass. BJ stopped. He looked down at his chest with a surprised expression. He looked up with an evil smile and lunged at Elijah again, wrapped his arms around him and pushed off, taking him backwards down the stairs.

I ran down the stairs where BJ was anchored atop Elijah.

"Elijah."

He grunted.

"Hold on, baby."

I leaned against BJ with my back, pressed my feet against the wall, and pushed. Elijah lay faceup with the gun still in his hand. I reached for it. He lifted it and let me take it. When I looked at it, I noticed the serial number had been filed off.

I checked BJ for a pulse. There was none.

Laughton stumbled down the stairs, holding his head.

"Where'd you get the gun, Elijah?"

He didn't respond at first. Instead he looked at BJ and up at me with watery eyes. "Ward gave it to me awhile back for protection," he whimpered, scrambling to get away from BJ's dead body. He hunched in the corner of the small landing. "I didn't mean to shoot him. I couldn't stop myself."

"Get Elijah out of here," I told Laughton, giving him Elijah's gun. "I'll call this in and wait."

"You really going to do this? Once you do, there's no turning back."

"What am I going to do, let him go to jail? BJ attacked him. It was self-defense, but you know as well as I do, it won't turn out that way."

After they left, I ran up and made sure the wall to the room was closed, put the pile of clothes back in the closet, and called it in.

CHAPTER 28

When I got to the house, it was dark except for kitchen lights. Laughton and Nareece were laughing about something until I walked in and they stopped. Nareece was on me, hugging me like it was her last official act on earth. When she turned me loose, she went to kissing my face and head and hands and arms.

"I'm cured," she said. "I don't want to move away from you. I want to live right here with you and Travis and Elijah. If it wasn't for Travis, we would have gone crazy all tied up in that basement like animals."

It was late, or rather early in the morning, so the kids were in bed.

"Can I make you some tea or soup or something, anything?"

"Go to bed, Reece. Those girls will be up before you know it, clamoring for your attention."

"So what's the story?" Laughton asked.

"I went there trying to come to grips with Calvin's death. When I got there, BJ was dead and the place was a mess."

Eventually I went to bed, but I couldn't sleep. Elijah lied about how he got the gun, I knew it. And I did not believe he just happened by after being at the center the night Calvin was killed. And, all of a sudden, he's never anywhere around, when it was not but a few weeks ago he was glued to Travis's hip.

I considered that I was being paranoid and that there was a perfectly logical explanation for why he lied. He said he had a girlfriend, which could explain why he stopped hanging around Travis so much.

Laughton and I needed to figure out what to do with the heroin in Calvin's closet, or rather, how to make it so the Mobile Street Crimes Unit found it and the flash drive. It would be one of the biggest drug busts in Philly history. I also needed to call Shea and find out if she knew about the secret room and Calvin's gun collection. If she didn't want to keep the guns, she could auction them off and use the proceeds to keep the center open. And what about Laughton, would he disappear again, or stay? Did I even want him to stay? I put the pillow over my head, trying to stop the flow of thoughts. My brain ached.

I wrestled with my bed until five thirty, then got up and put on running clothes and tiptoed past Laughton, sleeping on the couch in the den. I got about a mile from the house, when Elijah ran up beside me.

"I couldn't sleep either," he said. "I want to thank you for covering for what I did last night."

I can't run and talk, so I nodded at him.

I slowed my pace, thinking he wanted to talk more, but instead, he ran ahead of me and disappeared around the next corner.

Always so polite. My stomach gurgled, making me feel like I needed to use the bathroom. I picked up the pace.

The conversation with BJ before Elijah killed him replayed in my head. He never admitted to killing Calvin or that he had anything to do with Ward's death. He talked about Calvin being self-righteous and Griffin being too soft, but he never said he killed them. The look on his face, the smile, just before they fell, flashed in front of me. I slowed to a walk.

I was two blocks from the house when I noticed the car following me. A gray coupe with tinted windows. The same car from the last time I ran. This time it pulled half a block up and stopped. A fat white man got out and stood with his arms across his chest like he was waiting for me.

My first thought was to sprint across the street and through some yards to lose them, then decided I didn't have the energy, so I stopped when he stepped in front of me as I tried to pass.

The car window went down.

"Do you know who I am?"

I nodded my head yes. Angelo Bonanno, hit man for the Cosa Nostra. I testified in his son's murder case.

"Please, I am not here to hurt you in any way. In fact, I believe we can help each other. Can we give you a lift perhaps?"

No way was I getting in the car. "How about we walk?"

Angelo Bonanno got out of the car. I backed up a few steps.

"I imagine you think I'm here about my son's case. I'm not."

I didn't say anything. My nerves were shot. He started walking. I fell in beside him.

He reached in his pocket. I tensed. He came out with a picture.

"This is my granddaughter. She's fifteen years old. She's been missing for a couple of weeks now. I believe she is being held at the Blumberg housing projects by the gang who call themselves Berg Nation."

I glanced at the picture and kept walking.

"Please, Miss Mabley." He stopped walking and touched my arm to do the same. I stopped. "Please look at the picture. I know what I am, and I know you know what I am. My granddaughter has no part in the life her father and I are in. She and her mother live apart, on their own."

I took the picture from him. I stared at it, remembering the faces of the two young girls who were being brought up the stairs to Ward Griffin's place when Calvin and I were going down with Karin. One of them was the girl in the picture.

"Why are you showing this to me?"

"I have been watching the projects and the people in them. I know that they are dealing heroin out of that place. I know they are responsible for several deaths, including Calvin Bernard's."

He said Calvin's name as though he had a closer connection than I would like to imagine.

"You seem surprised. Bernard was a kind of friend, that's all I will say about that. I was working with him to disrupt the flow of heroin into the city."

He waited for me to respond. I didn't.

"This is the man who killed Calvin. We believe he is also the man who runs Berg Nation. It seems you are well acquainted with him, as is your son."

The picture he gave me was not of Ward Griffin or BJ. It was Elijah.

"You don't seem surprised."

"And how do you know all this?"

"Like I said, we've been watching."

"Mr. Bonanno."

"Angelo, please."

"If you know your granddaughter is at Blumberg and you know the man who is running the show there, why don't you just go in there and get her out?"

We walked some more, with his car following.

"I think you know the answer to that question. Things aren't like the old days, and I'm too old to even begin to stir the pot and ignite a war between the young men of Berg Nation and my family. I love my granddaughter, and I will do whatever it takes to get her out of there, but I do not want a bloodbath that might end up getting her and a lot of others killed."

I held out the pictures to him.

"Keep them." His car pulled up to where we stood. The fat man got out and opened the back door for him. He stepped off the curb to get in. "I hope to hear from you."

Elijah's blubbering about how sorry he was for shooting BJ played and replayed in my head. I folded the pictures and stuck them in my waistband and walked the rest of the two blocks to the house. Laughton had the television news on.

"You are serious about this triathlon, aren't you?"

"Did Elijah come back?"

"No, he's not here."

I ran down my conversation with Bonanno to Laughton. When I finished, we sat for a while, listening to the six-thirty newscast.

"Getting in the middle of the gangs and the crime family is not a good idea."

"I have to make this right, Laughton. Elijah is out there free, because I thought he was a victim. If he is who Bonanno says he is, he's the worst kind of ruthless, and I'm scared to death of what he'll do to get what he wants."

"*We* thought he was a victim and *we* have to make it right."

I settled on the couch in the crux of his arm. "We know he's looking for the heroin, and if he doesn't find it, he'll probably have to answer to the Mexicans. He's about out of options. Desperate. So, we dangle the goods again and find out if he is who Bonanno says he is."

I showered and dressed and took Laughton to the hotel to do the same. Then we made the call. Elijah answered on the first ring.

"I'm so glad you called, Miss Mabley. I am so sorry things have turned out the way they have. I had no intention of hurting you or Travis or anyone else in your family. Mine was a simple task of getting to Mr. Bernard and his compadre, BJ."

I shuddered at the reality of what was happening. "You killed Calvin."

"He hijacked my junk and wouldn't give it up."

"And Kenyetta and Sam?"

"Circumstance. Kenyetta found her long-lost sibling, a heroin addict. She tracked her to one of the apartments here. Her and Sam. Wrong place, wrong time. They saw and heard some things I couldn't let them leave with. Thing is, everybody's getting into heroin again, so it is so easy to convince people that someone is a user. If it's any comfort, they didn't suffer at all. They just went to sleep."

I squeezed out every ounce of strength I had to keep from screaming out the agony that clobbered my gut. Laughton squeezed my hand. I took a breath.

"So you killed Calvin for the shipment he intercepted? So he's dead, and you still don't have it."

"Ah, but you do, and I think you are willing to make an exchange of some kind so that we all come out of this in a good way."

"Did you kill your brother too?"

"Ward was a little slow, but good at carrying out orders, being the face of Berg Nation so I could operate under the radar and keep things going. There's millions to be made working with the Mexicans. Ward couldn't handle prison, so he killed himself." He let his words sink in before continuing. "So how is this going to work?"

"You have a young white girl there who I want to take out."

"I have several young white girls. Which one?"

"I'll know her when I see her."

"Ah, so you want to come to the kingdom. Fine. You bring the product and we can make an exchange."

"I'll come, but I want the girls brought outside. We can make the exchange outside."

"So the police can make a bust? I don't think so. Only under the cover of night, and you come alone. And Miss Mabley, you should know, I have eyes everywhere in Blumberg. It's a shame they're going to destroy this place, means I'll have to find another base of operation. Maybe it'll be in your neck of the city."

I hung up, feeling like I had crawled through a sewer pipe.

CHAPTER 29

Thousands of police officers from across the country attended Zoila's funeral at the Cathedral Basilica of Saints Peter and Paul, the largest Catholic church in the city. Her three sons, one daughter, and husband of thirty years sat in the front pew, accepting visitors as they passed to view the poster-sized portrait of Zoila in full police uniform, displayed next to a closed casket.

Sounds of sniffles, shushing of children, cracking of wooden pews adjusting to the weight of mourners followed her oldest granddaughter to the lectern.

"Nana was a terrible cook, but that didn't stop her from giving us cooking lessons. She hated girly things like tea parties and playing with dolls, but that didn't stop her from having a tea party for me and five of my ten-year-old friends, or coaching me through being a model at an American Girl Fashion Show. The only black model in the show. Nana said you have to step out of your comfort zone now and again to grow. I feel the growth coming on, Nana."

Santiago, Zoila's partner, joined us at our table at the repast. "She was a good cop and a great person," he said. "It's hard to accept that she went out that way. It was an accident. She swerved to miss hitting a dog in the road and lost control. A damn dog."

I was relieved to know Zoila's passing was an accident. Still, Zoila's was the fourth funeral I had attended in as many weeks. It made me consider the sense and nonsense of my life. I watched Zoila's family interacting, toddlers running around laughing and playing, babies being passed from one to another, adults hugging, kissing, laughing, and at the helm, her husband, invisibly conducting with enduring grace.

When I got home, the house was quiet except for the twins, who were in the den playing the game of Life, my and Travis's old-time favorite, and watching television. Nareece was not in the kitchen. I went upstairs to change and knocked on her door in passing. When she didn't answer, I cracked the door and called her name at the same time. She was standing in front of the mirror putting makeup on. I went in and plopped down on her bed.

"You got a hot date or something?"

"Just tired of looking tired, is all."

"You look fine. As beautiful as ever."

"Thanks for the vote of confidence, but I'd say you're a little biased." She stopped what she was doing and sat with me on the bed. "I'm sorry about your police friend."

"She was a good cop. And that's about the thousandth time that's been said today."

Nareece picked at a scab on one of her fingers.

"What's going on, Reece?"

She pulled the crusty layer away from her skin, making it bleed.

"I know that guy BJ is dead, but I'm still freaked out about the whole thing. I want to know that it's over and there's no worries about anything else like that happening. I mean, Elijah's gone now, and I know there's something going on with him, but I also know you're not going to share anything with me even if there is."

"It's done. You don't have to worry about any of that. Everything is fine." *It will be after tonight*, I thought. I lifted her chin so she looked me in the eye. "Trust me."

After I changed clothes, I went to the kitchen and made a sandwich. I didn't eat anything at the repast and my stomach was protesting the neglect. Nareece came in the kitchen as I was slapping together a mayo-and-chicken sandwich.

"Travis been around?" I asked through a mouthful of sandwich.

"He left this morning around eleven. Said he was going to help Elijah move some of his stuff from his brother's place into a new apartment."

I stopped chewing. Pulled my phone from my hip and called Travis. I heard the faint ring of his phone. Nareece went into the dining room and came back with Travis's phone still ringing. "I know that boy's going to be ticked off when he realizes he forgot . . ."

That's all I heard before I was out the door. I called Elijah as soon as I got in the car.

"Not to worry, Miss Mabley. Travis is on his way home. He doesn't know anything about what is going on. He was helping me pack up the moving truck. Like I said, we have to find a new location. But I wanted you to know how easy it would be for me. Reassurance that our little exchange will go off without any problems. Until tonight."

I pulled over into the breakdown lane on I-76, leaned out the door, and puked.

Travis called as I pulled into a parking space at the Rittenhouse. It was Saturday and he had the program at Calvin's center to run.

"Elijah seems really broken up about his brother committing suicide. I guess it doesn't matter how bad somebody is, if he's your blood, you love him anyway," Travis said.

I closed my eyes against his words.

He had no idea I had skirted the law for his supposed-to-be friend, who killed Travis's best friend and his girlfriend; who had everything to do with almost killing his niece, and who killed Calvin. I considered that if I told him what was going on, he would go off and confront Elijah and get himself killed. Then I remembered that he is my son. I raised him.

"Travis, I know we should be talking face-to-face right now, but there's no time. I need you to listen good to what I'm about to tell you." And I ran down to him all there was to tell about Elijah and his brother. When I finished, there was silence on the other end.

"Why are you just telling me this now, Ma? What do I have to do or how old do I have to get . . . ?"

"Travis, I didn't find out for sure about Elijah until this morning. Then Nareece told me you went to help him move or something. This is our first conversation today." I let a few seconds pass for him to calm down. "Travis, I need you to stay there with your aunt and the girls. You know where the gun is and you know how to use it. I'll call you when it's done."

"When what's done?"

"I'll tell you the whole long story when I get home. Right now I gotta go."

"Laughton with you?"

"He is."

"He best make sure he brings you home."

"For sure."

When I got to Laughton's room, Hamp was there and two other men, Lloyd and Sully, who worked for Calvin. I never paid much attention to all the men who worked for Calvin, except for BJ. The others were bodies that moved around when and where Calvin told them to move. Nondescript. Now here these two were willing to put their lives on the line for the sake of the young men and women at the center, who Elijah threatened with Berg Nation and the drugs he intended to distribute in their neighborhoods. They swore Calvin's legacy would prevail.

"This was all because of my gambling and you trying to help me figure out how I could pay a debt I was stupid enough to make. Now a lot of people have died. I know I'm not responsible for their deaths, but somehow I feel like their deaths are responsible for my life."

"Beautiful words, Hamp," I said and gave him a hug. "I didn't know you had them in you."

"There's much you don't know about old Hampton Dangervil." His laugh, or rather cackle, sounded like Dulcey was in the room. I quelled him with a look. "I know, we've been together too long." We laughed.

"You know we're going to have to stop meeting like this," Laughton joked when we were in the car alone, driving to Blumberg. "For seventeen years we did our job, messed around a little, loved a lot. It was all good. It was all quiet. Then all hell breaks loose and we're operating in these life-and-death situations. It's crazy."

"I'm thinking about quitting and moving out of the city. So what if we get rid of Elijah? If not him, someone else will come looking for revenge some kind of way. That's not something I want to stay on my brain all the time, wondering if my family is safe."

"I hear you, but running away never solves anything."

"I won't be running away. I'm saying I'm worried about my family."

"How about *we* pack everybody up and move somewhere?"

I jerked my head sideways to look at him. "We're about to walk into the lion's den and you're talking mess like that."

Laughton stayed silent.

I turned front again. From the corner of my eye, I saw him look at me. "Maybe *we* might can do just that," I said.

⁂

Blumberg was much different than when I had been there a month ago. The buildings were empty, the residents relocated. The news talked about the city's plans to gut the low-rise buildings and implode the two towers to reconstruct new public housing, but I had been ignorant of the timeline. And this was not a side of town I frequented. Berg Nation members seemed the only inhabitants, unauthorized as they were.

Driving through it felt like a scene from *The Walking Dead*, with shadows moving in front and behind us as we passed. There were no lights except from the full moon that hung over the towers, and the flickering of what I figured was a flashlight, here and there. Rap music played in the vicinity.

When we turned the corner on Sharswood Street and pulled to the curb of one of the towers, Elijah was out in front with five other men. The music was louder.

He bent down so he could look in my window and nodded at Laughton.

"I don't see the girls," I said.

He looked back and waved toward the men. One went into the building and came out with a young white girl who stumbled forward as though under a spell. I recognized her as Bonanno's granddaughter.

"Let her get in the car."

"Ah, Miss Mabley. That would be too easy for your man there to take off with the little lily and leave me with nothing." He opened my door. "Why don't you get out and be with me, and then the girl can get in the car. After that, you can give me the package, and I will let you get in the car and go home."

He patted me down for a weapon, then motioned for his men to bring the girl forward. I opened the back door and ushered her inside. She was half-clothed, dirty, emaciated, and loaded. When she was in the car, Laughton pulled from the curb. Elijah grabbed my arm.

"He's taking her out. He'll be back with the package."

Elijah kept ahold of my arm and pulled me with him so that he stood with his back against the building and me in front of him, rap music sailing over the breeze.

I prayed Sully, Lloyd, Hamp, and whoever else they had with them had done their jobs, as I leaned back and rammed Elijah with an elbow to the jaw that wrenched him sideways, followed by a high kick that bounced his head off the brick wall. I ducked around the side of the building as shots were fired. Laughton was there waiting in the car. I grabbed for the door handle but couldn't reach it, as Elijah grabbed me around the waist and pulled me to the ground.

Laughton was out of the car pointing his gun at us. Elijah had a gun to my head.

Laughton fired. Elijah fell.

I got in the car and Laughton drove out of the complex onto Jefferson and turned down a side street, pulled over and parked. We could hear the echo of gunfire.

Bonanno's gray coupe pulled in behind us. I got out and helped the girl out of the backseat. Mr. Bonanno got out of his car and approached me. I released his granddaughter and got back in the car. Laughton drove off.

CHAPTER 30

It was ninety-three degrees at six in the morning when my age group jumped into the Schuylkill River for the half-mile swim. I wasn't the first one out of the water, but I wasn't the last one out either. By the time I got to the transition area, I could hear the twins squealing, "There she is. There's Auntie." They hung on the railing that enclosed the transition area, shouting, "Hurry up, Auntie. Hurry." I dried my feet some, and struggled to pull socks on. Failing the attempt, I dropped them and stepped into my bike shoes. "Hurry, Auntie, Hurry!" I probably tied faster to get away from them, love them as I do. I lifted my bike off the railing and walked it out of the transition area to the street and got on.

I sucked in the air that blew in my face and let the coolness of the wet triathlon suit spur me forward. An hour later, I turned the corner back to the transition area. My head swirled from the heat, touted as the hottest and most humid day ever for such an event.

I jumped off the bike, lifted it onto the bike rack, changed into running shoes, and jogged out for the last leg of the event: a three-mile run. Everyone was seated along the road leading out. The twins jumped up and down, screaming, "Go, Auntie, go." Nareece worked at wrangling them in, Dulcey and Hamp sat in folding chairs holding hands, and Travis waited on the corner of the first bend. When he saw me, he stepped out and ran along with me for a few hundred feet, then backed off. I looked for Laughton but couldn't find him.

All I could think was next time I would just donate money for research and leave the tree-athlon, as Dulcey says, to the very ones who plowed over me swimming, whizzed by me on their bikes, and were running past me now like I was standing still.

I slowed at the first water table and grabbed two cups of water, gulping them down without stopping forward movement. My body felt like it would cave at any minute, my lungs screamed at the abuse. I breathed in the thick air as deep as I could and pushed forward.

The sidewalks along the street for the last half mile were three and four deep with spectators cheering us, the triathletes, on. Something about knowing the finish line was just around the corner renewed my strength. I picked up the pace and rounded the corner like a pro, and stepped over the finish line. I wasn't the first one to finish, but I wasn't the last one either. As I crossed the line, a race volunteer placed a ribbon laced with a weightless medal around my neck.

"My Auntie won a medal!" the twins screeched at anyone and everyone who stood around, listening or not. "You did it, Auntie. You won the race." They each bent over and took a leg and lifted me up. Nareece yelled at them to put me down before they dropped me, as she, Dulcey, and Hamp rushed toward us.

They were almost in full standing position, with me hanging out in the stratosphere above their heads and 'most everyone else's who stood around us. Then a runner bumped Helen and the victory stance tumbled. I dropped. Laughton rushed in for the save. Thank you, Jesus.

By the time we got home and I showered and fell out for a few hours, it was two o'clock. I had a three o'clock appointment at Dulcey's. She was going to fix me up for a celebratory dinner at the hotel—celebrating that I lived through the triathlon.

When I walked into the shop, the chatter and laughter was loud. I stopped at the doorway, taken aback by the display of bald heads—Dulcey's and the other hairdressers, Marsha and Tracy.

I became the focus of everyone's attention as the door closed, before everyone burst into laughter.

"If you could see the expression on your face, girl," Dulcey said.

I looked around at Dulcey, who sat behind the counter doing something on the computer. For weeks she had walked around looking like the crypt keeper from *Tales from the Crypt*, refusing to shave off the little bit of hair that stuck out of her head. She said it was hers and she wasn't giving it up. Now she was smiling and bobbing a bald head. I went to her and rubbed my hand across her smooth head.

" 'Bout time you decided to be bald and beautiful."

"You can bet it won't be my decision, at all," she retorted, with a slight chuckle. "I came in this morning to these two looking like they husbands." She stopped what she was doing and looked up at me, tears filling her eyes. "God's way ain't always what I want to hear, but I know I'm going to beat this thing, *and* grow some hair back." Dulcey got up and went to her hair station. I followed her, but stopped at Tracy's chair and then Marsha's, both of whom had shaved their heads bald.

"You have got to be kidding me." I checked to make sure Tracy did not have on one of those caps they use in the movies to make someone look bald. Tracy tipped her head back to allow me full access.

"It's actually quite liberating, girl. I don't have to think about it at all—no washing, blow drying, curling, perming, wrapping, *nothing*. Just shine this bad boy up with some tea tree oil and keep steppin'."

"Tea tree oil, my ass," I said.

"Girlfriend is on a roll now, rejuvenated, because she ain't worried about her hair going away anymore. And look at her, she's fine as she wants to be."

I looked over at Dulcey, who was putting on makeup in her mirror. She blushed. Dulcey *blushed*.

I wasn't the only one who noticed. "Miss Dulcey, is that you blushing over there?" Marsha said.

Dulcey waved her hand in Marsha's direction. "Girl, hush."

The client in Tracy's chair shook her head and said, "No way I'm shaving my head. I love you to death, Dulcey, but my husband would sure enough kick my behind out of the house, and I would not blame him at all because I know I would scare myself to death with a bald head. And, Lord, Muriel, you got all that pretty hair women would die for."

A moment of stiff silence.

"Don't you worry, Miss Jordan. Tracy is going to make you your usual beautiful self," Dulcey said.

"C'mon, Muriel, you in or out?" Marsha piped in. She gestured for me to take a seat in her chair.

"Girl, you better bring yourself over here and set your behind down," Dulcey threatened.

I sauntered over to Marsha's chair.

"For my girl? I'm all in." I plopped down in her chair. "Buzz it," I said.

COLD FLASH

Carrie H. Johnson

About this Guide

The suggested questions are included to
enhance your group's reading of
Carrie H. Johnson's *Cold Flash*.

Discussion Questions

1. Nareece acts out because Travis does not refer to her as his mother, rather he continues to call her his aunt. Do you think her feelings are justified? Do you think Travis should be calling her Mom? Do you think Muriel was right in letting him make his own way with Nareece?

2. Were you sympathetic toward Dulcey's husband Hampton? Did his love for Dulcey feel authentic to you?

3. Do the characters in the book remind you of people you know? Do you like them or disapprove of them? Who do you like? Who do you dislike? Why?

4. Some mystery writers/readers do not like the idea of a mystery having a romantic subplot. Do you feel the love aspect—with Muriel, Calvin, and Laughton—enhanced or detracted from the story? Do you think Muriel and Laughton should be together?

5. When Calvin confesses to Muriel that he is married she is mortified, but still sleeps with him. Does this change your perception of Calvin's character? Muriel's character? Should Muriel have walked out after learning Calvin lied?

6. Muriel accepted Travis's friend Elijah with open arms despite suspicions about him from the beginning. Should she have been more suspicious about him and his brother and their involvement in Berg Nation sooner?

7. Muriel and Nareece's relationship is strained, especially where Travis and the twins are concerned. Nareece is adamant about moving out and getting her own place. Do you think this is a

wise choice for her? Do you think Muriel should stop "rescuing" Nareece and encourage her to go her own way?

8. Muriel is about keeping her family together and safe under the same roof. Do you think she is masking her own insecurities with this desire? Why or why not? What insecurities do you see in Muriel's character?

9. Muriel is resistant to her new partner, Fran. Despite Muriel's antagonistic attitude toward him, Fran has her back throughout the story. Do you think he earned Muriel's trust?

10. Are you satisfied with the book's ending? Why or why not?

DON'T MISS

HOT FLASH

In this thrilling debut novel from Carrie H. Johnson, one woman with a dangerous job and a volatile past is feeling the heat from all sides . . .

Available wherever books are sold.

Enjoy the following excerpt from *Hot Flash* . . .

CHAPTER 1

Our bodies arched, both of us reaching for that place of ultimate release we knew was coming. Yes! We screamed at the same time . . . except I kept screaming long after his moment had passed.

You've got to be kidding me, a cramp in my groin? The second time in the three times we had made love. Achieving pretzel positions these days came at a price, but man, how sweet the reward.

"What's the matter, baby? You cramping again?" he asked, looking down at me with genuine concern.

I was pissed, embarrassed, and in pain all at the same time. "Yeah," I answered meekly, grimacing.

"It's okay. It's okay, sugar," he said, sliding off me. He reached out and pulled me into the curvature of his body, leaving the wet spot to its own demise. I settled in. Gently, he massaged my thigh. His hands soothed me. Little by little, the cramp went away. Just as I dozed off, my cell phone rang.

"*Mph, mph, mph,*" I muttered. "Never a moment's peace."

Calvin stirred. "Huh?"

"Nothin', baby, shhhh," I whispered, easing from his grasp

and reaching for the phone from the bedside table. As quietly as I could, I answered the phone the same way I always did.

"Muriel Mabley."

"Did I get you at a bad time, partner?" Laughton chuckled. He used the same line whenever he called. He never thought twice about waking me, no matter the hour. I worked to live and lived to work—at least that's been my story for twenty years, the last seventeen as a firearms forensics expert for the Philadelphia Police Department. I had the dubious distinction of being the first woman in the unit and one of two minorities. The other was my partner, Laughton McNair.

At forty-nine, I was beginning to think I was blocking the blessing God intended for me. I felt like I had blown past any hope of a true love in pursuit of a damn suspect.

"You there?" Laughton said, laughing louder.

"Hee hee, hell. I finally find someone and you runnin' my ass ragged, like you don't *even* want it to last. What now?" I said.

"Speak up. I can hardly hear you."

"I said . . ."

"I heard you." More chuckles from Laughton. "You might want to rethink a relationship. Word is we've got another dead wife and again the husband swears he didn't do it. Says she offed herself. That makes three dead wives in three weeks. Hell, must be the season or something in the water."

Not wanting to move much or turn the light on, I let my fingers search blindly through my bag on the nightstand until they landed on paper and a pen. Pulling my hand out of my bag with paper and pen was another story. I knocked over the half-filled champagne glass also on the nightstand. "Damn it!" I was like a freaking circus act, trying to save the paper, keep the bubbly from getting on the bed, stop the glass from breaking, and keep from dropping the phone.

"Sounds like you're fighting a war over there," Laughton said.

"Just give me the address."

"If you can't get away . . ."

"Laughton, just . . ."

"You don't have to yell."

He let a moment of silence pass before he said, "Thirteen ninety-one Berkhoff. I'll meet you there."

"I'm coming," I said and clicked off.

"You okay?" Calvin reached out to recapture me. I let him and fell back into the warmth of his embrace. Then I caught myself, sat up, and clicked the light on—but not without a sigh of protest.

Calvin rose. He rested his head in his palm and flashed that gorgeous smile at me. "Can't blame a guy for trying," he said.

"It's a pity I can't do you any more lovin' right now. I can't sugarcoat it. This is my life," I complained on my way to the bathroom.

"So you keep telling me."

I felt uptight about leaving Calvin in the house alone. My son, Travis, would be home from college in the morning, his first spring break from Lincoln University. He and Calvin had not met. In all the years before this night, I had not brought a man home, except Laughton, and at least a decade had passed since I'd had any form of a romantic relationship. The memory chip filled with that information had almost disintegrated. Then along came Calvin.

When I came out, Calvin was up and dressed. He was five foot ten, two hundred pounds of muscle, the kind of muscle that flexed at his slightest move. Pure lovely. He pulled me close and pressed his wet lips to mine. His breath, mixed with a hint of citrus from his cologne, made every nerve in my body pulsate.

"Next time we'll do my place. You can sing to me while I

make you dinner," he whispered. "Soft, slow melodies." He crooned, "You Must Be a Special Lady," as he rocked me back and forth, slow and steady. His gooey caramel voice touched my every nerve ending, head to toe. Calvin is a singer and owns a nightclub, which is how we met. I was at his club with friends and Calvin and I—or rather, Calvin and my alter ego, spurred on by my friends, of course—entertained the crowd with duets all night.

He held me snugly against his chest and buried his face in the hollow of my neck while brushing his fingertips down the length of my body.

"Mmm . . . sounds luscious," was all I could muster.

The interstate was deserted, unusual no matter what time, day or night.

In the darkness, I could easily picture Calvin's face, bright with a satisfied smile. I could still feel his hot breath on my neck, the soft strumming of his fingers on my back. I had it bad. Butterflies reached down to my navel and made me shiver. I felt like I was nineteen again, first love or some such foolishness.

Flashing lights from an oncoming police car brought my thoughts around to what was ahead, a possible suicide. How anyone could think life was so bad that they would kill themselves never settled with me. Life's stuff enters pit territory sometimes, but then tomorrow comes and anything is possible again. Of course, the idea that the husband could be the killer could take one even deeper into pit territory. The man you once loved, who made you scream during lovemaking, now not only wants you gone, moved out, but dead.

When I rounded the corner to Berkhoff Street, the scene was chaotic, like the trappings of a major crime. I pulled curbside and rolled to a stop behind a news truck. After I turned off Bertha, my 2000 Saab gray convertible, she rattled in protest for a few moments before going quiet. As I got out, local news anchor Sheridan Meriwether hustled from the front of the news truck and shoved a microphone in my face before I could shut the car door.

"Back off, Sheridan. You'll know when we know," I told her.

"True, it's a suicide?" Sheridan persisted.

"If you know that, then why the attack? You know we don't give out information in suicides."

"Confirmation. Especially since two other wives have been killed in the past few weeks."

"Won't be for a while. Not tonight anyway."

"Thanks, Muriel." She nodded toward Bertha. "Time you gave the old gray lady a permanent rest, don't you think?"

"Hey, she's dependable."

She chuckled her way back to the front of the news truck. Sheridan was the only newsperson I would give the time of day. We went back two decades, to rookie days when my mom and dad were killed in a car crash. Sheridan and several other newspeople had accompanied the police to inform me. She returned the next day, too, after the buzz had faded. A drunk driver sped through a red light and rammed my parents' car head-on. That was the story the police told the papers. The driver of the other car cooked to a crisp when his car exploded after hitting my parents' car, then a brick wall. My parents were on their way home from an Earth, Wind & Fire concert at the Tower Theater.

Sheridan produced a series on drunk drivers in Philadelphia, how their indiscretions affected families and children on both sides of the equation, which led to a national broadcast. Philadelphia police cracked down on drunk drivers and legislation passed with compulsory loss of licenses. Several other cities and states followed suit.

I showed my badge to the young cop guarding the front

door and entered the small foyer. In front of me was a white-carpeted staircase. To the left was the living room. Laughton, his expression stonier than I expected, stood next to the detective questioning who I supposed was the husband. He sat on the couch, leaned forward with his elbows resting on his thighs, his head hanging down. Two girls clad in *Frozen* pajamas huddled next to him on the couch, one on either side.

The detective glanced at me, then back at the man. "Where were you?"

"I just got here, man," the man said. "Went upstairs and found her on the floor."

"And the kids?"

"My daughter spent the night with me. She had a sleepover at my house. This is Jeanne, lives a few blocks over. She got homesick and wouldn't stop crying, so I was bringing them back here. Marcy and I separated, but we're trying to work things out." He choked up, unable to speak anymore.

"At three a.m."

"I told you, the child was having a fit. Wanted her mother."

A tank of a woman charged through the front door, "Oh my God. Baby, are you all right?" She pushed past the police officer there and clomped across the room, sending those close to look for cover. The red-striped flannel robe she wore and pink furry slippers, size thirteen at least, made her look like a giant candy cane with feet.

"Wade, what the hell is happenin' here?" She moved in and lifted the girl from the sofa by her arm. Without giving him a chance to answer, she continued. "C'mon, baby. You're coming with me."

An officer stepped sideways and blocked the way. "Ma'am, you can't take her—"

The woman's head snapped around like the devil possessed her, ready to spit out nasty words followed by green fluids. She never stopped stepping.

I expect she would have trampled the officer, but Laughton interceded. "It's all right, Jackson. Let her go," he said.

Jackson sidestepped out of the woman's way before Laughton's words settled.

Laughton nodded his head in my direction. "Body's upstairs."

The house was spotless. White was *the* color: white furniture, white walls, white drapes, white wall-to-wall carpet, white picture frames. The only real color came in the mass of throw pillows that adorned the couch and a wash of plants positioned around the room.

I went upstairs and headed to the right of the landing, into a bedroom where an officer I knew, Mark Hutchinson, was photographing the scene. Body funk permeated the air. I wrinkled my nose.

"Hey, M&M," Hutchinson said.

"That's Muriel to you." I hated when my colleagues took the liberty to call me that. Sometimes I wanted to nail Laughton with a front kick to the groin for starting the nickname.

He shook his head. "Ain't me or the victim. She smells like a violet." He tilted his head back, sniffed, and smiled.

Hutchinson waved his hand in another direction. "I'm about done here."

I stopped at the threshold of the bathroom and perused the scene. Marcy Taylor lay on the bathroom floor. A small hole in her temple still oozed blood. Her right arm was extended over her head, and she had a .22 pistol in that hand. Her fingernails and toenails looked freshly painted. When I bent over her body, the sulfur-like smell of hair relaxer backed me up a bit. Her hair was bone-straight. The white silk gown she wore flowed around her body as though staged. Her cocoa brown complexion looked ashen with a pasty, white film.

"Shame," Laughton said to my back. "She was a beautiful woman." I jerked around to see him standing in the doorway.

"Check this out," I said, pointing to the lay of the night-gown over the floor.

"I already did the scene. We'll talk later," he said.

"Damn it, Laughton. Come here and check this out." But when I turned my head, he was gone.

I finished checking out the scene and went outside for some fresh air. Laughton was on the front lawn talking to an officer. He beelined for his car when he saw me.

"What the hell is wrong with you?" I muttered, jogging to catch up with him. Louder. "Laughton, what the hell—"

He dropped anchor. Caught off guard, I plowed into him. He waited until I peeled myself off him and regained my footing, then said, "Nothing. Wade says they separated a few months ago and were trying to get it together, so he came over for some making up. He used his key to enter and found her dead on the bathroom floor."

"No, he said he was bringing the little girl home because she was homesick."

"Yeah, well, then you heard it all."

He about-faced.

I grabbed his arm and attempted to spin him around. "You act like you know this one or something," I practically screeched at him.

"I do."

I cringed and softened my tone five octaves at least when I managed to speak again. "How?"

"I was married to her . . . a long time ago."

He might as well have backhanded me upside the head. "You never—"

"I have an errand to run. I'll see you back at the lab."

I stared after him long after he got in his car and sped off.

The sun was rising by the time the scene was secured: body and evidence bagged, husband and daughter gone back home. It spewed warm tropical hues over the city. By the time I reached the station, the hues had turned cold metallic gray. I pulled into a parking spot and answered the persistent ring of my cell phone. It was Nareece.

"Hey, sis. My babies got you up this early?" I said, feigning a light mood. My babies were Nareece's eight-year-old twin daughters.

Nareece groaned. "No. Everyone's still sleeping."

"You should be, too."

"Couldn't sleep."

"Oh, so you figured you'd wake me up at this ungodly hour in the morning. Sure, why not? We're talkin' sisterly love here, right?" I said. We chuckled. "I've been up since three anyway, working a case." I waited for her to say something, but she stayed silent. "Reece?" More silence. "C'mon, Reecey, we've been through this so many times. Please don't tell me you're trippin' again."

"A bell goes off in my head every time this date rolls around. I believe I'll die with it going off," Nareece confessed.

"Therapy isn't helping?"

"You mean the shrink? She ain't worth the paper she prints her bills on. I get more from talking to you every day. It's all you, Muriel. What would I do without you?"

"I'd say we've helped each other through, Reecey."

Silence filled the space again. Meanwhile, Laughton pulled his Audi Quattro in next to my Bertha and got out. I knocked on the window to get his attention. He glanced in my direction and moved on with his gangster swagger as though he didn't see me.

"I have to go to work, Reece. I just pulled into the parking lot after being at a scene."

"Okay."

"Reece, you've got a great husband, two beautiful daughters, and a gorgeous home, baby. Concentrate on all that and quit lookin' behind you."

Nareece and John had ten years of marriage. John is Vietnamese. The twins were striking, inheritors of almond-shaped eyes, "good" curly black hair, and amber skin. Rose and Helen, named after our mother and grandmother. John balked at their names because they did not reflect his heritage. But he was mush where Nareece was concerned.

"You're right. I'm good except for two days out of the year, today and on Travis's birthday. And you're probably tired of hearing me."

"I'll listen as long as you need me to. It's you and me, Reecey. Always has been, always will be. I'll call you back later today. I promise."

I clicked off and stayed put for a few minutes, bogged down by the realization of Reece's growing obsession with my son, way more than in past years, which conjured up ugly scenes for me. I prayed for a quick passing, though a hint of guilt pierced my gut. Did I pray for her sake, my sake, or Travis's? What scared me anyway?

Also Available

THE STRIVERS' ROW SPY

Suspenseful and evocative, Jason Overstreet's debut novel glitters with the vibrant dreams and dangerous promise of the Harlem Renaissance as one man crosses the lines between the law, loyalty, and deadly lies . . .

Available wherever books are sold.

Enjoy the following excerpt from *The Strivers' Row Spy* . . .

1

Middlebury College, Vermont
Spring, 1919

It was graduation day, and the strange man standing at the top of the cobblestone stairwell gave me an uneasy feeling. It was like he was waiting on me. With each step I climbed, the feeling turned into a gnawing in my stomach, gripped me a bit more, pulling at my good mood.

I glanced at my watch, then down at my shiny, black patent leather shoes. First time I'd worn them. Hadn't ever felt anything so snug on my feet, so light. Momma had saved up for Lord knows how long and had given them to me as a graduation gift.

Again I looked up at him. He was a tall, thin man, dressed in the finest black suit I'd ever laid eyes on, too young, it appeared to me, to have such silver hair, an inch of which was left uncovered by his charcoal fedora. Even from a distance he looked like a heavy smoker, with skin the texture and color of tough, sun-baked leather. I had never seen any man exhibit such confidence—one who stood like he was in charge of the world.

I finally reached the top step and realized just how imposing he was, standing about six-five, a good three inches taller than I. His pensive eyes locked in on me and he extended a hand.

"Sidney Temple?" he asked, with a whispery-dry voice.

"Yes."

"James Gladforth of the Bureau of Investigation."

We shook hands as I tried to digest what I'd just heard. What kind of trouble was I in? Was there anything I might have done in the past to warrant my being investigated? I thought of Jimmy King, Vida Cole, Junior Smith—all childhood friends who, God knows, had broken their share of laws. But I had never been involved in any of it. The resolute certainty of my clean ways gave me calm as I adjusted my tassel and responded.

"Good to meet you, sir."

"Congratulations on your big day," he said.

"Thank you."

"You all are fortunate the ceremony is this morning. Looks to be gettin' hotter by the minute." He looked up, squinting and surveying the clear sky.

I just stood there nodding my head in agreement.

He took off his hat, pulled a handkerchief from his jacket pocket, and wiped the sweat from his forehead. "You can relax," he said. "You're not in any trouble." He put the handkerchief back in his pocket and replaced his hat. He stared at me, studying my face, perhaps trying to decide if my appearance matched that of the person he'd imagined.

He took out a tin from his jacket, opened it, and removed a cigarette. Patting his suit, searching for something, he finally removed a box of matches from his left pants pocket. He struck one of the sticks, lit the cigarette, and smoked quietly for a few seconds.

Proud parents and possibly siblings walked past en route to the ceremony. One young man, dressed in his pristine Army uniform, sat in a wheelchair pushed by a woman in a navy blue dress. He had very pale skin, red hair, and was missing his right leg. Mr. Gladforth looked directly at them as they approached.

"Ma'am," he said, tipping his hat, "will you allow me a moment?"

"Certainly," she said, coming to a stop. She had her grayish-blond hair in a bun, and her eyes were some of the saddest I'd ever seen.

"Where did you fight, young man?" asked Gladforth.

"Saw my last action in Champagne, France, sir. Part of the Fifteenth Field Artillery Regiment. Been back stateside for about two months, sir."

"Your country will forever be indebted to you, son. That was a hell of a war effort by you men. On behalf of the United States government and President Wilson, I want to thank you for your service."

"Thank you, sir."

"Ma'am," said Gladforth, tipping his hat again as the woman gave him a slight smile.

She resumed pushing the young man along, and Gladforth began smoking again—refocusing his attention on me.

"I don't want to take away too much of your time, Sidney," he went on, turning and exhaling the smoke away from us. "I just wanted to introduce myself and tell you personally that the Bureau has been going over the college records of soon-to-be graduates throughout the country.

"You should be pleased to know that you're one of a handful of men that our new head of the General Intelligence Division, J. Edgar Hoover, would like to interview for a possible entry-level position. Your portfolio is outstanding."

"Thank you," I said, somewhat taken aback.

"I know it's quite a bit to try to decide on at the moment, but this is a unique opportunity to say the least."

"Indeed it is, sir."

He handed me a card. "Listen, here's my information. We'd

like to set up an interview with you as soon as possible, hope-
fully within the month."

He began smoking again as I read the card.

"Think about the interview, and when you make your
mind up, telephone the number there. We'll have a train
ticket to Washington available for you within hours of your
decision. Based on the sensitivity of the assignment you may
potentially be asked to fulfill, you can tell no one about this interview.

"And, if you were to be hired, your status in any capacity
would have to remain confidential. That includes your wife, family,
and any friends or acquaintances. If you are uncomfortable with
this request, please decline the interview because the conditions
are nonnegotiable. Are you clear about what I'm telling you?"

"Yes, I think so."

"It's imperative that you understand these terms," he stressed,
throwing what was left of his cigarette on the ground and stepping on it, the sole of his dress shoe gritting against the concrete.

"I understand."

"Then I look forward to your decision."

"I'll be in touch very soon, Mr. Gladforth. And thank you
again, sir."

We shook hands and he walked away. Wondering what I'd
just agreed to, I headed on to the graduation ceremony.

I picked up my pace along the cobblestone walkway, thinking about all the literature and history I'd pored over for the
past six years, seldom reading any of it without wishing I were
there in some place long ago, doing something important and
history-shaping. I may have been an engineer by training, but
at heart, at very private heart, I was a political man.

I wondered, specifically, what the BOI wanted with a colored agent all of a sudden. I was certainly aware that during its
short life, it had never hired one. Could I possibly be the first?
I thought it intriguing but far-fetched.

"Don't be late, Sidney," said Mrs. Carlton, one of my mathematics professors, interrupting my reverie as she walked by. "You've been waiting a long time for this."

"Yes, ma'am." I smiled at her and began to walk a bit faster. I reminded myself that Gladforth hadn't actually mentioned my becoming an agent. He'd only spoken of an interview and a possible low-level position.

"It's just you and me, Sidney," said Clifford Mayfield, running up and putting his hand on my shoulder, his grin bigger than ever.

"Yep," I said, "just you and me," referring to the fact that Clifford and I would be the only coloreds graduating that day.

"The way I see it," he said, "this is just the beginning. Tomorrow I'm off to Boston for an interview with Thurman Insurance."

Clifford continued talking about his plans for the future as we walked, but my mind was still on the Bureau. Working as an engineer was my goal, but maybe it could wait. Perhaps this Bureau position was a calling. Maybe if I could land a good government job and rise up through the ranks, I could bring about the social change I'd always dreamed of. I needed a few days to think it through.

Moments later I was sitting among my fellow classmates, each lost in his own thoughts inspired by President Tannenbaum. He stood at the podium in his fancy blue and gold academic gown, the hot sun beaming down on his white rim of hair and bald, sunburned top of his head.

"You are all now equipped to take full advantage of the many opportunities the world has to offer," he asserted. "You have chosen to push beyond the four-year diploma and will soon be able to boast of possessing the coveted master's degree. . . ."

Momma had told me from the time I was five, "You're going to college someday, Sugar." But throughout my early teens I'd noticed that no one around me was doing so. Still, I studied hard and got a scholarship to Middlebury College. My high school English teacher, Mrs. Bright, had gone to school here.

"It seems," Tannenbaum continued, "like only yesterday that I was sitting there where all of you sit today, and I can tell you from my own experiences in the greater world that a Middlebury education is second to none. . . ."

I'd left Milwaukee, the Bronzeville section, in the fall of 1913 and headed here to Vermont. I had taken a major in mechanical engineering with the goal of obtaining a bachelor's and then a master's degree in civil engineering. I would be qualified both to assemble engines and construct buildings. Reading physics became all consuming, and I'd spent most of my time in the library, often slipping in some pleasure reading. Having access to a plethora of rich literature was new to me.

"I want you to hear me loud and clear," President Tannenbaum went on. "This is your time to shine."

As I looked across the crowd of graduate students and up into the stands, I saw Momma in her purple dress, brimming with joy. She was so proud, and rightfully so, having raised me all on her own. For eighteen years it had been just the two of us, Momma having happily spent those years scrubbing other families' homes, cooking for and raising their children. But now that I had turned twenty-five, I would see to it that she wouldn't have to do that anymore.

It was time for my row to stand. As we progressed slowly toward the stage, I became more and more painfully aware of my wife's absence. I'd first laid eyes on Loretta in the library four years earlier when she'd arrived at Middlebury, making her the third female colored student here.

I'd approached her while she was studying, introducing myself and awkwardly asking her if she'd like to study together sometime. She'd just given me an odd look before I'd quickly changed my question, asking instead if she'd like to have an ice cream with me sometime in the cafeteria. She said yes and it was easy between us from that day on.

"Sidney Temple!" called out President Tannenbaum, the audience politely clapping for me as they had for the others. I walked onto the stage, took my diploma from his hand, and paused briefly for the customary photograph. I looked at Momma as she wiped the tears from her eyes.

I longed for Loretta to be sitting there too, witnessing my little moment in the spotlight. Before coming to Middlebury she'd spent one year at the Pennsylvania Academy of the Fine Arts and another at Oberlin College. But she'd finally found her collegiate home here and earned a degree in art history.

Her graduation, which had come three weeks prior to mine, had been a magical affair. Unfortunately, that celebratory atmosphere had come to an abrupt halt. Today she was grieving the loss of her father and was back home in Philadelphia arranging for his funeral. His illness had progressed during the last year, and he'd rarely been conscious the last time we'd visited him together. I figured that would be the last time I'd see him and had said my good-byes back then. Still, it was comforting to know that Loretta had insisted I stay here and allow Momma to see me graduate.

With the ceremony over and degree in hand, I headed to the reception the engineering department was having for a few of us. My mind raced to come up with a good reason for visiting Washington, D.C.—one that I could legitimately tell Momma about. As I arrived at the auditorium, she was waiting outside. We embraced.

"I'm so proud of you, Sugar."

"I couldn't have done it without you. I love you, Momma."

The pending trip to Washington crept into my mind even during that long motherly hug.

A week later I was standing in the train station lobby in downtown Chicago on my way to the nation's capital. I'd said my good-byes to Momma back in Milwaukee earlier that morning. My "good reason"? I'd told her I'd been asked to interview for a position on the Public Buildings Commission, a government committee established in 1916 to make suggestions regarding future development of federal agencies and offices. It was the first time I'd lied to her, and the guilt was heavy on me.

The Bureau had sent an automobile to pick me up at Momma's place in Milwaukee and drive me to Chicago. It was a wondrous black vehicle—a 1919 Ford Model T.

When my train was announced, I headed to the car where all the colored passengers were sitting. Unlike the South, here in Chicago there were no Jim Crow cars I was required to sit in, but I guess most of us just felt comfortable sitting apart from the whites, and vice versa. Was the way things were in public. But it was a feeling I never wanted my future children to have.

All the folks on the train were immaculately dressed, and I felt comfortable in my cream-colored three-piece suit and brown newsboy cap. We gazed at one another with curiosity, each probably wondering, as I was, what special event was affording us the opportunity to travel such a distance in style. The car was paneled in walnut and furnished with large, upholstered chairs. It was the height of luxury.

I began studying the brand-new Broadway Limited railroad map I'd purchased. Ever since my first year of college, I'd been collecting every map I could get my hands on. It had become a hobby of sorts, running my finger along the various lines that connected one town to another, always discovering a new place various rails had begun servicing.

The train passed by West Virginian fields of pink rhododendron, then chugged through the state of Virginia as I reflected on its history and absorbed the landscape with virgin eyes. This was the land of Washington and Jefferson I was entering.

Connect with Us

Visit us online at
KensingtonBooks.com
to read more from your favorite authors, see books
by series, view reading group guides, and more.

Join us on social media

for sneak peeks, chances to win books and prize packs,
and to share your thoughts with other readers.

facebook.com/kensingtonpublishing
twitter.com/kensingtonbooks

Tell us what you think!

To share your thoughts, submit a review,
or sign up for our eNewsletters, please visit:
KensingtonBooks.com/TellUs.